ELIZABETH LAVENDER'S

THE SPINNING OF DECEPTION

BOOK 1 OF THE SUNSPEAR SERIES

Ebook ISBN: 978-1-951741-00-6

Paperback Print ISBN: 978-1-951741-01-3

Hardcover Print ISBN: 978-1951741-02-0

First Printing: October 2019

ACKNOWLEDGEMENTS

Special thanks to Pam Hotz, Patty Ellis, Rebecca Latimer, and Rachel Latimer, who read the manuscript and gave valuable feedback. Also, thanks to Tracy Feaster for helping ease the frustration of the web for me so I could do that part of this project. Also, thanks to those at Arcane Book Covers for taking my concept and transforming it into something that amazed me. Many thanks go to family and friends, whose constant enthusiasm about the book encouraged me daily to continue to write the story. Special thanks to my husband and my two kiddos for their patience and encouragement as I continue to write the story. Thanks also to my husband and my older son for making editing suggestions, most of which I accepted.

And thanks goes to you, the reader I have just met you, but the story is written for you. I have come to enjoy creating this world and this cast of characters. They have quite the journey ahead of them. Many challenges stand before them, and many battles must be fought. I hope you will find value in following the journey before them and become entwined in their story. Stay with me the whole journey and see where it leads them. I believe you will find it was worth the trek

CHAPTER ONE

Dante breathed heavily. The sun beat down as a bead of sweat dripped from his sandy brown hair and slid down his face. How long had he been out here, he wondered. Surely enough for one day. Suddenly, he heard a noise—a rustle in the leaves. He spun around in time to see a Horned Dragon Lizard crawl from the bush. The purple-green, oversized lizard appeared deceptively harmless, but Dante knew better. It was fast for its size, and the creature's striped, poisonous tongue could stretch far beyond itself, leaving its victim helpless with one paralyzing lick. It delivered a slow and painful death. Thankfully, he had no firsthand experience, and he vowed not to find out today.

Dante assessed his surroundings and smiled. He stepped back carefully, his brown eyes never leaving the lizard. He gave the vine from the Zora Tree a tug and broke off a low-lying limb. The lizard inched closer as if anticipating an easy prey and a won match.

Dante felt his muscles tighten as he got ready. The lizard lunged with a burst of speed, stretching its tongue toward him. Dante whipped the vine out, caught the animal's tongue on it, then took the jagged point of the branch and plunged it deep into the creature's body. It shook for a moment before stilling.

Now, he could put a close on this day. Thirty minutes later, he emerged from the woods into the open courtyard.

"Did you enjoy a relaxing stroll in the woods?" a man holding a staff asked as he approached Dante.

Dante tried to keep from laughing. "I should know better when you tell me it's a great day for a leisurely stroll in the woods. I suspect you knew, though, Seth."

Dante smiled. Seth was an Elder who had trained Dante as far back as he could remember. Seth came from a long line of Elders spread across the colonies, assigned to train and guide young warriors. However, Seth recognized Dante as *especially gifted*, and so he expected more from him. It was reflected in the stare Dante received from the Elder now.

"Come, Seth. It's almost dinner."

"That was as close to a whine as I've heard from you in some time, Dante," Seth teased. "You can make time to practice with your sunspear before dinner. If you search hard enough, you can locate someone to spar with."

Right on cue, a lean figure walked up. His blue eyes took in Dante with amusement. "You're back. Lana wondered if she needed to send a search party. Quite the walk you took."

"Ha-ha. Always the funny one, Caleb. You can tell my cousin to forget the search party. I started to wonder too. Everything I met wanted to attack, maim, or send me to a slow death. Another great walk."

"Ah, sounds like a Seth suggested walk. Dante, you know my wife would be coming through the woods herself if she thought you couldn't handle it. She's relentless." He laughed.

"She's an army by herself for sure." Dante grinned.

"One of the many reasons I married her. Are you done or not, Dante?"

"Well ..." he began, but Seth interrupted.

"Actually, he wishes for someone to spar with him before dinner with his sunspear."

"And I came just in time, right? Yes, of course, I would love to help you, Dante," finished Caleb, laughing.

Dante groaned, and Seth smiled.

Dante crafted his spear when he reached a certain point in his training, as all chosen warriors must do. Some called the weapon a moonspear, some a sunspear. All sunspears displayed a stone embedded in the handle, which caught natural lights, like the moon, stars, and the sun in such a way it gave the appearance of radiant light reflecting from the spear. It was not shaped like a traditional spear. Instead, it sported a sharp point at one end with the underside fashioned much like a sword. At first, only the handle with the stone of the spear could be seen. When ready for battle, it responded to the warrior and grew to its full length. More than once, Dante asked Seth how the sunspear worked, the way it responded to the holder. Seth's answer was always the same. "Sunspears are gifts from the Ancient One, forged by the chosen warrior as instructed by the written knowledge. Some things will always remain a mystery, my boy. But keep in mind, many times power is more about the wielder than the weapon."

Dante usually regretted asking in the first place because he got several reminders about the responsibility associated with his training and wielding the sunspear. Finally, it ended with another exhausting round of training much like he had accomplished today.

Seth handed Dante his sunspear, and Dante took it, weighing it in his hand. It responded without hesitation, expanding to its full length, Dante muttered, "You know my walk would have been much easier with this."

"I am sure it would have been, but you found other resources around you that worked so you returned without injury. With the sunspear, you would not have used your surroundings to get out of the predicaments you encountered," Seth reminded him.

Dante groaned again. At least he learned the point of the training today.

"Are we going to do this, or are you going to chat all day, Dante?" Caleb stepped forward with his sunspear poised for a fight.

Dante turned to attack Caleb, and they began.

Without warning, another sunspear interrupted Dante's and Caleb's sparring.

"You two are intense. You know you can hurt someone with those things if you're not careful," teased Lana. She walked to stand beside Seth before moving closer to watch the two men battle. When they continued, she used her own sunspear to get their attention. Her long red hair reflected the last bits of the sun as it began its final descent for the day.

Caleb smiled at her. "Sorry, Lana. We overdid it, but I was helping out your cousin."

"I see. I'm calling this battle a draw because it's time for dinner. Now," she stressed.

"Seth, now, can we stop?" asked Dante, avoiding eye contact with Lana.

Seth smiled at them and bowed to Lana. "Even I know when I'm beaten."

They all laughed, and Caleb took Lana's hand as they went inside for dinner. The tantalizing aromas of dinner met them long before they arrived at the dining hall. It was a beautiful area inside the fortress on the planet of Oriana despite the damage it had endured throughout the years. Banners of red and purple velvet and satin hung in many of the halls, determined to hold onto glories of the past. They were torn in places but refused to come down. The banners were a constant reminder of a hope that someday their world could be great again, and the dangers of the present could be left behind. Today, they sat in the smaller dining area while they ate.

"This chicken is dry, Lana," remarked Caleb.

"Yeah, great, Caleb."

Caleb and Dante glanced over at each other. The food tasted fine, but she was somewhere else today.

"Hey Lana," Caleb waved a hand in front of her face, "what's going on? I insulted your cooking and no punch in the arm or smart remark?"

"Something is stirring within the Dark Lord's forces. The attacks keep coming. They're on the move again."

"And we'll answer them in battle, if need be, no matter how many times it takes, Lana," Seth assured her.

"Yes, you're right." Her brown eyes stared off into the distance.

Dante and Caleb knew whatever report Lana had received from her advisors troubled her. No doubt Caleb would know the report's details as the top commander in the fight against the Dark Lord's army.

Dante sighed and stared out into the night. The Dark Lord spread his terror throughout every world and brought death, fear, and enslavement. He had his army and, at the helm, the Black Dragon Commander, who did most of the work for him the last several years. Dante still found it hard to swallow after all this time. In another time, his mother called the commander husband, and he and his brother had called him father. Now, throughout every world, the name of the Black Dragon Commander was spoken in fear, his actions sparking hatred and grief for the trail of destruction he left behind. Lana and Caleb lost their family in one of the attacks, but thankfully, the Elders protected Lana and Caleb from the same fate. The Elders safeguarded Dante similarly, something not forgotten to this day by Dante's father. According to Seth, without the Elders' intervention, Dante would be helping his father on the path of destruction he now saw around him. Although Dante rejected his father's dark path, he felt a strange sense of responsibility when he viewed the terrible destruction. He peered at Lana and sensed her deepening concern over the Dark Lord's movements. Dante didn't feel hungry anymore.

CHAPTER TWO

SIX YEARS EARLIER

O n the planet Merletta, Denisa sat down in the girl's room, watching the child sleep. The ten-year-old played hard earlier and had given in to a catnap, a strange occurrence for her.

Denisa leaned down and kissed her little girl on the forehead, sighing as she wondered aloud. "What will happen next, sweetheart?" She closed her eyes and a whispered voice answered.

"He will come, and you will know what to do." Denisa knew the voice, and with it came a vision of an approaching man. The voice and vision were clear. She would be waiting.

⎯ℓℓ⎯

On the other side of town from Denisa, the Elder Alika sat in his study. He leaned over, absorbed in reading a manuscript, and stopped to let the words encourage him. He heard what sounded like a gentle breeze come through his study, followed by the whispered sound of his name. Maybe he imagined it. No, he smiled. He heard it distinctly now.

"Go to her, and she will be ready." A vision appeared with the voice. He knew what he must do.

Alika sat back in his chair. He would need to make the preparations. A moment later, a slim girl of fourteen years of age came into the room. She had shoulder-length blonde hair that framed her soft face and a quiet manner about her.

"Did you need something, Alika?" she asked.

"Yes, Alena. Please shut the door."

Alena did as she was told and sat down, sensing something amiss.

"Alena, I'll be leaving first thing in the morning to begin a special task. I don't know how long I'll be gone. Let's be ready for the possibility the others will need to take over. You'll be assisting me with the task."

"So, am I coming with you tomorrow?"

"No, first, I will evaluate the situation and then contact you in a few days. Be ready to join me."

"What do I tell the others?"

"Less than I told you. Simply, I am called away to a task. I believe I could be gone for some time, and I will probably require your assistance. They should take over indefinitely," Alika stated thoughtfully.

Alena stared at him with her large brown eyes. "Could this be *the* task?"

"Yes, which is why it must be handled with care." His eyes met hers and held their gaze.

*

The next morning, Denisa knelt outside over the flowers in her garden when she sensed a presence. She looked up to see Alika approaching her.

She smiled. "I expected you."

Alika nodded. "I know."

"Come quickly, inside."

They entered the home and made their way to her daughter's room. The little girl eyed the visitor curiously. Finally, she smiled at him as one who understood if her mother accepted the visitor, she should too. Alika sensed the strong bond of trust and understanding between them as soon as he stepped inside the room. The incredible beauty of the little girl struck Alika as well. She was slender, with the frame of a ballerina and shimmering long light brown hair that fell in waves. She possessed gentle, beautiful blue eyes, the color of the ocean.

Denisa smiled at her daughter. "Come here, sweetheart."

Her daughter was at her mother's side in an instant, waiting for an explanation.

"This is a special teacher who will help you with additional training I want you to do. I know you'll do well for him, as you do for me. He'll help you in areas which are beyond me."

"I understand, mother. I can't wait to learn more and become stronger."

"I'm sure we'll work well together. You are eager to learn," said Alika to the little girl.

"Oh, I am," the little girl replied, smiling up at Alika.

"Sweetheart, why don't you read again for a moment while I talk further with your teacher?"

Her daughter nodded and returned to her reading.

Denisa turned back to Alika, and they sat at the table to speak privately. She seemed hesitant to get her thoughts out, and choosing each word with care, she spoke, "My husband is out at the moment. He does not tell me much of his business, but I am aware of his dealings. Therefore, we must keep my daughter's training from him. He leaves our daughter to me anyway, as he stays busy with his business. Normally he wouldn't notice, but this would be different. Do we understand each other?"

"Perfectly. Another student, a young girl, will be assisting me with your daughter's training as well. She'll be joining me in the next few days. I'll make sure she understands the arrangement."

"Be certain she does, for my daughter's sake. My husband's work is troubling, but more of late. He has a terrible temper if crossed." Denisa stared down at her hands and then fixed her eyes on her daughter.

"I understand your fear, and you're right. We'll do this as you wish to train your daughter, but she will be kept safe."

"Thank you. I'll explain to my daughter so she understands the necessity of keeping her training only between us. She's used to me arranging these matters for her. She's also accustomed to leaving her father unaware of certain details. It's an unfortunate reality of her world. She'll see it as a bonus when she learns a young girl is assisting you with her training. Give me a few minutes with my daughter to explain the arrangement, and you can get acquainted with her."

Alika nodded to Denisa as she knelt beside her daughter. The little girl listened intently and nodded, understanding as she always did.

Alika understood Denisa's misgivings. He wished he could say her fears would prove unfounded. He sighed. The woman knew about her husband; she didn't need to dig further to confirm in her heart the truth.

CHAPTER THREE

PRESENT

The Dark Lord stared into the distance, soaking up the inky gloom of night. He sat in the stronghold's grand hall. His forces continued their ghastly work. He heard the timed pace of his Black Dragon Commander approaching, so he did not bother to turn.

"How are the operations proceeding?" he inquired.

"Dark Lord, we're working on the prototype. If we're successful on a smaller scale, we will know how to proceed. It will be easier to create our army soon," said the Black Dragon Commander.

"Excellent, you are doing well with supervising the operations, as expected."

"Soon, they will join us. They will all see."

"Of course, they will. You were wise enough to see the truth years ago. We will succeed in this together, my friend."

"How I long for the day, Dark Lord."

"I know you do, and your efforts will find success. I knew when I chose you."

A beeping sound interrupted any further discussion.

"Something demands your attention, commander. I will leave you to attend to it. I suspect it involves the enterprise at hand."

The Commander briskly turned and took his leave of the Dark Lord. Once he walked away, his thoughts drifted. After all this time, he found it strange many people remained blind to the world around them and how it operated. Those in the colonies gave the man the name Dark Lord, but the Black Dragon Commander decided long ago, they simply didn't understand as he did now. After all, the Elders taught him for years as well. Then the betrayal came, like a dagger edging closer, digging inch by inch, and the final plunge in his back sealed it. It cost him everything. His son dead, his wife gone, and his other son stolen from him to serve the very ones who drove the dagger. The one everyone called the Dark Lord helped him, exposed the truth. He once foolishly believed the lies of the Elders—numerous worlds still clung to them. He would help the Dark Lord, and they would be victorious. Deep down, he believed he could convince his son of the truth and get him back too. A second beep interrupted his thoughts, and he realized he still needed to address the issue with the project.

The Dark Lord watched his Commander leave the room. A figure materialized from the shadows behind him, a slender woman with long, jet black hair cloaked in black. Her eyes turned from shades of black, orange, and red.

"Here, my Dark Lord. Your favorite." She handed him a cup.

He smiled and took it from her, drinking the liquid greedily, a unique concoction he enjoyed each evening. He affectionately called it liquid fire and was convinced it gave him the extra energy he liked.

The woman smiled. "He serves you superbly as always."

The Dark Lord's eyes danced. "Yes, and he will continue to. He is fully convinced our cause is just. My hold on him cannot be broken."

The Dark Lord settled back and smiled at his conquest.

CHAPTER FOUR

Two men sat deep in conversation as they sipped their drinks.

The black-cloaked figure spoke, "What is their conversation?"

"The items are coming through. I assure you they will arrive," said the other man.

The cloaked figure eyed the man, sizing him up before continuing, "What about their movements?"

"Scattered, trying to organize, but the effort will result in nothing," The other man waved his hand to dismiss the whole matter.

"You underestimate their efforts. I prefer to make my own judgments."

"I can be helpful to you. Give me greater responsibility in these operations. I'm capable of more than what you believe." The other man leaned forward as if it would manifest his request into existence.

The cloaked figure stiffened at this and stared straight at him with pools of darkness. "Don't presume to tell me what I will do or what I believe. Once you prove your usefulness, I will tell you if you have a further role. So far, I am not convinced you are up to the meager task before you. Get me what I need and accurate information for a change, Draco. You will learn your place in this arrangement. This meeting is over."

The cloaked figure saw himself out.

Draco watched him go. He stood with his body still shaking and his eyes flashing with anger. Once the door shut, he threw the drink against the wall. It shattered to the floor, tiny shards of glass scattering everywhere.

Denisa busied herself in another room, but she came running at the sound of the shattering glass.

"What in the world happened?" she surveyed the scene and turned to her husband.

"The glass fell." Draco continued to glare at the wall with stormy eyes as his hands clenched the table.

"When you threw it?" Denisa demanded.

Draco turned on her, his eyes icy cold, but he didn't say anything.

"Your business puts you in a cross mood, Draco. Will you continue down this path?"

Draco approached her with lightning speed, closing the gap between them. He forcefully took her face in his hand. "My business is my own, and you will stay out of it if you know what is best, darling."

Denisa glared at him defiantly. "Understood, darling."

She backed away from him, turned, and walked from the room. She could see the cloaked man's ship lift off through the window of the den. She felt great darkness surround the man and wished it would depart with him. She knew the dark path Draco chose and the dangerous position she found herself in because of it. Denisa would continue to be careful. The safety of her daughter remained her first priority. She shivered. The cloaked figure haunted her dreams. She'd known as soon as he entered the door this evening, though Draco tried to hide his presence, as he did each time. She closed her eyes, but when she opened them again, the darkness stayed.

Denisa went to her daughter's room to check on her and found her reviewing her earlier training.

"Mother, are you all right?"

"Of course, sweetheart." She hugged the child.

The girl returned the hug and kissed her mother on the cheek. "It's okay, Mother. I felt it too."

Denisa pulled her daughter close again.

CHAPTER FIVE

"All of them will be here today?" asked Dante as he walked alongside with Seth toward the meeting room in the fortress.

"Yes, Lana indicated all the commanders for the five other regions should be arriving shortly," answered Seth.

"Hopefully they'll churn up a few suggestions on our next move against the Dark Lord's forces. We're at an impasse."

"It does appear so. However, your cousin values our counsel, and your abilities with the sunspear prove helpful on occasion too." Seth grinned at him.

"I suppose so. I have a fairly good teacher." He grinned back.

Dante and Seth walked into the meeting room. Seth went ahead and sat down as Caleb strolled up to greet Dante.

"Are you ready for this?" Caleb mumbled.

"No more than you. Lana is the only one who gets into this. The only one I really spend time with is Ryan."

Caleb's face brightened. "Oh yeah, Ryan *will* be here. You're right, though. I command the rest, and they still don't say much to me." They laughed.

Commander Ryan was second in command to Caleb and a close friend, leading him to visit the fortress the most out of the commanders.

Dante stared off in space. "I wonder if Lana received any new information."

"No, she didn't say anything that hasn't already been reported from the previous attacks." Caleb studied Dante. "What are you thinking?"

"Something's not right about what we're seeing from the attacks." He started to continue, but the commanders from the other regions began arriving. Caleb and Dante received a look from Lana that said she expected them to greet the commanders with her.

Caleb nodded as they walked over to the other commanders. "I thought so too. We'll talk more later."

Everyone took their seats, and Lana started straightaway. "Our colonies expect attacks from the Dark Lord, but the increase in numbers demands attention. Furthermore, bits of intel hint something big is in the works, but so far, there's no reliable data."

The commanders started talking at once, despite Lana's efforts.

Commander Austin, representing area three, spoke, "It's getting difficult on all fronts, and we're spread too thin."

Followed by Commander Conrad from area two, "The attacks are coming quicker, and they're too many. It's going to be hard to keep up with the current approach."

Commander Aegeus spoke next from the fourth area: "The Dark Lord's army only gets stronger. If they're working on something else, we must get to the bottom of it, quickly."

"We can't do that if we're focusing all our energy on their attacks," Commander Cephas, from area five, added.

Commander Gabe, of area six, interjected, "Well, we may need to concentrate our attention on finding out what they're working on and stopping it. Then focus less on other areas."

"Are you suggesting leaving the colonies defenseless?" Commander Ryan from area one said, sounding horrified.

Commander Gabe sighed. "We may be forced to make hard choices soon."

Lana's eyes flashed with a fire that matched her red hair, and her voice rang out through the hall. Even Dante and Caleb jumped. "No! We will not sacrifice one of the colonies. Not one! We cannot leave a colony to be massacred by the Dark Lord. Not on my watch."

The room was silent. No one dared say a word for several moments.

Caleb spoke calmly but with authority, "We've all seen the aftermath of the Dark Lord's destruction, and some of us experienced it more personally." He glanced at Lana and Dante. "We all know we can't let the Dark Lord take a colony. On the other hand, we've got to discover what he's got his hands into now and put a stop to it. We use every resource, and come up with a plan to cover it all. It'll be difficult, but we will find a way. We always have, and this is no different."

Commander Ryan glanced at Lana apologetically and fixed his eyes on Caleb. "You're right, and we stand with you against the Dark Lord. None of us meant to sound otherwise." He shot a glance at Commander Gabe as he said it and fixed his eyes back on Caleb. "Please, Commander Caleb, what is your plan?"

"I don't know fully, yet." Caleb started to continue, but his words were interrupted by a signal from Lana.

An advisor entered the room and consulted with Lana animatedly. Lana grew tense and nodded to the woman after giving her a few short instructions.

Lana turned to the group. "Our choice is made for us. We received a distress call from the planet Jorie. The Dark Lord's fleet approaches it. Caleb, coordinate with the rest of the commanders to take care of those in the air. Dante and Seth, coordinate your efforts on the planet's surface."

Caleb nodded. "Let's move, people." The group jumped from their seats, dashing after him.

The ships speedily arrived at Jorie. It was the beauty of space travel, courtesy of the Ancient One's perfect order. At least that was the way Seth always explained it to Dante. Travel portals or pockets occurred at regular intervals in space. When a pilot reached one of these portals, they simply entered the location in their ship. The ship would go to the new location once it entered the portal. Individuals could obtain small devices to use if traveling on foot to do the same thing. Children learned from an early age about travel portals and how these regular intervals reflected the order found in creation by the Ancient One.

Caleb's voice came through the speaker. "Be ready, guys. We'll reach the portal in about a minute."

After passing through the portal, the planet came into view along with a squadron of the Dark Lord's ships. At the rear, a larger ship appeared, perhaps a command ship. The black ships had raven-like wings, and the front was fashioned in the style of a dragon head. It appeared terrifying when a civilian saw them headed toward their colony, but that was the idea.

CHAPTER SIX

"She is mastering more and more," said Alika to Alena as he watched the teenager practice her stances with the spear. She alternated, working with a spear, then with a sword.

"Alena will practice with you now," continued Alika.

"Sounds great, Alika," the girl replied with a smile.

He continued to watch her. His student was light on her feet, moving with quick, catlike ease. She dodged, somersaulted, jumped —whatever she needed to avoid getting hit—as if it were as natural as walking to her. Something else stood out, though, and Alika sensed this upon the first meeting of the child. She understood, sensed beyond her years what laid below the surface. Her mind constantly worked, making sense of it, and a calmness permeated her entire spirit, always reflected in her deep blue eyes. She absorbed the teachings into her being, signaling she already understood their importance.

Parts of her somewhat unorthodox training surprised him.

"You could find yourself in unique situations and must be ready for anything. You may need to communicate with someone or try to get information. Do this without being detected."

"I can see how that could be useful, Alika. What do you want me to do?"

"Let's start with something simple. How about tapping into a nearby system."

Before he could name something, the teenager piped in with a suggestion. "How about The High Tower?"

"My dear, we should start simple. Anyway, it's connected to the defense of the colony. It's locked down. There's no way access it." Alika stopped talking as he noticed the teenager.

Her face wrinkled deep in concentration, and within seconds, she tapped rapidly on the data pad. It lit up minutes later, and dozens of pictures inside the tower appeared on the screen. She glanced at Alika's amazed face and smiled. "Which picture do you want?"

That was when Alika realized he had just gotten schooled by his student.

The teenager also learned all the parts of a ship and worked on one as part of her training. She soon knew every inch of it and how all the parts worked together. In addition, she became proficient in making repairs and improvising if she couldn't get the needed part. With Alika or Alena accompanying her, the teenager trained as a pilot too.

The girl finished sparring with Alena.

Alika smiled at his pupil. "Why don't you rest momentarily while I speak with Alena?"

The girl nodded and sat under a nearby tree.

Alena settled next to Alika. She struggled to catch her breath as her eyes sparkled in wonder over their student's progress too. "She's doing so well. Are we pushing her too hard? We're filling her with so much training."

"I wondered the same, but we must continue at this pace. There are dangers always in training, but we cannot delay. I anticipate she will be using everything she's learned soon."

"Alika, do you know something?"

He shook his head. "Not for sure. Yet I feel an urgency for her training, and it's from the one that gave me this task."

CHAPTER SEVEN

Draco sat in his chair, puzzled at the other man. He could not figure out what happened. He also anticipated getting a communication soon that he dreaded. Draco, looking perturbed, demanded, "The shipment went where?"

"To the planet Nuri." The man purposely avoided Draco's gaze.

"And the other shipment?"

"I don't ever see that it shipped. A similar shipment went to the planet Nuray, so perhaps the shipment belonged to the other place. It appears a mix-up occurred." The man focused intently on the data pad in front of him.

"There's always a mix-up. Leave the paperwork here as usual, and get out of my sight, now."

The man happily saw himself out. He had experienced his employer enough after these types of conversations and didn't stay around any longer for what came next.

Draco stomped back and forth in the room, enraged. He assured them he could complete the job, get the shipments to the correct location, and acquire whatever supplies they wanted. They expected all this from him. Sometimes he delivered, but most of the time, this is where he found himself. The shipments arrived at the wrong place, didn't ship at all, were stolen while in shipment, or any manner of other mix-ups. It didn't make sense. The boxes didn't have the contents on them in neon lights during transport. He knew the more mistakes with the shipments, the more ground he lost with the cloaked one.

He pounded the table in frustration. A few minutes later, the whole room laid waste, the aftermath of his all-out tirade. Torn papers mixed with broken glass littered the floor and the table was toppled over. He sat in his chair, his eyes stormy and his mind racing in anger.

Suddenly, as he sat there, his mood changed. A shiver of shock passed through him, and he caught himself. He laughed at the thought, so ridiculous at first. It couldn't be, but he entertained it further. It would explain it, but he refused to give her such credit. Still, perhaps it was worth pursuing.

Draco got up and went outside, hastily placing a call on his data pad.

"Yes, it's me. I may be doing a disposal soon. I will do that part of the job on my own, but I need you for the rest. The day after tomorrow. Yes, I should know by then. Of course, the normal price."

Draco came back inside and got to work.

———ete———

The next day, he peeked up from his data pad as he heard a knock on the door, and one of his employees stepped inside.

"How about the shipment?" Draco asked him casually.

The man looked at him, puzzled. "Which shipment? Draco, there are a lot of shipments going in and out of here."

"I sent one out yesterday and labeled it *important weaponry materials*."

"I don't remember seeing it. I know I didn't take care of it, but I can double-check. We could be behind."

"Huh, strange. I will just place the shipment again."

The man watched him. He knew Draco's temper, and he felt relieved but nervous about the calm way Draco took the news of the missing shipment. "Are you sure? Let me try to track it down for you, Draco."

Draco rose and smiled at the man. "That won't be necessary. I've discovered where the missing shipment went, and I'm taking steps to remedy it. Thank you for your help." He showed his employee to the door, leaving him to walk away bewildered.

"Time to prepare for tomorrow." For the first time in a while, he felt like things were looking up for him. He even felt mildly cheerful.

Sunlight poured through the room, teasingly promising a new day of ease.

Draco got up leisurely and stayed in for most of the day. Today he acted differently. Normally, even if he remained in for the day, he spent it engrossed in his work and avoided his family. This morning he ate breakfast with his wife and daughter, but he still barely spoke two words to either one. Once done, Denisa dismissed her daughter, who knew to go to her training. Her daughter understood more than a constant disagreeable mood plagued her father, and it became abundantly clear to her with each passing day why she kept her training a secret from him. Denisa feigned finishing her food for several minutes, ensuring her daughter time to slip away to her training without Draco noticing. Once sufficient time had elapsed, she stood and walked out of the room. She felt Draco's eyes follow her.

Denisa went into the living area and tried to appear busy, but an uneasy feeling refused to leave her. After reading the same passage six times and still not comprehending it, she gave up. She turned to leave the room and jumped in surprise. Draco stood in the doorway, staring at her.

He smiled at his wife. "Denisa, there's something I am dying to discuss with you."

Outside, less than a mile away, Alika and Alena conducted training with their student. The teenager sparred with Alena when she stopped abruptly. She backed away a split second from sustaining a nasty hit from Alena's spear, or at least Alena thought the teenager escaped in time. The teenager's expression changed to one of horror, and she steadied herself on a nearby tree. Alena ran to her side, with Alika close behind.

Alena checked her, but she didn't spot a hit through the protective gear or any blood on the girl. She was puzzled at the girl's reaction and turned to Alika.

"What is it, child?"

She gaped up at him with the same look of horror on her face, and her voice shook. "I saw a picture, a vision. She's in trouble."

"Who?" Alena asked.

Alika answered for his student, addressing Alena, "Her mother."

The teenager nodded her head, with tears swimming in her eyes. "We must help her now."

Before either could stop her, she jumped on one of the speed gliders and was off like the wind.

"Wait, child," Alika called to her, but to no avail.

Alika grabbed a bag out in a panic and handed it to Alena. "Remove your cloak, put this garment on over your clothing and the helmet." Alika continued as he changed his attire as well. "We will be one of Draco's employees today to preserve the life of our student."

"What about her mother?" Alena asked, jumping on the second speed glider they'd brought.

He sighed sadly in response, and Alena felt a lump in her throat as the two of them raced forward, trying desperately to catch up to their student.

***

Denisa struggled to remain calm. She knew something was wrong all morning with Draco. He studied her the whole time but tried to appear not to do so. She attempted to brush it off or reason it away, but none of it worked. Now she could not deny it. Somehow, he had uncovered it, despite her careful workings.

"What did you wish to discuss, Draco?"

"Don't you know, Denisa?"

"I'm sure I don't, and you're the one who wanted to talk to me. Discuss already."

"All right, since you insist on playing dumb, it's about my business enterprises. Why don't you tell me about them?"

"I'm beyond confused, Draco. That is your realm, and I want nothing to do with it. I believe all was made clear to me some time ago." Denisa stared at him defiantly.

A sadistic laugh escaped his lips. "Well, darling, I must hand it to you. What a marvelous performance you've given for some time now. I suppose that's how you fooled me for so long." Draco's eyes turned cold and dark. "I made it abundantly clear you should stay out of my affairs, but it didn't work. My shipments keep getting mixed up, going to the wrong places, or never getting shipped at all. They're important shipments, and the failures are piling up with the wrong individuals. I kept wondering how this could continue to happen for so long? It never once occurred to me, my clueless wife, whose only concern is tending to the house and our affairs and that worthless child of ours, could be the source of my problems. To your credit, you hid your tracks extremely well. Now it's time for me to remedy this situation."

Denisa glared at him. "How dare you! You blame your failure on me? It's no fault of mine. I warned you long ago of the path you chose. You brought that man into our house and everything which follows behind it. I've no part of it with you."

Draco deliberately advanced toward her as he spoke, "I chose my path, and I warned you about interfering. You chose to do so anyway. Your interruption ends today."

Fear crept through Denisa as she backed away from Draco, but she realized too late she had sequestered herself in a corner. Something shiny peeked out from inside Draco's cloak, and she felt sick. He planned it, and she realized the terrible reality of her current predicament. She tried to escape, but he trapped her. Her eyes frantically searched her surroundings until they landed upon an ornate metal candle holder atop the dining table. She reached for the candle holder and tried to strike Draco, but he grabbed her hand, knocking the weapon to the floor. He grabbed her roughly around the waist as she struggled to break free, then tossed her on the floor in front of him. He held her down, pulled out the knife, and without hesitation, plunged it deep into her stomach. A pool of crimson spread from where he delivered the fatal blow, and his clothes splattered with his wife's blood.

As he rose, he laughed as he towered over his dead wife. "Don't take it personally, darling. Simply the cost of business."

"Mother!" the voice keened from across the room.

Draco turned to see his daughter standing in the doorway, breathless, staring in horror at the scene before her.

CHAPTER EIGHT

T he girl ran and knelt over the body of her mother, sobs racking her frame. She lifted her mother's limp form and held her close, but it was too late. No life lingered in her mother's body, and a heaping pool of blood lay spilled on the floor.

In one doorway, four uniformed men entered alongside a cloaked woman with jet black hair. She surveyed the scene and gave Draco a nod of approval.

Moments later, Alena and Alika slipped into the room in uniform unnoticed.

The cloaked woman smiled at Draco. "You saw this through. A pleasant surprise. I thought I might be forced to take care of this for you too."

Draco regarded her with annoyance. "I told you I'd take care of it. I only need you for the disposal."

"You are a great disappointment thus far to your boss, so he sent me to be sure this was done correctly for a change. So watch your tone, Draco. Although you are convinced this solved your issue, others do not share your opinion. They're more aligned with your late wife's estimation of your incompetence." She snickered.

Draco shook with anger and started to protest.

The cloaked woman's eyes shot daggers at him. "Don't. I can be encouraged to dispose of two bodies today."

She motioned to her companions. "Get on with this. Other business summons us today, so clear this body from here. We'll leave Draco to clean up this mess."

The men reached forward to haul the corpse away, but the girl still held her mother, lost in a daze. The men glanced at the cloaked woman, but she rolled her eyes at their seeming helplessness.

"Must I do everything myself?"

She didn't need to, though. Alena and Alika stepped forward, wrenching the girl from her mother.

"Well, someone knows how to do their job. I thought I had two bodies to dispose of, after all." The cloaked woman looked pleased with them.

The four men hauled the body up, carrying it from the room, while the cloaked woman glared at Draco. "We'll be leaving now. Our part is done. Get to cleaning this up, Draco."

On her way out, she passed the girl struggling against her captors. "Oh, come dear, stop with the tears. I'm sure she thought of how much she would miss you as she took her last breath. No worries, though. You still have your father." She laughed and departed.

Alena and Alika loosened their grip on the girl once the cloaked woman and her companions left. The girl faced her father. Alika saw uncontrollable hate and rage flashing in the girl's eyes, something he had never witnessed from her. Worse, a darkness radiated from her that neither Alena nor Alika had ever felt. Alika's heart sank. It appeared that all the teachings and training he had bestowed upon the child had been lain to waste in a single moment.

"How could you? You killed her and laughed as you did it. You threw her out like trash. Like you always treated her. I hate you," she spat the words at him.

"The feeling is mutual. As for your dearly departed mother, I should have done this a long time ago." Draco glared at his daughter with equal hate.

The girl moved toward her father. "You won't get away with this. You'll die for what you did today. I'll make sure of it."

"Oh, and you're going to be the one to avenge? You are nothing but a child, a waste of one at that. I do not fear you. If you had come a moment sooner, I could have eliminated both of you."

The girl had heard enough, and she launched herself at him in fury. She vowed to tear him to pieces for what he did. He grabbed one arm and began to bend it back. She screamed as fierce pain shoot through it, but she forced herself to ignore it. She could rip him apart with the other arm, and either way, she already felt his grasp loosening on the one arm. He would pay. To her surprise, she felt hands grab her roughly, pull her back, and throw her to the ground. Two of Draco's employees stood ready and waiting to repel here again if necessary.

Draco knelt in front of his daughter with mocking eyes. "This looks familiar. I suggest you heed this warning better than your mother unless you want to leave through the backdoor for disposal as she did. You will do as you are told and stay out of my way. If not, you see where it leads." He rose to his full height, looking down his nose at the pitiful creature he called daughter. "Get up now, to your feet before me, you worthless child."

The girl just stared up at him, making no move to get up. One of Draco's employees hollered at her, "You heard your father. Get up, girl," as both employees yanked her up to face her father. The girl turned back at her captors in surprise. For the first time, she realized it was Alena and Alika who held her.

Draco smiled. "Much better. Now, look at me."

The girl remained focused on the ground, lost in her grief and confusion.

Draco's smile disappeared. "I said, look at me." He lifted the girl's chin and slapped her. She gazed at him with tears streaming down her cheeks. "Your mother no longer lives to shield you. I have no use for you. Do not defy me. I will not hesitate to end your life."

Draco turned and walked off. His daughter used the last bit of her strength to break from her captors and attack Draco one more time. Her escape was only momentary, and they caught her. Draco turned to face his daughter again, looking simultaneously amused and angry.

Her captors pushed her to her knees, pulling her arms behind her forcefully. One knelt beside her, growling, "This time, don't try anything. You'll learn respect."

Draco smirked. "That is a proper position for you. Perhaps you can be taught yet."

His daughter lifted her face, her eyes glowering nothing but hate. She made one final lunge for him. One of her captors sighed, positioned himself in front of her. He delivered a sharp blow to her stomach, leaving her to fall unconscious into the arms of the other captor, who let her drop to the floor.

Draco looked at his two employees with delight as if he wanted to clap for them. "You two did exceptionally well controlling her. I must admit, this day proved most entertaining."

The two nodded. One of them spoke, "Not a problem, Draco, except she will try to go after you again. Let us get her in line for you. I promise, we can break her for you, and she won't cause you any more problems."

"Well, I saw your results firsthand today. She's all yours. Do as you wish with her as long as she stays out of my way. I don't care to know your methods. I wish I could get someone as skilled to help me with other things around here, like my business enterprises. Actually, I'm not concerned now. I expect, after today, things will go smoother there as well."

"Maybe it will, for you. You're in a tricky business, though. People in your line of work encounter more problems with getting the shipments where they need to go than you would think. They simply don't discuss them; it would be bad for business. The more sensitive the shipment, the harder it gets, but you know how that works. You're the businessman—too risky a business for me. Don't want to make the wrong person mad. Why this is much safer work, right?" The man chuckled, and his associate smiled.

Draco laughed. "Yes, stay where your talent lies, right?"

"Of course. We'll haul the girl to her room, so we don't have to knock her out again. She'll learn soon enough, Draco." He began to help his associate carry the girl to her room before casting his gaze at the shattered glass and blood littering the floor. "After I get the girl taken care of, do you want me to clean this up for you?"

"I like you more and more."

⸺ꝫꝫ⸺

The girl woke up in her room, feeling like she'd been run over by a ship. She opened her eyes to find Alena sitting at her bedside, peering anxiously at her. The girl noticed Alena motion to her side, and Alika approached her. Could it be one big nightmare? No, the brutal truth slammed into her as all the images flooded back, and she hurt too much in every way. She couldn't understand why the two people she trusted the most betrayed her as they did today. Now they hunched over her as if they cared. Anger burned through her again, and she started to sit up. She couldn't, though. Her head began to spin, but it didn't matter. The rising fury carried her over the wave of nausea. She sat up in bed and faced her two teachers with daggers in her eyes. "Has this been the plan all along with my father? Is this a sick game you're playing?"

Alika watched her. "Is that what you believe?"

"You treated me as your prisoner. My father just killed my mother before me, and he smeared it in front of me over and over again seconds after. He beat me in front of you, and you let him. You dragged me away. You became his new best friend. Yeah, I heard it. You even cleaned up after him. Are you serious? After all that, you really wonder why I think you played me all this time?"

Alena gazed at her this time. "Yet, do you think after all the time we spent with you, all the training, that is who we are?"

The girl continued seeming to ignore them, her rage gaining momentum and her head still spinning. "I was right, you know. My father deserved to die for what he did. I had him. With all the training, I could have overpowered and ended him right there for killing Mother. He should die. You should have let me kill him, but you stopped me. Why would you do that? You are supposed to help me. I trusted both of you."

Alika continued to look at her steadily. "We did help you. You cannot see it in your turmoil."

The girl continued at a breathless speed, but tears began to stream down her face uncontrollably. She tried to hold onto the anger, but she no longer could. She attempted to process the avalanche of emotions pouring through her, but it overwhelmed her.

"Why didn't I get there in time? Just another minute, and I could have helped her, but I didn't. Mother and I could have killed him. But would you have stopped us? I don't know what side you're on anymore. I can't trust you. I don't understand after all this time we spent together. Now both of you are acting concerned for me. None of it makes sense. My poor mother. Did you see all the blood? Of course, you did. You helped him clean it. Why would you do that? He laughed after he killed her. He made a joke. Did you hear him? And the cloaked woman too. I should kill her as well. They all just threw mother out with the garbage. I can't ..." The girl could no longer continue and began to sob.

Alena stroked the girl's hair. Finally, the girl quieted again.

Tears streamed down Alena's face as she whispered to the girl, "Do you believe we could ever betray you?"

The girl gazed at both of them with tears still pouring from her eyes, her voice pleading, "No, but I can't understand what happened today. Help me, please."

Alika reached over and clasped the girl's hand. "Child, your mother gave me the task to train you. She knew the dangers of it from the beginning because of your father. That is why everything was done as it was from the start. However, she understood you should be trained, so she determined it worth the cost. Today my responsibility in training you meant ensuring your safety, which, in this case, meant saving your life. Yet it had to be done in a way where nothing would be discovered. Your mother took great lengths to hide it, and so it could not be uncovered today. We said and did a great many things we didn't want to, but it was necessary to gain your father's confidence. He spoke correctly when he said your mother is no longer here to shield you. We took the steps necessary to safeguard our appearance in the household and preserve your life."

The girl tried processing what Alika said. It made sense. The words hurt, but she understood. Even though it did, one question burst out.

"My father deserved to die for what he did. Even if everything ended up being discovered, I don't care. Why didn't you let me kill him?"

"Draco chose his path, and it will lead to his own destruction. You won't be the one to strike the blow. Assuming we allowed you to do so, you would strike him down in revenge. It went against everything you were taught." Alika took a deep breath. "Child, a great darkness overwhelmed you as you faced your father, about to kill him. With Alena's assistance, I taught you, but ultimately you must choose your path. Your father chooses a path of great darkness, and he is its slave. You are at a crossroads. It is time to choose which path you will take. If you choose to continue on the one path, we can resume your training. But if you travel the path of darkness, we cannot."

She sighed deeply and looked back up at her teachers, her eyes vacant. "I understand. Give me time to think."

Alika rose from her bedside. "Child, your mother wanted you trained because you have a special purpose to accomplish. She knew that beyond today. Do not dismiss it."

Alena hugged the girl, and both Alena and Alika left the room. As they turned back, the girl continued staring straight ahead in her bed. Once the door shut, the girl collapsed down in her bed and sobbed again.

Alena eyed Alika, worried. "What do you think she's going to decide? She sees her father. Surely, she couldn't choose such a path, Alika?"

He sounded tired. "I don't know. I never thought she would consider it. But the look in her eyes today, I'm afraid for her."

CHAPTER NINE

The girl cried until she thought no tears remained but more flowed. Alena and Alika checked on her the next morning, but she did not answer. They knew she lingered still in the room, but she was not yet ready to emerge. They left her alone, giving her the time she needed. During these three days, the girl wavered back and forth, like one of the flowers in the wind she would glimpse in her mother's garden. She knew what she needed to do and what her heart told her. Then she would see Draco's laughing face leaning over her mother's body, and only one path stood before her. At that moment, she'd willingly throw away the training, the teachings, all of it to the darkest corner of the universe if she could be the one to avenge her mother's death. The afternoon of the third day, the girl found herself collapsed from exhaustion after crying again. She awoke, and it was pitch dark in her room. Too dark for the hour. She summoned the light but still nothing. She sat up and felt cold in her room. Not just cold, freezing. Then she sensed it. Darkness. Every time one of those people entered the house, or her father entered the room, she felt the same darkness. She hated the darkness. She saw or sensed no one in her room, but she could see nothing after all. Surprisingly, though she felt the darkness, she did not feel the usual reaction to shrink from it. It seemed foolish to fear it as she had in the past.

She heard a whisper, a haunting voice, "Yes, there is nothing to fear. Come."

She heard another voice before always encouraging her, echoing the teachings of Alika, Alena, and her mother, but this voice was different, unfamiliar.

"You feared the darkness too long. You do have a purpose, one yet to be unlocked, but discover it on your own," the voice said.

The girl stood from her bed. No light entered the room, but somehow it appeared easier to see in the darkness. Either she became more accustomed to the darkness, or it was not pitch dark anymore. Inside, the girl knew neither explanation could be possible, but she ignored it.

"You are right. With your training and will, you can avenge her death. She was innocent of this slaughter done to her, so be strong and make him answer for her murder. You know it to be true. You are capable of so much more. They are holding you back. There is a path for which you do not see yet. Let me show you," the voice continued.

Before the girl realized it, she answered out loud, "How?"

"Fearing darkness are tales told to scare children, nothing more. The path of darkness does not lead to destruction, as you were told. It is full of power and glory. Come to me, cloth yourself in it, and I will help you gain what you truly seek."

The girl peered down, and it seemed as if there was a path she could see even in the darkness before her. She stood there for what seemed like forever, staring at the path in the darkness. She took a deep breath and tentatively stepped forward. Instantly, a fiery pain spread over the bottom of her foot that threatened to seize her whole body. Almost simultaneously came wetness. She understood. It must be the edge of her spear or sword she practiced with a few days ago. How was it possible? She always put both under her bed to prevent such a thing from happening. She bled from the wound, and in the darkness, somehow, she could see a pool of blood forming around her foot. The girl felt sick with horror as an image of her mother's dead body materialized in the pool of blood. Her father's laughter echoed throughout the room though she knew he was not anywhere around. She stepped back, but it was still pitch dark and freezing cold. Even worse, the darkness hung in the room, but now it seemed to suffocate her. Then she remembered Alika's earlier words and understood. She couldn't get rid of it because it originated from her now. She felt the abhorrence for it return to her, as she always felt, but now she could not escape. It entrapped her, and she did not realize its strangling grip until now.

The cloaked woman's laughter joined in to fill the room. The girl was no better than her father, the cloaked lady, any of them. She had tossed aside everything like it meant nothing, much like they dumped her mother's body. She murmured, "No, no ..." Her mother had poured her life's blood out for her, to be trained, to be kept safe, sacrificed everything for her. This is what she did with such a precious gift?

"What have I done?" she whispered. She fell to her knees at the side of her bed and allowed the wracking sobs to consume her. Her bleeding foot no longer mattered, and she no longer felt the pain of it. She didn't know how to recover what she had lost.

"I am with you, always, wherever you are. *That* is why you do not need ever to fear the darkness," a voice softly reminded her.

She knew this whisper. The familiar, encouraging one she trusted from the beginning with her mother and continued with Alika and Alena. Her sobs quieted. She needed to hear it.

"You will pass through darkness; it must be at times. However, you must not become a part of the darkness. You must not clothe yourself in it. That is why you found yourself so hopeless. You allowed it to gain entrance," the whisper continued.

"But I don't want it anymore. I messed up. I know now which path to take," the girl pleaded.

"You already know what to do, child. I'm always here. Never forget."

She did know what to do. Immediately, she stood from her bedside and turned around. It was still pitch black, cold, and the darkness persisted there. Her voice became steady and firm. "I have no fear of the darkness because I do not walk alone in the darkness if I must pass through it. I chose my path, and I will continue that path, the one I know from the beginning. You cannot be a part of me because I do not belong to you. I hate you, and you will never be a part of me. Leave me now."

The unfamiliar voice returned, and a storm of voices rose with it. "No, you don't know what you're throwing away. The path you choose is full of pain. You will see. You can still come. Do you think it is so easy to get rid of the darkness?"

The girl answered back, and her voice reflected the same firmness. "The darkness will always lurk, trying to gain access, so it will never be easy. But I do not belong to you and never will. I will be rid of you. You spoke in half-truths, for it is your way. I understand the path I chose, and my choice stands. Now, I say, leave me. You are no longer welcome here."

Without warning, many voices screamed in rage, and a strong blast of wind tore through the room. Then a hiss of vapor in the air, and finally, silence.

The girl smiled. The chill left the room, and the normal darkness of evening came, but nothing more.

"It's gone," she whispered. The darkness has departed from the room because it was gone from her. She summoned the light, and the room lit up on cue. She realized her cut foot no longer hurt. To her surprise, she spied no pool of blood and no spear or sword on the floor. She checked under her bed, finding her practice weapons stored safely underneath, just as she had left them. She sat on her bed to examine her foot. Not a single mark could be found upon it. Tears streamed down her face, but different from the ones shed for the past few days. She went to the bathroom connected to her room and splashed water on her face. A half-drunk water bottle still sat on the dresser with an open pack of snack bread rations. She finished it along with more of another water bottle and was once again thankful for the preparations they always made with living under the same roof with her volatile father. A trip to the kitchen was not always advisable. She would finally get a real meal tomorrow, but now her exhaustion won over all else. She had stayed in her room these days, but she did not sleep at all. Tonight, she got in bed, and briefly hesitated to turn the light out, but she smiled and said, "Lights off." She did not fear the darkness because she was not alone in it. As she drifted off to sleep, she heard a familiar whisper.

"Sleep, my child."

And she did for the first time in days.

CHAPTER TEN

Alika and Alena knocked on the girl's door the fourth morning. This time the door opened for them. They found the girl showered, dressed, and looking out her window. She turned to face them. Her eyes held the usual calmness they had seen in her before the past days' events.

"Please, I'm ready for you to continue with my training."

"Are you sure you're ready?" Alena gently pressed her. She was anxious after the girl's ordeal.

"Yes, more than I ever thought, surprisingly."

"I believe you are," said Alika looking at her attentively, sensing a change.

"Let's sit." The girl proceeded to tell them of the preceding night's event. She paused when she finished. "Everything from last night, I was taught from the beginning by mother, by you, and Alena. I knew it, but I didn't until I grasped it last night. It's hard to explain."

Alika put his hand on the girl's and placed it over her heart as he spoke, "You owned it. It became yours last night. You understood it at this level."

"Yes, that's it!" exclaimed the girl. "And something else. I felt as if in the middle of a battle, more exhausting than a whole day with the sunspear."

"Yes, a different battle which required a much different weapon. You came to a crossroads and had to choose a path at a vulnerable time," said Alika.

"Yes, I'm glad I was given what I needed to come through it. I'm also relieved it's over."

"What are your thoughts now?" questioned Alika, his eyes gentle.

On the surface, it seemed a strange question. However, the girl understood the root of Alika's inquiry. She still grieved her mother's loss, but she didn't care about her father any longer and getting him back for what he did. His actions would catapult him ever quicker to his demise. From what she perceived and the cloaked woman's words, she believed his end approached soon. She accepted her focus needed to be completing her training. Although uncertain of what future lay ahead for her, she gained a whole new appreciation for the sacrifice made to ensure her training. So, she understood why they needed to know her frame of mind after the encounter they witnessed between her and her father.

Alika nodded after listening to the girl, satisfied with her answer. "We're ready to move forward in your training. Also, I know by now, you are familiar with how your mother caused havoc for your father's business enterprises. It's necessary for your mother's efforts to continue. As it does, the same individuals will become increasingly unhappy with your father, and his day of reckoning will come."

"I must be careful he doesn't move his focus to me when I take over for Mother. If so, he'll get rid of me before the others eliminate him."

Alena nodded. "We worked on that while you recuperated. Your father believes we're wonderful employees. We convinced him he needed cameras for these rooms, particularly since he experienced his daughter's temper. Of course, we control what he sees on his side of the camera. It will be creative, so he doesn't get suspicious. He doesn't realize there have been cameras around the house for a long time now. He underestimated your mother in countless ways. We also reconfigured the room doors to us, so we don't get any surprise visits from him. It ensures we have plenty of time to be back if need be. We hacked further into the communications he gets and those he sends out. Again, he won't be aware of what's happening with his shipping operations. He'll think things are going relatively problem-free with the occasional mishap and find out too late that's not the case at all. Your mother was already doing all of this to an extent, but we've enhanced it. We conveniently planted ideas in his head that he's not alone in his shipping problems. We're hoping he warms up to the idea that there are a fair number of *pirates* out there stealing shipments and selling them to the highest bidder."

"Wow, you two were busy."

Alika said, "Yes, and your father also stayed busy as you would expect. The official report he gave is your mother was outside, and he heard a scream. He rushed out too late and found her on the ground, bleeding out. A couple of men ran away from her body, and he could not catch them. As for you, you're so devastated by the news you refuse to leave your room for all your tears. Your father vowed to find the men who did this and bring them to justice."

"I would expect nothing less of him than to be sure he prepared a proper story. He's assured no one will pursue it. The galaxy is too full of trouble everywhere to investigate it. Of course, there are so many attacks across the galaxy with the warring powers; he could place blame there as well. I'm sad but not surprised in the least."

They were all quiet momentarily, and the girl got up. "A new day of training awaits. Let's get started."

They set off, following the girl's lead today.

—ele—

"A fine job, child," commented Alika.

"Yes, excellent. I'm excited for you," agreed Alena.

The girl held the weapon up. She had spent two whole days completing the sunspear. Now would be the task of learning to use and control it. She turned to Alena and Alika. "Are you sure I'm ready?"

Alena and Alika both smiled and said in unison, "Yes."

"Starting tomorrow, you and Alena will practice exclusively with the sunspears. Alena got her sunspear a bit earlier than you, but not by much."

"I'm sure she'll teach me as much as she has done already."

"It'll come as easy to you as the rest does. There's no doubt in my mind," said Alena with a smile.

CHAPTER ELEVEN

Dante and Seth exited the ship with a squadron of their troops. The pilot took the ship back to join the battle in the air.

Dante sized up the field. There were about eighty of the Black Dragon men approaching, primarily machines. Their helmets resembled the face of a dragon, and their fake armor was akin to black scales. Dante nodded to Seth. Their squadron should be able to take the Black Dragon army head-on with those numbers. Dante signaled the squadron, and they attacked. Seth and Dante stayed close to each other to monitor any changes in the Black Dragon Army. Dante spun around with his sunspear. The Black Dragon men tried to raise their swords to hit Dante, but he caught them first with the point of the sunspear. The weapon found its mark time and time again. Nearby, Seth swung his staff, and many of his enemies met the razor-sharp edge of it. Dante finished dismantling one of the Black Dragon men with his sunspear then stopped. He pulled himself from the battle and looked pointedly at Seth.

"Did you hear it?" Dante shouted.

"Yes," Seth yelled back.

Dante pointed over the nearby hill. Seth nodded in the affirmative.

"Fall back," Dante hollered to the squadron.

The men followed Dante's commands. They understood now, waiting with bated breath for Dante's and Seth's plan to unfold.

Dante took a scanner out, and Seth came to stand beside Dante.

"Four for sure. I can't tell beyond that," Dante said.

"Not bad even with more troops behind them," Seth mused.

"No, it's not," Dante mumbled. He was happy about it, but something continued to nag him about the attack. "You want me to take care of them while you and the squadron cover me?"

"Yes, let's get to it."

Seth turned around to the army and signaled them while Dante got closer. Seth and the army stepped forward, pushing on a metal device on their arm. With a motion, each device opened to form a shield in front of them. They got closer to deflect the shots, enabling Dante to reach his target.

Over the hill, all four of the photon tanks charged ahead to destroy anyone in their path. They were big and ugly, like everything else in the Black Dragon Army. They had the same dragon shape to them but also resembled a tank. The shaft that the photon blast erupted from gaped in the shape of a dragon mouth.

***

Meanwhile, Caleb was at the helm in the sky with his squadron, trying to eliminate the Black Dragon's forces attacking the planet.

"Okay, everyone, you know your assignments. No trying to get the command ship involved unless necessary. My ship will keep an eye on it. Let's go."

Caleb would try the strategy anyway. They had to knock out the squadron ships first if they stood any chance against the command ship. Fighting both at the same time could end up too costly for his group. Of course, the battle strategy might not be sustainable for long, but they would see. Caleb spun the ship in and out between enemy ships, dodging and blasting simultaneously. He had always been one of the best pilots around, and so the blasts found their mark. His squadron pinpointed their targets as well. He'd trained with many of them.

Everything seemed to be going as planned for Caleb's squadron. They took minimal damage, with only a couple of ships leaving the battle rather than getting shot out of the sky. The Black Dragon lost several ships, and others sustained heavy damage. Caleb saw them fly from the battle to avoid the total loss of the ship. Likely, the Black Dragon ship's pilot was mostly machine, like what Seth and Dante had fought on the surface. Evidently, the Black Dragon was trying to save resources as well. Caleb felt confident so far about the damage they placed on the Black Dragon.

Out of nowhere, he heard a massive blast in the sky. Caleb groaned. "There went hoping the command ship stayed out of it. Guess it's time to divide our time between finishing off the rest of the squadron and giving the command ship a little share of the fireworks."

His co-pilot sighed in agreement. "All right, everyone, you heard Caleb. The command ship demands some of our attention."

Dante reached one of the tanks, moving fast before they got too close to Seth and the others. He climbed up to the top, but not before one of the Black Dragon men spotted him and started to climb up to yank him off. He caught Dante's foot and almost succeeded in pulling him back to the ground. Dante hit the man with the sunspear, freeing himself from his enemy's grip. However, once Dante turned, the end of the tank shaft narrowly missed slamming into him. The men inside the tank realized something was happening on top. His time was running out. He cut a hole through the top of the tank and jumped inside, taking out the two Black Dragon men and commandeering the tank's operation. Turning the machine around, he aimed the cannon at one of the opposing tanks. He fired three times before turning his attention to the third tank and repeating his assault. He had pushed it hard enough and climbed swiftly out the top of the tank. As expected, the last tank operator saw the other machine firing on its own, and a couple of minutes later, the fourth tank blasted it into pieces. Dante got out in time, unbeknown to the fourth tank operator, who counted Dante among the pile of flaming rubble.

"One more to go," said Dante as he got up from the ground. He glimpsed something shiny out of the corner of his eye and moved to the side, barely in time to avoid the edge of a sword from a Black Dragon soldier that had sneaked up on him.

"Really, there's no time to deal with you." He returned the blows from the Black Dragon soldier as the tank crept closer to Seth and the others. With a quick blow to the waist with the sunspear, Dante finished off the Black Dragon soldier and ran for his target.

Dante got to the tank and used his sunspear to dislodge one of the tracks, slowing that vehicle to a crawl. He worked fast as they would be checking to see why it stopped. He used his sunspear to punch a hole in the fuel line and threw the firestone inside the hull. Once he turned to clear it, he discovered a circle of Black Dragon men closing in around him. He had to clear the tank, but he didn't want to find the end of a Black Dragon sword either. He rushed them at full speed. The move surprised them, and Dante used it. They prepared for Dante to attack them head-on, but instead, he plunged his sunspear into the ground and catapulted himself over their heads. He landed smoothly behind them with his sunspear and ran. Immediately, a giant explosion ripped through the silence as the tank burst into a ball of fire. The Black Dragon soldiers had stood too close to the tank and were lost in the fireball. Dante doubled back to Seth and the squadron now that he took care of the tanks.

He expected to see an army of Black Dragon soldiers remaining, but found little work left for his sunspear. Dante glanced at Seth, puzzled, but told himself Seth and the squadron had made fast work of the Black Dragon troops. "I guess I took longer with the tanks than I thought."

"No, that was one of the fastest times yet, Dante. These are the days you should thank me for all those extra training sessions." Seth chuckled. "There does appear to be a scattered few still fighting," Seth said it with the hesitancy Dante felt. "They retreated over the hill, but there is nothing there as far as I could tell. We could check it out before our ship comes to get us." Seth stopped, seemingly still in thought.

Seth and Dante realized it at the same time.

"I'm betting the space over the hill is big enough for a transport ship," Dante said.

They both ran toward the hill, and Dante motioned for the squadron to follow them.

Seth and Dante now could see the ship lifting off the ground from about a fourth of a mile away after the last soldier entered it. Seth, Dante, and the squadron could only watch helplessly.

Dante got his data pad out. "Hey, Lana, Caleb, a transport ship left here with Black Dragon soldiers. So, you have company. I don't know where they're going. They could be adding to the air battle or going somewhere else to attack."

"Got it, Dante. I'll get back to you. Caleb says it's kind of strange here now. I'm not sure what the transport ship adds to the scene."

"Strange as in?"

"Not sure, but we'll be in touch. Sit tight."

"What do we do now, Seth?"

"You heard the lady, sit tight."

Up in the sky, Caleb tried to follow his own strategy, as did his squadron.

"Caleb, we tried getting shots in at the squadron and the command ship. Not working out for us, though," reported Commander Ryan.

"Yeah, I see that. Okay, everyone, different strategy. Strive to avoid getting your ships hit. Pull back. Return fire only to get a fighter off your tail, off a friend's tail, or if you can get a clear shot."

Caleb turned to his co-pilot. "I thought the command ship was joining the fight, but it doesn't look like it. It appears to be trying to take the heat off the squadron, and the squadron is headed back toward the command ship."

His co-pilot nodded. "They're conserving their ships, which doesn't make sense. They possess a ton more resources than us."

Caleb said, "I agree, but this is beginning to be a familiar scene."

Then they heard the transmission from Seth and Dante. Lana asked, "Caleb, did you hear them?"

"Yeah, I don't know what the extra ship means for us, but we'll see soon enough, Lana."

"Anyone's guess. Just watch and see if you spot it."

"Tell Dante we'll get back to them when we know more."

"Already did. Love ya."

"Back at you, sweetheart."

"Do you see anything?" Caleb asked his co-pilot, but they spotted the transport ship at the same instant. It sought to go unnoticed. It didn't engage any of the ships and made no effort to become a part of the battle at hand. Instead, it headed straight toward the command ship to position itself directly behind it. Caleb noticed all the squadron now clustered themselves beside the command ship, and all turned to leave together. They headed toward the portal.

"Should we pursue?"

"No, I like to know what I'm walking into first."

His co-pilot nodded in agreement.

"Lana, did you see all that?"

"Yeah, Caleb, and I'm not sure what to think either."

"We'll get Dante, Seth, and the squadron off the planet, and we'll see you."

The Black Dragon command ship and the rest of the squadron passed through the portal. The admiral on the command ship waited for enough time to lapse before motioning to one of his officers.

The officer nodded. "There's no sign they followed us, sir."

"I'll inform the Black Dragon Commander," said the admiral.

The admiral walked away and into his chamber. He opened a channel to the Black Dragon Commander.

"Admiral, I trust everything went well," said the Black Dragon Commander with a smile.

"Yes, sir. We used little of our resources and will begin repairs on the ships. We lost a fair amount of troops, but we didn't send many just as planned. The rest left in the transport ship. We did lose all four of the tanks, so there is no salvaging them."

"Strange, you would think the tanks harder for them to beat."

"Sir, I believe, from the report, it was someone with a sunspear who defeated them. One report identified the individual as Dante."

"I suppose that explains where our tanks are going. No matter. What is the rest of the report?"

"We left, and they did not follow. With our resources, we could put a crushing blow on their forces."

"However, you didn't. I understand it took everything in you not to do so. Remember why we mounted this attack today. Admiral, have patience and follow this to the endgame. They have no idea?"

"No, sir, they do not. Done and secured according to your wishes."

"You accomplished your goal. I am happy, and that should make you happy. Continue to make me happy, admiral." said the Black Dragon Commander with a slight edge to his voice.

"Yes, sir," said the admiral with a forced smile as he swallowed the lump in his throat. He was relieved when the transmission ended. He had seen the Black Dragon Commander unhappy, and he knew he needed to keep the Commander happy if he wanted to stay in one piece.

The Black Dragon Commander would transmit the update to the Dark Lord shortly. The commander sat back in thought over the information. He always felt mixed reactions when he heard of his son battling on the other side. It angered him greatly, more than he wanted to admit. Yet, something else stirred. He couldn't help but feel a sense of pride at the boy's skills, even if it continued to be at the expense of his army's hardware. His son was certainly impressive. He vowed to get him to see and use his skills here. The Black Dragon Commander reminded himself to take his own advice and be patient. The Dark Lord and his army would destroy the Elders and everything they held dear, but Dante would not be destroyed. His son would see the truth, and they would be on the same side. The Black Dragon Commander determined to see this to its endgame as well.

CHAPTER TWELVE

Alena and the girl finished a round of sparring and sat with Alika to rest.

The girl sat down and looked out, seeming lost.

Alika studied her face. "What are you thinking, child?"

The girl focused back on Alika and Alena. "There's something I need to ask you. The visions. They're becoming more frequent, but they aren't like the others."

"In what way?" asked Alika.

"A couple of ways. I don't feel the need to act on them, like in the past. It's as if I'm truly a spectator. Also, I don't think they are set in the future. A great deal of it is from the past. Somehow, some of it ties into my past, but I don't recognize other parts of it." She paused. "And some is not my past at all."

"Are any of the visions alarming?" inquired Alena.

"I don't know how to answer that question—not alarming like the vision with Mother. Some images would be disturbing to most, but the galaxy is in a rather ugly place now. The words sound rather meaningless, after watching my father murder my mother and all the things he has his hands in too. I always knew, and as time went on, I understood more. She let me know in ways to keep me safe." She stopped to regain her composure. "So, the other reason is the visions confirm things I started to piece together on my own. As far as the visions of other people, I'm confused as to why I'm being shown them."

"Do you know the people in the visions where you're not involved?" asked Alena.

"I know of the individuals by name. Others I saw in person, but in many cases, only briefly."

"My guess is you need to keep watching, as you will use the information from the visions later, so at this point you are a mere spectator. I feel sure it will not always be the case with certain individuals in the visions. Continue to absorb the visions. Their purpose will be revealed at the proper time, and you'll know when to move on the visions," said Alika.

"I'm certain you're right about the visions involving other people's past." The girl replied and looked at Alika and Alena, waiting expectantly.

"It's time to piece together the visions involving you, to finish what you have already started," said Alika. His student had been patient, and it was time to give her the information she needed.

The girl told them what she saw, and Alika and Alena assisted in processing through it with her. The more answers the girl confirmed, the more she understood why everything had been done as it had. Her training continued, and the vision sharing sessions became a regular part of her time with Alika and Alena.

⁓ℓℓ⁓

The next day the girl found herself training in a nearby clearing with Alika and Alena. They had come here many times before, but it felt different today. The girl studied a point beyond the clearing.

Alika noticed her focus. "What captures your attention today, child?"

"I don't know." The girl mumbled, staring at the point beyond, but she began walking toward it.

Alika and Alena followed. Then they stopped and watched.

The girl continued to walk, and she saw a figure ahead. It called her to come closer, but the girl didn't feel threatened. In fact, she understood to approach the figure. The familiar voice she knew well encouraged her to come nearer. Without warning, she felt something change around her. It felt warmer, followed by sounds like the hissing of vapor. She realized it was getting hotter, and waves of heat turned into flames. Her spirit urged her forward, but she saw the flames in front of her. The figure became almost invisible among them. The girl's focus shifted to the fire and the fierce heat radiating from it.

"Why are you not coming?"

"I can't. The fire is hot."

"You did not think so before."

The girl was confused. The flames only now appeared. Why did the voice act as if the blaze was there from the beginning? "I'm scared." The girl continued to stare at the fire.

The voice made no response.

She glimpsed inside the flames, and while she could no longer see the figure, she knew it stood there somewhere. The girl stared at the fire again. Filled with doubt and fear, she hesitantly stretched her hand out, eyes focused on the flames, even as they stung her eyes. Fierce pain captured the end of her hand and she pulled it back, yelling in agony. She instinctively wrapped the end of her cloak around her fingers and fell to her knees. Immediately, Alika and Alena ran to her side.

"What happened?" asked Alena as she knelt beside the girl.

"My hand ... the flames burned it." The girl choked out, trying not to cry, but the pain was intense. She removed the cloak to uncover her severely burnt flesh and gasped at the sight. She glanced around frantically only to see nothing. No flames, no figure, and no sign of any fire in the clearing, other than her charred hands.

"Oh!" Alena gasped when she saw the girl's burns. "Let's get back to the house to tend to this." Alena helped the girl up.

"Come, child. She's right. We need to get relief for your hand." Alika saw the confusion in the girl's eyes.

They returned to the girl's room and cleaned up her hand in silence. They sprayed a substance on it, and her hand started to heal. Still, both Alena and Alika agreed one of the portable chambers would be a wise idea for the next couple of days to ensure the wound healed properly. The girl inserted her hand into what resembled a sturdy clear bag. It sealed at once on her hand above where the burn started. There was a small valve to insert the needed medicine, which they did.

The girl sat on her bed with Alika and Alena beside her. Her hand felt better as her skin regenerated, but nothing else felt good. Confusion overwhelmed her again. She thought she had progressed so far in her training, and now she was at the beginning again.

"Did you see the figure today?"

Alika and Alena exchanged a look. Alena answered for them. "Yes, we saw a figure before you."

"Did you see the flames today?"

Alika answered this time, "What do you think?"

The girl studied them. "I don't know. I'm not sure why I asked because it doesn't matter. It was my test, not yours, and I failed. I know it's important. I need to be alone to figure it out."

"If we can help …" Alena left the rest unsaid as she squeezed the girl's uninjured hand before exiting the room.

Alika stood up and smiled at the girl. "Don't be disheartened. You've learned more than you believe. This is a hard lesson, but you're right in that it's worth the learning, child."

The girl stared straight ahead in her bed, lost in her failure. Alika and Alena closed the door behind them. Tears streamed down her face. She began to understand why she failed and knew it was a test she would see many more times. She also realized, next time, the cost would be much higher than a burnt hand. Again, the girl found herself collapsed on her bed in tears.

The girl did not leave her room for two days. Alena and Alika left her alone. They would know when she was ready. The girl, for her part, did much struggling. She found this part of her training as difficult as any. It drained her on a different level. She could spar all day with Alena, and it did not deplete her anywhere close to the same level. However, she could not fail again. It was not a simple training exercise. It represented much more, and so her failure shook her to the core. The encounter exposed an unpleasant truth in her again, forced her to face it, and wrestle with it. Later, it could cost dearly. She didn't need a vision to show her this truth.

On the third morning, Alena and Alika heard movement in the girl's room to indicate she was up and ready. They knocked as before and heard the girl's voice indicating for them to enter the room. She stood up, already showered and dressed.

She turned to them, her blue eyes again at peace, and smiled. "Thank you for giving me time."

Alika smiled. "I believe you used it well."

The girl nodded. "I hope so."

"Can we examine your hand?" Alena asked.

"Sure, it feels much better."

They sat, and the girl stretched her hand out for her mentors. Her hand appeared totally healed, and it didn't hurt anymore. Alena scanned it with a medical scanner for confirmation.

"Everything healed properly—no sign of infection. The skin tissue regenerated as normal. I don't think it will even leave a scar."

An unspoken awareness hung in the air. There would not be a sign of the incident on her hand, but it would be there, burned into her memory.

CHAPTER THIRTEEN

The girl continued training with Alena, developing her skills with the sun-spear. The girl also resumed the other parts of training, including becoming an excellent pilot. None of them discussed the incident involving her burned hand. They knew it would be a lesson revisited.

Two weeks later, the girl found herself in the same clearing with Alena and Alika. They arrived back from one of the training sessions on the ship. Upon approaching the clearing after hiding the ship, a familiar sensation came over her.

She turned to Alika and Alena and nodded. They understood and stopped. They would wait for her.

The girl focused on the clearing again. A short distance ahead, she spied the same figure from two weeks ago, beckoning to her. The girl walked firmly forward, her eyes locked on the figure. Suddenly, the girl felt it become warmer, and she heard the slight hiss of the vapor as before. Yet this time, her entire focus stayed in front of her.

A snake-like voice hissed, "The flames will burn you alive. How can you be so foolish? Turn back." It was the unfamiliar voice that spoke to her from the darkness in her room.

The girl did not respond to it, or even acknowledge it. She continued walking.

She could feel the heat, but she knew her entire focus must be getting to the figure, trusting the voice beckoning her to come. She saw the flames in front of her now, but this time she walked forward, keeping the firm pace she started. Even as she stepped through it, she knew she should be burning up. She didn't, though. It was like the hottest summer day she had experienced. The figure wavered in the heat waves sometimes, but the girl could always see the form. Finally, the girl stood before it, drenched in sweat but untouched by the flames in all other respects. At once, the temperature become normal around her, and the hissing of vapor ceased. The girl did not need to look around her to know the fire vanished.

The figure was a tall, slender lady with blonde hair pulled back on each side and golden pins in the shape of a dove. She wore an ankle-length turquoise dress with a white cloak on top.

The figure smiled at the girl. "You found your way this time."

The girl stared at her hand, remembering her past failure. "Yes." She started to say more, but the lump in her throat stopped anything further.

"Oh, come, child, you did well. You reached me, so you understand part of the lesson. I am here to help you with the rest."

The girl looked intently at the woman, listening.

"You walked through the flames. They did not burn you as before but were as hot as the last time. The fire would consume your whole body this time, but you stayed focused on coming to me. You trusted the voice which commanded you to do so. You were not distracted by anything else, including the flames or the competing voice persuading you to turn back. Although, I perceive you understand that part."

"Yes."

"I believe you discerned what this is about as well. It's not the passing of a test or getting through a wall of flames. You have a purpose, something you keep being reminded of by those around you. You will need to remember all your teachings, including this lesson, to fulfill your purpose. What you see may not be a wall of flames to conquer, but it will feel as such. The darkness will always attempt a ploy to distract you from hearing the voice you know to trust, but you must focus on the One voice in the midst of the struggle."

"In my room that night after Mother was killed, the darkness said the path I chose would be hard. I said it spoke in half-truths, and that was one of the few things it said which was true. Yet I know this is the right path."

"You're right. You chose a difficult path. There will be struggles to overcome, harder than you can imagine. Take this knowledge and use it in the trials to come."

As the girl watched, to the side of the figure, a scene with trees appeared. A window opened, but it displayed solidly somehow. The girl watched, transfixed at the paradox. A flame emerged upon the trees and began burning. Within a few seconds, the entire scene was reduced to a pile of ash, eaten up by the blaze, casting a shadow on everything in the clearing. The flame disappeared.

A sinking feeling settled on her as she regarded the pile of ashes. She continued to watch, and the flame appeared again on the other side of the figure. At first, the girl only saw the flame. Then she saw something gradually form in the bright orange flickers. She stared entranced by the demonstration, wondering what the flame contained. It began to sparkle, and a beautiful diamond resulted. It caught every angle of the sunlight. The flame continued to burn, but it could do no damage to the diamond. If anything, the diamond sparkled more as it caught the light from the inferno. Gradually, the flame diminished until it could barely be seen in the diamond and then disappeared altogether.

The blonde woman peered at the girl with a smile. "Just like the flame, your struggles will do one of two things to you. They will burn you up, reduce you to nothing more than these ashes," she paused. "Then, there is the diamond, formed from heat and pressure. It is necessary for the diamond to endure the heat and pressure to reach its true form. The heat and pressure do not hurt it. Rather, nothing can break it because those conditions refined it, made it strong."

The girl could only look and nod.

"You will receive plenty of opportunities to decide which of these you will be. There are many struggles ahead for you, and many tears will spill from your eyes on this path you chose, child. Yet, which will you be, the rubble burned up by the flame or the diamond refined by your struggles?"

As the woman spoke, the ash reappeared on the ground to one side, and the diamond hovered on the other side.

Memories of the past swept over her, and she looked down. She shook her head as she gazed back up at the woman. "I know what I want to be, but I fail so much. I'll do it again. I'm afraid."

The girl heard the voice she knew, "And I'll pick you up again because I am always with you. You are never alone."

The lump in her throat returned, but for a different reason. She did know. She didn't simply get thrown aside.

The woman smiled at her. "Sometimes, you need a reminder. You knew the answer. Your heart desires to be the diamond in the flame of your struggles. If you find yourself losing your way for a time, you know how to find the path again. Always remember how you got through the flames. Focus on the voice of the One whom you know to trust, and you will get through whatever struggle lies ahead for you."

The girl watched in surprise as the figure reached for the diamond, and it came to rest in her hand. She was amazed further when the woman handed her the diamond.

"This is yours to keep."

The girl took the diamond. It was in her hands for an instant, and it disappeared. The girl peered up at the figure, puzzled.

"It remains with you. It will appear back to you when you need it. You will understand when the time comes."

"Does it do something out of the ordinary?"

"It is simply a diamond in one sense, as the sunspear is a weapon given by the Ancient One. Any power beyond what is given to the wielder is because the Ancient One chooses to do so. At the intended time, it will fulfill its purpose for you only."

"I understand. Thank you."

"I must take leave of you now, child. I delivered the message needed for today. Remember it along with the lessons of the past already given to you. You'll need them all for the struggles to come. Be the diamond in the flame of your struggles, and follow the voice of the One who is always with you."

The figure left her.

The girl rejoined Alena and Alika and recounted everything with them that transpired with the messenger.

CHAPTER FOURTEEN

Lana walked out to greet Caleb, Seth, and Dante.

Lana hugged Caleb and then searched his eyes. "What do you think our next move is?"

Caleb was thoughtful as he absently played with a strand of Lana's hair. "The commanders just got back, but the four of us should talk first before we involve them. They're tired, so they would be fine taking a breather."

Dante spoke up, "Commander Ryan would be perfect to work with them while we talk. He wouldn't mind while we compare notes."

Seth nodded. "He's a close friend and well-respected by his fellow commanders. He can run discussion among them of what they saw during the recent battles, and perhaps uncover something we missed."

"Dante and I were planning to talk with him earlier, but then the attack started." Caleb glanced at Lana, waiting to see if she agreed.

Lana nodded. "We'll see you inside."

Caleb gave Dante a friendly shove. "Come on, let's go say hi to Commander Ryan."

Caleb and Dante approached Ryan. Ryan turned around with a smile. He was in his mid-twenties, just like Caleb and Lana. He was good-looking with dark brown hair and matching brown eyes. His eyes could reflect the decisive demeanor needed for the role of commander but off the battlefield quickly switched to the more playful stance with his friends. "Commander Caleb and ..."

Caleb rolled his eyes and stopped him. "Come on, Ryan, stop with the formal stuff. Lana is not around with the other commanders to hear you."

Ryan laughed. "All right, Caleb, Dante, what have you two been doing besides beating up on the Black Dragon?"

Dante laughed too. "Well, I prefer long walks in the woods."

"Really? Who's the lucky girl?"

Caleb grinned. "He can't be roped any easier than you for any length of time. Those are Seth urged strolls he's talking about."

Ryan shook his head, still laughing. "Should have known. Dante, how long has he been your teacher? What did you do this time to make him mad?"

"Can't even remember. He just prescribes it now because he can. He says I should be grateful since it keeps me battle ready. These attacks eat into our time these days."

Ryan sighed. "No joke, and Lana isn't kidding about the attacks coming faster lately. My dad mentioned coming along today but figured he should stay behind. You don't know where the next attack will strike."

Caleb smiled. "Hang in there. We know we can count on you."

"Always. I got your back."

"Well, we need your help with something," said Dante.

"What's up?"

Caleb replied, "How about running a discussion with the commanders? We keep seeing the same pattern in the air battle. Like they're holding back. You saw how that command ship did?"

"Yeah, I've seen it, and it feels off to me as well.   I don't have the answer."

"I was tempted to follow through the portal today."

"Too risky. I'm glad you stayed put."

"Yeah, I guess. It gets stranger." He turned to Dante.

Dante nodded. "Seth and I caught them getting a whole batch of their troops out in a transport ship."

"Why would they be doing that?"

"To conserve their resources?"

"I got that. Still, why would they be doing that? They're not exactly hurting for troops."

"That would be the other puzzle."

"I wonder how long that one has been going on. If it's been every time too. Strange is right." Ryan shook his head.

Caleb sighed. "Yeah, we know. If you could check in with the commanders and see if they have any ideas that would be great. Maybe they saw something we didn't. I need to go over some details with the other three before we come back together."

"Consider it done. I'll take notes on the data pad. Anything that comes out at me in the brainstorming, I'll send it to you. Let us know when you're ready to come together again."

"Appreciate it, Ryan," said Caleb.

"Anytime. You two better get back for your meeting. Lana will be coming out to drag both of you inside, personally," Ryan said, laughing.

"Come on, Caleb, you know Ryan's right." He gave Caleb a friendly shove forward as they laughed.

"Are you two boys ready?" Lana asked in mock sternness as the two entered, still laughing.

"Always for you, Lana." Dante smiled.

"We're good to start, sweetheart." Caleb flashed his wife a reassuring grin.

"Where do we begin?" pressed Lana.

Seth spoke, "Something bothered Dante about these attacks. He mentioned it to me before the incident today."

Caleb agreed, "Yeah, Dante tried telling me, but the meeting started. We didn't get a chance to finish, so Dante go ahead."

"We're used to all-out attacks in the past. The attacks are personal for us after what they did to our homelands, our families. They've always wanted to do as much damage and hurt as many people as possible, but these attacks are different. Each time they possessed the means to cause a lot more destruction to our fleets, come with a much larger force. They don't. That part doesn't make sense. It feels like we're missing something."

Caleb chimed in, "I couldn't put my finger on it, but Dante nailed it. This last fight, they did the same thing as before, down to limiting their damages and conserving their ships. That tactic makes sense with our limited resources. For them, no. I thought about following them through the portal today, but I was afraid we'd fly into a trap. Maybe their whole army stood on the other side waiting."

Seth finished his unspoken thought, "But you knew they didn't. I believe the other side of the portal would reveal a mirror image of what you left. I think you're both right."

"It sounds like the attacks are for another purpose," Lana wondered aloud. "It's like being stuck in a rut. We're used to how they always attacked in the past. Now we see a different view from them, but we're still cramming them in the same mold, and it's what they want. We must view this differently to solve it."

"You hit on it, Lana. The other problem is there's not enough pause between attacks to solve it—we're repairing ships and getting resources together for the next attack. It's frustrating. I mean, this is the first time Caleb and I put together what troubled us about the attacks. While you're in the middle of battle, it's impossible to figure out this puzzle. Our focus is keeping the colony safe, which is what it should be. We need a way to do both," said Dante.

Caleb agreed, "He's right, and the Black Dragon knows they have us in a corner."

Lana and Seth stared at each other. "It's a distraction," Seth concluded.

"But a distraction we can't resist, because they know full well, we won't stand by and let them massacre a colony," Lana said.

"So why are they carrying out the attacks?" Dante wondered out loud.

"I need a water refill. Let's take a few minutes and come back." Caleb motioned to Dante to walk with him. "Do you mind sending something to Ryan to give him a heads up on what we're thinking, see if it gets the other commanders' thinking caps buzzing? I don't want them coming in with no idea of what's going through our heads."

Dante agreed. "I'll do it now."

A few minutes later, they sat back down.

Caleb spoke up, "Computer, pull up all the planets in the last six months with recent attacks by the Black Dragon and display them with the dates." On cue, a holographic image covered the back of the room.

"What do you see, Caleb?" questioned Lana.

Caleb sighed. "Nothing, I stared at it more times than I want to admit. I hoped a pattern would jump out at me, but I'm getting nowhere. The planets are light-years from each other. Sometimes the Black Dragon Army returned to a system they attacked previously, but to a different planet. There doesn't appear to be any reason for their choice of attack."

"It's here in front of us. Caleb is right. We're missing it," Dante murmured.

They watched Lana as she studied the starry projection. The question displayed on her face as clear as the hologram on the wall.

"I don't know yet. I'm still thinking," said Lana continuing to stare at it. "Caleb, did the other commanders discover any connections between the planets?"

Caleb's eyes registered surprise.

Lana smirked. "Come, sweetheart, surely by now, you sent something to get a feel for how the discussion is going and give them an update on ours so far."

Caleb recovered and looked at his wife mischievously. "Can't get anything past you, right? I delegated the task to your dear cousin, Dante." He turned to Dante. "How's it coming, Dante?"

Dante tried not to laugh as he watched the exchange between the two. He checked his data pad. "They agreed with our assessment and saw the same sequence during the battle. Our conclusion makes sense to them. They discussed a possible connection between the attacked planets but came up empty too."

"Distance doesn't bind them, the times of the attacks aren't consistent, and the populations of the colonies are all over the place. I don't see it. How do we figure it out?" Lana's face changed as she turned to them. "Tell everyone to rest tonight, and we'll assume we have a couple of days before the next attack. The shortest time between attacks has been three days in the past six months, right?"

Caleb nodded. "That's what I'm seeing."

"Hopefully, they won't change their timetable. I'll think more tonight, but I want us and the commanders to take a trip tomorrow. I don't know if it will help but staring at the data is useless. We also know in the middle of the battle we won't solve this puzzle."

Dante was perplexed. "Where are we headed tomorrow, Lana?"

"To get a fresh perspective on our puzzle. Climbing out of the rut, cousin."

Caleb and Dante glanced at each other and shrugged.

Seth nodded at Lana. "I think you're onto something."

Morning came too soon for Lana. They all met in the hall. The commanders looked at Lana expectantly, and she became less sure of her decision. They wanted the answer to the attacks, and they thought she had uncovered it. She hadn't. Moreover, she didn't know if this would work or how to explain her plan for today. She understood something different must be ventured. It was a feeling. No, rather, it originated from the wisdom of those who always guided her in the past.

"You received the briefing on the discussions between myself and those around me," Lana motioned toward Dante, Seth, and Caleb, "as we know the discussion that took place between you." She gestured toward the commanders. "Thank you, Commander Ryan, for leading the discussion. We all came to the same conclusion and stand at the same roadblock. We tried the traditional methods to determine the connection between the attacks and their true purpose but got nowhere. A different approach is needed. Indulge me for a moment."

She turned to Commander Ryan. "If I visit your colony, what do I need to see? What do you love about your colony the most? Not what a guide will tell me, but what a local knows from living there. I will give you five minutes. Oh, and Commander Ryan, please, nothing sensitive to get you in trouble with your advisors or officials. We do want you to be able to return home after this demonstration."

Everyone laughed, including Ryan.

He was off and running about the colony he spent his life protecting. Everyone listened, entranced as he described the beautiful mountains and the cascading waterfall at the end of one of the paths. On the other side of the colony rolled the sea waves upon each other, and the sun would shimmer off the surface as it made its descent for the day. It painted a picture every evening for the colony in soft hues of red, orange, and pink. He told them about a little place only the locals knew, which served the best food to be found in the galaxy. Then he couldn't forget the lady in town who knew the colony's whole history, the storyteller.

Lana lost track of time, and five minutes went long past as she became swept away like everyone else. She glanced down and caught the time. "Whoa, commander, your storytelling was perfect, absolutely perfect."

"Are we going to Commander Ryan's colony for the day? You did say you planned a trip today?" teased Dante.

The comment emitted laughter from everyone again.

"It's tempting, but no. The point is Commander Ryan told us what data couldn't tell us, because he's a local from the planet. Someone who breathes the air of the planet and knows the ins and outs of it possesses the answer to our mystery. That person just doesn't realize it. We need to return to the scene of the last few battles and talk to the officials and the locals. We should reexamine the battleground now, not in the middle of an attack."

Commander Conrad commented, "Your plan makes sense. Although, I'm wondering on the practical side, what do we ask? I mean, we could be at it for a while."

"I don't have that clear-cut answer for you. It's going to be talking to them about the planet and the attack. It's one of those things when you hear it, you'll know it. I realize that's not the response you wanted. It pushes against every battle strategy instinct in you. Regardless, what we see from the Black Dragon Army doesn't fit, so we're going to feel uncomfortable solving our puzzle. This is where we are in the process."

Seth spoke next, "Your leadership skills will be tested. Part of leadership is listening with discernment. In this situation, it will involve a different discernment than you are accustomed. It's not determining between a right or wrong decision. It will be discerning whether the information is a part of the puzzle. The piece may appear useless at first glance, or you could go through a fair number of worthless ones before you locate the component you need. I urge you, sound judgment and patience are needed in this endeavor."

"Thank you, Seth. Very nicely put," Lana said.

"I heard and saw it lived out with wise leaders not long ago. I will not forget them."

A lump formed in Lana's throat, and she nodded at Seth. How she missed them and wished they were still here.

They decided to visit the last three planets of the attacks. Lana, Dante, and two of the commanders went to one of the planets. Caleb and two of the other commanders headed to another planet. Seth, Commander Ryan, and one of the other commanders left for the last planet.

CHAPTER FIFTEEN

Lana and Dante arrived at the planet with the other two commanders. They were all dressed casually. The idea was to talk with the officials of the land while also being approachable to residents. Their first stop was to check in with the colony's representative.

"It's a pleasure to see you, Lana. Thanks to your group we only had minor repairs and a bit of cleanup from the attack. What can I do to assist you today?" the representative queried as he walked with them.

Lana gave a prepared but vague answer, which didn't really disclose why the group had arrived. However, she did it with such skill the representative thought he understood the reason for the group's visit. The colony representatives in each of the regions said they were loyal to the Freedom Fighters. Still, the dreaded possibility always lurked of a traitor to the Freedom Fighter cause. Lana couldn't risk the Dark Lord realizing their group's closer examination of the attacks and growing suspicions. So, the group came simply to inspect the damage, see if anything from the battle could help them strategize better for the next attacks, and give general reassurance to the colony if another attack occurred. The representative showed them around politely for about thirty minutes, answered their questions, gave them clearances for the day, and left for a meeting back at his office.

Dante asked Lana, "Where do we go now?"

Lana turned around thoughtfully. "Let's go to where you, Seth, and the rest of the squadron battled."

Dante tried unsuccessfully to hold back a groan. "That would be on the other side of the city."

"Then take in all the sights on our way there, Dante."

A bustle of activity commenced at this time of the day. They came to an open marketplace area, a common sight in most colonies. The colonies consisted of modern indoor shopping areas, but many locals preferred to purchase certain items in the open marketplace areas like this one. The areas also created a chance for locals to catch up with friends for the week. For visitors to the colony, it provided an excellent way to get a feel for the local culture of the particular colony. It could also be a place to obtain valuable information. They made small talk with clerks who stopped them, but they didn't discover anything useful. They reached the edge of the marketplace area to find themselves walking through the colony's residential section.

Suddenly, they heard a high-pitched voice, "I knew it was her, Mommy."

They turned to see a little girl running toward them from her home, her eyes locked on Lana. A lady followed close behind her, smiling.

The child screamed in excitement, "You're Princess Lana! I knew it was you!"

Lana smiled. It sounded strange. She didn't get called by that title much anymore, and it took her a moment to register the words. After the destruction of her homeland by the Dark Lord's army and the massacre of her family, she didn't feel like a princess anymore. A princess without a kingdom. However, none of that mattered to this little girl.

Lana knelt down to the girl. "What's your name?"

"My name is Emily, and I'm six years old."

"It's nice to meet you, Emily. Is this your mother?"

"Yes, this is my mommy."

The lady stepped forward. "My name is Else. Sorry about my daughter. She saw you from a long way off, and I couldn't hold her back any longer."

Lana laughed. "No need to apologize. She's charming. It was an incredible welcome."

Emily piped in, "Why are you here today? Can you stay with us?"

"I'm not sure how long we're going to be here. We came to check on you after the attack from the Dark Lord's army the other day, to make sure everyone is okay."

Emily's face fell a little. Her voice sounded sad with a touch of anger as she remembered the attack, "The Dark Lord is awful. They tore stuff up, and our friends had to fix it. They look so scary too and made so much noise when they did all the fighting. I was afraid at first." Her voice brightened again. "But then Mommy said the good guys were fighting for us, and we would be okay, and I felt less scared. She said the good guys flew ships in the sky, and she said we had the Elders and you," Emily pointed to Dante, "with the sunspear taking down the bad guys. We're okay, though, because you chased away the bad guys."

Lana got up as the wave of emotions threatened to overcome her. The little girl was so sweet. Lana didn't want her to be frightened, but this was the way of the world with the Dark Lord's army.

A mixture of sadness and anger ripped through Dante as he listened. Innocence stolen so young. The child shouldn't be afraid. His father and the Dark Lord created such a brutal world for this child. It was wrong in countless ways. He remembered the way his father was before, the person he loved as a child. These moments pained his heart, to look in a child's eyes full of fear and know the same man ignited it.

The two commanders continued to watch and listen.

Emily gazed up at Dante. "Did you really destroy those tanks and bad guys with your sunspear?"

Dante stepped forward and smiled at Emily. "I did, but I got help from the rest of the squadron. My two friends here used their ships to get rid of the bad guys in the sky. We all worked together. We'll do it as many times as we need to so you and your mom stay safe. Okay, Emily?"

"I know. Mommy helped me when I got the most scared. When they stayed far away, I was okay. I only got really scared when they were right outside. I thought they would come in our house."

Lana looked from Emily to Else. "I'm confused. Dante and the others fought them on the other side of town."

Emily shook her head. "No, Black Dragon soldiers passed by here."

Lana made sure she heard correctly, "You saw Black Dragon soldiers pass by your house during the battle?"

Else nodded. "Yes, Emily is right. They came right through here."

Lana glanced at Dante and the others. "Dante, all the fighting occurred on the other side of town. We decided none of the Black Dragon soldiers got past that line."

Dante's face reflected the same confusion. "We were wrong it looks like. If some reached this point undetected, I wonder what they were doing?"

Lana focused back on Else and Emily, "Can you tell me more about the Black Dragon soldiers you saw? Were there many or just a few? Could you tell where they headed? The information may be important."

Else replied, "They were a small group, not like the normal attack squadron. They came through and didn't bother anyone. It sounds strange saying that about a Black Dragon soldier. Maybe like they didn't want to be noticed or engage anyone. During the attack, we just assumed they were a part of it. Honestly, I don't know why they came this way, because they didn't behave like they normally would. We stayed down as soon as we saw them pass, and then the fighting started. We didn't budge until we received the signal to come out. My husband was at work in full lockdown while the attack happened."

"You saw them pass before you heard the fighting start?"

"Yes, we got the alarm to go into lockdown as our colony's scanners spotted the fleet coming out of the atmosphere, and almost immediately, the small group of troops passed by. Several minutes went by before we heard the fighting start."

"Did you see what direction they went, and can you tell me what's there?"

Else pointed to the right. "They went down that road. This is the last of the residential area. Then you start heading into more of a warehouse area, and further down there are a couple of industries, plants of some sort."

Emily smiled. "When I grow up, I'm going to be brave, so I can fight the bad guys too."

Lana knelt in front of Emily again and smiled at her. "You are already a brave little girl. Hopefully, we can get rid of the bad guys, so you never worry about it again, Emily."

"That would be nice. I wish you could stay for my tea party. My house is right next door. My tea set has unicorns on them."

"Emily, that is the best offer from someone in a long time. I'll make a deal with you. Once we get rid of the bad guys, I'll come back and join you for tea."

Emily squealed, "Oh, yes, yes!"

"In the meantime, I want to give you something. Here is my butterfly scarf." Lana tied it loosely around Emily's neck. "Of course, you need the matching hairpiece." She took a silver-colored butterfly from her hair and put it in Emily's. "They are much prettier on you anyway. Why, you look like a princess! If you ever feel scared again, let these remind you of us and keep being the brave little girl you are. Remember, the Ancient One watches over you and me and my friends here. He lets us help with protecting you from the bad guys, and we're going to keep doing it, okay?"

Emily nodded and wrapped her arms around Lana in a big hug. Lana hugged the little girl back, kissed her on the forehead, and got up.

Commander Gabe approached, and tears glistened in his eyes. He knelt before Emily.

"Hi, Emily. I'm Commander Gabe. Lana is right. You are a very brave little girl. I know I'm braver because I got to meet you today," said the commander trying to steady his voice.

Emily smiled at him and patted his shoulder. "You're already brave. You shot all those ships out of the sky to protect us."

He smiled. "Yes, but I forgot something important, and you helped me remember it. Now I can protect everyone much better. Thank you, Emily."

"You are welcome, then." Emily said proudly.

He nodded, got up, and stood behind Lana again.

They waved goodbye to Emily and her mother. Once they were out of sight, Commander Gabe stopped the group. He faced Lana, and tears filled his eyes again. The other commander's eyes were moist as well.

Commander Gabe spoke, his voice full of emotion, "Lana, I owe you an apology. The thought I even suggested leaving the colonies unprotected feels me with shame after meeting Emily. We cannot leave them to the Dark Lord. There are precious ones everywhere at every colony, like Emily and her family. I needed this today if it served no other purpose. Please forgive me, Lana, for earlier."

She clasped the commander's hand briefly and said, "There was nothing to forgive, but all right, it's forgiven. I'm glad good came from today." She smiled. "Let us follow the road and see where it leads."

Lana turned to Dante. "Please send an update to the other two groups. See if they learn a group went unnoticed behind the line during the battle too. If so, have them follow up on it. It may be nothing, but it's the best lead so far. I'd assume if they found something, we would know by now."

"I imagine you're right. I'm on it."

⸎

Once Caleb's and Seth's groups got to a quiet location, they listened as Dante shared the information.

Caleb asked quietly, "You got all that out of a six-year-old and her mom?"

Dante said, "It was all Lana who got it going."

"She connects with others like few are able to do," Seth admitted. "It may give us the lead we needed. We will see where the information takes us here."

"Us too," Caleb said. "Everyone is nice here, but we spent most of our time reassuring them we'll be here if the Black Dragon army comes back. This could give us a direction to nudge the conversation when talking with the residents."

⸎

Lana and the others saw the residential area ended. They spied businesses and further down warehouses. Beyond those, there appeared to be a plant, as Emily and her mother recollected.

"Let's check out these warehouses first," Lana said.

Lana and one of the commanders spoke with one foremen while Dante and the other commander spoke with the foreman at the adjacent warehouse.

"So, what's the story?" asked Dante once Lana came back with Commander Gabe.

"He said the warehouse materials here are low tech, mostly for the colony's needs."

Commander Gabe added, "He also remembered hearing footsteps outside during the lockdown, though. Sounded heavy, like military grade, so it fits our Black Dragon profile."

Dante nodded. "Same story here. Thankfully they didn't encounter any visitors in their warehouse that day. We did ask about the buildings further ahead."

"The foremen told us those warehouses ship out the products from the plant," finished Commander Cephas.

Lana smiled. "It looks like Emily put us on the right road."

The group proceeded to the warehouse, and a guard greeted them at the gate. Further up, they saw a couple of guards at the door of the building and more walking the grounds.

"Someone feels they must secure the building, and this is only the warehouse," Dante said to the group.

Lana agreed. "Which makes me wonder what goodies are in the warehouse. Let's go chat with the guard."

Initially, the guard talked readily with them. Yet, when they asked about the attack, he became noticeably nervous.

"Did you see anyone come close or enter the building?" Lana quizzed.

"It was chaotic with the alarms blaring. The whole place went into lockdown. Nobody was supposed to enter the building," said the guard as he avoided their eyes.

"We discovered enemy troops breached the perimeter during the attack and headed this way to approach the building," said Lana.

The guard grew pale as one who understood he no longer kept his secret, "I'm supposed to protect the building no matter what, you understand."

Dante jumped in, "We're not here to cause you trouble. It was lockdown, with a whole Black Dragon Army on the surface. There's no way anyone should expect you would stand here and try to fend them off as they headed straight toward you. Please tell us how many you saw, where they went, and what they did. Anything you can tell us may help."

The guard studied them for several seconds and sighed. They refused to give up. "About twelve of them came through, and you're right. I left my post and hid. They went first to the warehouse, and I believe they headed to the plant next. I don't have a clue what they did afterwards. I'm sorry, you must think I'm awful for letting them come into the warehouse."

Commander Gabe reassured the guard, "No, we don't. You were ill-equipped and outnumbered to handle a group of Black Dragon soldiers and scared, understandably, considering the circumstances. There is no reason to apologize. The information you supplied us will help. Thank you, sir."

Commander Cephas nodded. "Absolutely. Can you tell us what type of items the plant makes and what the warehouse ships out?"

"Honestly, I'm not sure. I'm told the plant produces mostly metal items, using industrial materials from the warehouse, along with a few high-tech pieces. However, there are a couple of areas in the plant, which include specialized labs. Enough that we don't handle those shipments from the plant. My guess is they contain sensitive chemicals in them or advanced technology. I wish I could be more helpful, but that's all I can tell you."

Lana said, "You were extremely helpful. Can we take a look inside the warehouse?"

The guard shrugged. "Help yourself. I see you have unlimited clearances for the day. Probably unnecessary, though. I mean, you kind of pull rank around here,

Lana." He smiled. "We're thankful to all of you. We realize those attacks could always end differently. About leaving my post ..."

"Don't worry," Dante reassured him, "how we came by this information is on a need-to-know basis, and our team is the only one who needs to know."

The guard nodded, clearly relieved again.

"Dante, could you ..." Lana began as they walked toward the warehouse.

"Already on it, cousin. I'm letting the others know now."

Dante communicated the information, and they heard him say, "Hey, and only our team knows about the guard leaving the post. He was petrified about anyone finding out, so none of this comes back on him. I agree. I don't know who expected him to fight off a squad of troops coming at him, but they're insane. He helped us enormously today with the information." Dante sighed. "My guess is all the guards at these places report the same story as the last one, or they turned up missing after the attacks."

Lana and the group finished at the warehouse and proceeded to the plant. Despite their unlimited clearances, they sensed they didn't get a full tour. After gathering information from conversations with those in the warehouse and plant, they did unsupervised investigating. They were sure the Black Dragon Army came for items inside the plant and warehouse but piecing it together would be challenging.

"Time to regroup?" Dante suggested.

"Yes, tell the others to do so once they finish. If they're still getting information, they should continue. However, when the fountain runs dry, tell them to head back. We need to compare notes and put it together." She peered up at the sky and sighed. "We can't be sure when the next attack will come."

CHAPTER SIXTEEN

The piercing eyes, a chilling mix of bloodshot red and abyssal black, hungrily hunts for the one prey it had stalked for ages, and finally it waits no longer to claim its prize. She shivers inside as terror engulfs her, and it creeps closer. A monster so strong, so hideous that embodies it. She begs to forget, but it marches ahead to its task. This time not for her though. A cloak is heard swishing, approaching. She knows whose form hides behind it. Vapors hiss. A voice is heard with every syllable dripping in cruelty. "Last time he fails me." Another voice promises to carry out the gruesome death sentence. "It will be done, Dark Lord.' The eyes speeds closer, the cloak rushes toward her, and red and black mingle together like streaks of paint racing across her vision. If only the streaks were just that and not the precious red liquid emptying from the veins of life. Cruel laughter combines with the toxic smoke, and the cloak rips away to reveal a body mangled and covered in blood, to be used as a sickening fuel to satisfy a master's final rage.

The girl awoke with a start from the vision, breathing heavily. She stood up in bed, her eyes wide open. Morning arrived, thankfully. She hurriedly got herself ready.

"Alena and Alika, I need to talk to you as soon as you get up," said the girl as she knocked on their doors.

They came into the girl's room. Her eyes were untroubled, but filled with a new urgency. "It's time. They're coming, and I know when to expect them."

There was silence from Alika and Alena as the realization of her words sunk in, but there would be no hesitation from them.

She continued, "My father's day of reckoning is upon him. We must make the preparations."

Alena and Alika nodded.

⁓ℓℓ⁓

The Dark Lord sat in his oversized chair. His eyes stormed with rage. He thought about the last communication with that wretched Draco after yet another failure to deliver. His regular evening drink nor the comforting words from his beautiful companion provided no calming of his mood. Draco angered him to the upmost with his excuses for the continued failures. The creature seemed utterly unconcerned with how he persisted in testing his goodwill, and that part infuriated him the most. Didn't he know he could be destroyed in a moment? Draco was worthless and warned for too long of his accumulated failures.

The Dark Lord smiled as he considered his Black Dragon Commander, the opposite of Draco in every way. Everything he asked the Black Dragon Commander he did with no mistakes. If only all his help were so efficient. His mood soured again as his thoughts reverted to Draco. His eyes grew blacker, and his anger reignited.

"Black Dragon Commander, I need to see you in my room."

"Yes, Dark Lord, I can be there in about ten minutes from my present location."

"I will see you shortly, commander."

Before the promised timeframe, the Black Dragon Commander entered the Dark Lord's room.

"Please, sit as I have a task for you. You are aware there is trouble with items getting to us due to the consistent failures of the one named Draco. You are present in many of the communications with him, even led them when I could not do so. So you see as well."

"Yes. You were furious with him this last time, but he ..."

"Waved it off. Again. Yes, I noticed. In fact, I cannot get it out of my mind. The man has been warned, and he repeatedly fails me. He believes he can laugh in my face, and I will continue to tolerate it? A message needs to be sent in person, and I want you to do it."

"Do you need me to give him a demonstration of your power? Perhaps then he will cooperate as you wish."

"I contemplated that, and I concluded he's not capable of doing what I ask. He had numerous opportunities to prove himself and failed. I tolerated his incompetence for this long, because he's not the only one assisting us with securing what we need for our operations. The others can do their job with great efficiency. Our operation is at a delicate stage, and we cannot continue with this nonsense from Draco. It is time to take care of any loose ends before it costs us. We warned him on numerous occasions, and he seems unconcerned with provoking my anger. A grave mistake on his part. Besides, my patience is no more with him. There is only one way he will fail me no longer." The Dark Lord's meaning was clear.

"You were more than patient for far too long, Dark Lord. He drove you to this course of action. I confess, it's a shame with the location."

"Yes, the well-kept secret in the shipping business, except to our allies. I spent considerable time establishing it which is the other reason I put this off as I did. You're right though, I've endured Draco long enough. I can always count on you to see it my way. Today will be the last time he fails me." A sinister smile formed on the Dark Lord's face.

"It will be done, Dark Lord. When do you wish it to occur?"

"Finish the present task and afterward take care of Draco. Be sure to get footage of your work for me. I thought about seeing to Draco myself because he angered me so, but I changed my mind as I do admire your work, commander."

"As you wish, Dark Lord. Three days should give enough time to finish the present task and make the preparations to take care of Draco." The Black Dragon Commander got up and nodded to the Dark Lord.

The Dark Lord nodded back and smiled, dismissing the man to tend to the tasks at hand.

All three had been up early.

The girl stared out in the distance along with Alena and Alika for another minute and turned back around. "That was the last one."

"Everything went as we hoped," said Alika.

"It feels like we are on our own now," said the girl quietly.

"It appears sparse, but ..." Alena said, meeting the girl's eyes.

"We're not alone. I know, I know." The girl smiled despite herself. She knew she couldn't get away with that one. She closed her eyes briefly and then turned to Alika and Alena. "It's time to get back."

CHAPTER SEVENTEEN

The Black Dragon Commander stood at the ship's command post as the ship inched closer to Draco's home. It had been a while since he visited a planet to carry out a task of this sort, but the Black Dragon Commander knew the long leash given to Draco would one day turn into the man's choke collar. The Dark Lord would only be pushed so far. Frankly, the Dark Lord surprised the Black Dragon Commander for how long he endured with Draco, despite what he had said. The Dark Lord gave clear instructions. Draco would pay with a long, painful death since his patience extended so far with him before he ultimately ordered Draco to be eliminated.

"Black Dragon Commander, we reached the portal. We will be upon the planet in a few minutes," said the officer.

"Take us through the portal, and land us as previously discussed. I'm afraid Draco will find himself ill-prepared for company today, but we will make quite the entrance on him regardless."

⁓ℓℓ⁓

Draco sat at his desk, going over paperwork. He eased back in his chair and took a sip of drink.

"Empty," he muttered, dragging himself up and pouring more. He sat back down when he heard sounds from outside the room. The racket grew louder until he could ignore it no longer. "Worthless child. I warned her. When I get my hands on her, I'll make her sorry for this latest disturbance." Full of impatience, he rose from his seat and walked to the door.

He opened the door into the large room and boomed in anger, "What is all this commotion?" His eyes darted across the room, and his face went pale.

The Black Dragon Commander stepped forward into the room. "I believe that would be me, Draco." Several of his men filed in behind him.

Draco tried to find words, but managed nothing.

The Black Dragon Commander smiled. "Sorry for the mess," he waved his hand toward a couple of Draco's employees who made the mistake of trying to stop the commander from entering Draco's household, "but my orders were to make this a surprise visit for you. I follow orders, unlike some of us, right Draco? We can put ourselves in terrible positions, I hear. Would you know anything about that, Draco?" The Black Dragon Commander continued to step forward as he spoke to Draco.

Draco stammered, "I don't understand. I mean ... I tried really. He said ...told me ... it was ok. No ..."

The commander shook his head. "At no point did the Dark Lord say your continued failures are okay, Draco. He let you know many times if they continued, we would be where we are now." The Black Dragon Commander stood within arm's reach of Draco, and the other men surrounded Draco.

Draco stared at the commander. No way out of this existed. Despite knowing his fate, his eyes darted around the room as if a portal would open and snatch him from his situation. His focus returned to the Black Dragon Commander for the other impossibility that somehow the commander would reconsider his case.

The Black Dragon Commander read his thoughts, and a low laugh escaped him. "Draco, you are a fool. You are a dead man as you stand by order of the Dark Lord."

Draco's eyes filled with new terror as the realization hit him. He tried to flee the circle, but the Black Dragon men grabbed and held him fast.

The Black Dragon Commander eyed him again as if not believing how foolish the man remained. "You cannot escape. You will die today. I have been told to make you suffer by the Dark Lord himself. Why you would push the Dark Lord for this long and think it could continue is beyond me."

"No, this can't happen."

The Black Dragon Commander ignored Draco. He motioned behind him, and a few more of his Black Dragon men stepped further into the room to receive instructions from him. Once done, two of them disappeared to another part of the house. The other two came closer to the commander for their task.

"Place the hood on Draco and begin your work as agreed. The Dark Lord wants him to suffer for his failures before he dies. I will deliver the final blow when you are done with him."

The two Black Dragon men nodded and walked over to Draco. Draco's screams could be heard through the very walls, but the two Black Dragon men did not stop. They would stop when the order was given, and the Dark Lord did not readily appease. Draco walked the final steps on the path of darkness he chose so long ago, and the mouth of destruction waited to receive him.

The Black Dragon Commander could hear commotion in an upstairs room, but he tried to pay it no attention. He knew what the chaos would be. A couple of minutes later, he heard screams, and then the noise ceased. Several minutes later, he glanced down at his data pad device. He quickly scanned the images, and the few bits of information flying across them as well.

"Fine. It's taken care of as I can see, and I heard too." The Black Dragon Commander listened to the update from the Black Dragon troops, but it proved unnecessary. The images showed the confrontation ended as expected. There was no point in bringing it down here. "No, leave it there. The Dark Lord's real interest was with Draco. We simply need to make sure there are no loose ends here, and that is done. We can manage here. Rejoin the rest of the troops outside after you make your final sweep." Strangely he found himself still staring at the data pad for several moments as in a trance, but then looked away and closed it, along with the bloody images sent from the two troops. Something tried to surface as it occasionally did, but he brushed it aside. He wasn't successful with doing so, but he forced himself to move forward.

He returned his attention to the scene before him and eventually saw something flash on his device again. He signaled for the two Black Dragon men to stop and move aside.

The Black Dragon Commander removed the hood from Draco. "The Dark Lord saw enough. He says it's time to mark the hour of your death."

Draco glared at the Black Dragon Commander full of hate, but he could not move. No strength remained from the torture he endured. He laid there, a barely conscious bloody mass.

The Black Dragon Commander pulled out his sunspear. He used it sparingly, but the Dark Lord specifically requested him to use it on Draco. It once had been the shiny silver color that shone in the light when his loyalty entwined with the Elders' cause. Now the blade changed with him. The sunspear turned a pitch-black metal as if dipped straight in the abyss. The Black Dragon Commander plunged the sunspear into Draco's chest and sliced through to his stomach. Blood rushed from his body and emptied on the floor. He was dead instantly.

"Our business is concluded now, Draco." He never had any use for the man, so he felt no remorse over his death. The Black Dragon Commander gestured to his men. One of them threw a firestone on the body, and it transformed into a pile of ashes.

The Black Dragon Commander ordered the rest of the Black Dragon soldiers with him, "You know what to do. Place the devices down here, and then make your way back. It will start at Draco's household. Our ships will do the rest as planned."

The Black Dragon Commander sat on the ship and watched calmly as the ships finished tying up the last bit of the Draco situation. It would be time to get back to the ongoing operation now that he had snuffed out this long-standing irritation for the Dark Lord. He let his mind drift to that operation. He did not care to watch them finish up this situation with Draco.

⌒⌒⌒

The girl caught her breath on the hill with Alika.

"It's done? She's dead?" asked Alika.

"Yes, dead. I took care of it myself as agreed, Alika." The girl replied as she peeled off the blood-soaked clothes to reveal spotless garments underneath. She didn't know how she felt. She thought she would feel strange after killing her, but she didn't. It had to be done. She knew they were right.

She added the blood-soaked clothes to the pile.

The girl threw a small firestone on it, and watched it become reduced to ashes. It seemed pointless, but they would take no chances. The wind scattered the ashes away.

"We're ready, Alika?"

"Yes, Alena just got on board. I expect she's starting the ship now."

"I figured. She ran a few seconds ahead of me."

The girl stared out and spotted the amber tongues in the distance, rising to touch the sky. More were joining it at an alarming rate.

"We must go now, child," Alika whispered.

"I know. The worse is yet to come. After everything that's happened, you'd think I'd be running to leave, but now it makes no sense." Her voice broke.

Alika put an arm around her shoulder. "That's not true. You spent your whole life here. To say goodbye is unimaginable, and not every memory is terrible, despite your father's efforts." He whispered, "We cannot delay any longer though, child."

"You're right," She whispered back as a tear slid down her face, and she took one last look before they climbed aboard the ship.

"Ready?" Alena asked in a gentle voice, talking to both but looking at the girl.

"We're ready, Alena," The girl answered as she watched the planet disappear in the cockpit window.

CHAPTER EIGHTEEN

Lana, Dante, and the two commanders arrived back at the fortress.

"How long before the others return?" inquired Lana looking at Dante.

"Guessing from their last update, about an hour."

"We can get a head start making sense of what we found until they get here," said Lana.

Dante smiled. "Lucky us. I'll get everyone something to drink before the fun begins."

His guess proved correct as both groups walked in about an hour later.

Caleb arrived first with the others behind him. "What are you guys doing?"

"All Lana's doing. She insisted we start without you."

Caleb took a second glance at the busy scene spread out on the table in front of them. "You know, I think we had a few more questions for those warehouse workers. I feel a strong urge to head back over there." He pretended to turn around and motion the rest of the group to do the same.

"Commander Caleb, nice try, but you and your group are needed here. Your interviews proved quite thorough, and I'm anxiously waiting to hear about them." Lana laughed at her husband.

"Wow, Commander Caleb, in trouble again and dragging the rest of us with you. Really?" Commander Ryan chuckled.

"A wise man once said to know when you're beaten." Caleb went over to his wife and gave her a hug and kiss.

Everyone laughed. The way the two of them played back and forth so easily put everyone else at ease. Nevertheless, everyone knew in the middle of everything they recognized the seriousness of a situation. The others suspected this was how the young couple kept their sanity, and it helped those around them to do the same.

"Now that all of us are ready to begin," Lana gave her husband a playful jab, "we need to figure out how best to sort what we found."

"It's a lot, and since we went in separate groups, I'm not sure of the best way. I was only half-joking when I saw everything spread out. I'm open for suggestions of the best way to do this, because we all know the clock is ticking," Caleb said.

"If we narrow it down to what stood out to all of us, we can organize the data easier," said Commander Ryan.

"Yes, now, I think we all agree with Commander Caleb's initial reaction when he saw so much information at once. We're trying to figure out what is important and how it ties together. It reverts back to the discernment element we spoke about before we left," stated Commander Gabe.

"We should find the consistencies in the plant and warehouse interviews and the snooping our teams did," said Commander Conrad.

Lana looked around and confirmed the group was in agreement. "How about thirty minutes for each group to pull an overview together." She saw the hesitation in their faces. "Remember not detailed, just the high points of what stuck out. How about forty-five minutes?" The group agreed.

Her husband teased her, "Technically, your group should be done since you started without us. So, what are you doing for the time?"

"Attempt to keep you on task," She tried unsuccessfully to appear stern with her husband as he leaned over and kissed her.

The three groups delved into their day's findings, checking notes from the data pad and recalling the day's events with the same goal.

Forty-five minutes later, they started listening to each other's findings. They discovered several things that coincided. Lana's discovery with Emily and her family helped the others find the connection they needed at the other colonies, and a similar pattern emerged. In each place, a small group of Black Dragon soldiers found their way beyond the battle line. It occurred before the actual battle started, but after the alert sounded of each Black Dragon attack, so the colony was already in lockdown. They targeted similar types of places once at the colony. However, that part turned out to be shrouded in mystery. Each group received varying degrees of information about what the Black Dragon soldiers did while in the facility. None of it seemed to be the colonists at the facilities being intentionally uncooperative. Rather, they followed the lockdown procedure and feared for their safety if they tried to intervene during the encounter. Facility workers in the warehouse suspected the Black Dragon men took items from the warehouse, but the warehouse officials could not confirm it. They did not appear to be missing anything, but they were still checking inventory. The Black Dragon men knew precisely where they wanted to go each time, accomplished whatever their purpose, and then left.

Even Lana felt the effects of the long day, and she knew the others did as well. "Dante and I can work on organizing our group's data further. Caleb can work on his group's data, and Seth can do the same this evening. Why don't the rest of you go on to sleep, and we'll see how far we get tomorrow? I'm getting nervous. I feel the clock ticking on us, as Caleb said earlier."

The others didn't want to abandon the four and gave half-heartened offers of continued help, but the six commanders were exhausted. So, Lana found no real objections to her gracious offer for them to call it a day. The six commanders retired for the evening, and the four of them dug in for longer.

Finally, Caleb put the data pad down and rubbed his eyes. "It's doubling on the data pad now."

"Your husband is right. It's time to take your own advice," Seth said, looking at Lana.

"I'm outnumbered, and you three happen to be right in this case. We put this aside until tomorrow." She tried, unsuccessfully, to stifle a yawn.

The next morning came too rapidly. The six commanders found the other four made considerable progress with the data before exhaustion overtook them. They concluded it was impossible to tell what, if any, items the Black Dragon left with from the warehouse and plant. In fact, it didn't appear anything was tampered with or missing. Maybe they left something behind or searched for something. Nothing appeared out of place, so it begged the question of why the Black Dragon soldiers entered the building. Of course, records could be altered easily enough with certain technology and the right expertise. Just because no one saw anything leave, it meant nothing.

"What do we do now?" asked Commander Aegeus.

"It does seem like our approach changes for the next attack," said Commander Austin.

"I believe it must." Lana knew what she thought, but she felt terribly uncomfortable with it. The strategy it demanded grated against every fiber in her.

Commander Ryan echoed her unspoken thoughts. "Only to a certain point, because we didn't obtain enough information yet. We can't let them know we figured out about their extra soldiers, until we track down what they're going after at these facilities."

Commander Gabe nodded. "As much as I would like to mow them down as soon as they set foot in the facility the next time, our best strategy is to let them leave unhindered. We should send a small force inside to uncover what they're doing."

Commander Cephas added, "Agreed. Intel is our greater need now, so we can properly answer the threat."

Commander Gabe continued, "The rest of the group must still manage the attacks as normal to keep the colony safe. Everything should appear we are fighting as before to avoid arousing any suspicions."

They all looked at Lana, Caleb, Dante, and Seth as they realized none of them said anything about how they wanted the next attacks handled.

"It came together fine, so I let you work it out. It's a solid plan," Caleb said.

Dante nodded. "Everything is covered."

"Nice work," said Seth with a smile.

Lana gave her final nod of approval. "You're right. Every bone in my body wants to give the order to stop them the second they enter the facility, but we need to see what they're doing once they're inside. One more time won't tip the balance in whatever they're doing, or at least that's my thought. If it does, I'll regret this decision. I agree with the rest of you, the information gleaned is important enough to take the chance. We'll plan accordingly, so everything remains covered, and we can run this operation as well. They'll get one more time to roam free in the facility."

Caleb spoke, "Let's start planning. This will play out a little different for us, but it shouldn't appear so to the Black Dragon. Alert your squadrons beforehand of any changes we make. We don't want any questions from them on the battlefield. We need to be specific on the small group we choose to do the other operation. Begin thinking about who in your squadron is best suited for it. It's essential it goes right. They must remain undetected during the operation, and their only purpose is to observe and get intel. Nothing else."

Everyone nodded in understanding and started pulling it together.

Eventually, they finished planning. Seth would run the special operation. They chose the team for it and briefed them on their assignment. Commander Ryan would be on the ground with Dante to provide help. Essentially, everyone else would continue as normal during the attack. After eating lunch, the commanders prepared to head back.

Before they left, Commander Gabe approached Lana. "Is it possible to speak briefly with the commanders, including your husband and Seth, before we leave? You and Dante are welcome as well, but I believe you know what I wish to say to them."

"Of course, feel free to meet with them, commander."

He nodded. Moments later, the group disappeared into one of the small rooms.

Dante reflected a puzzled look as he came to Lana.

"Dante, I don't believe Commander Gabe will go into battle again without seeing a six-year-old little girl named Emily."

A look of understanding came over Dante. "I believe you're right." He smiled and put his arm around her shoulder. "You did well, cuz."

Twenty minutes later, everyone strolled out of the room. There was a different mood springing from the group, a fresh determination to accomplish the task set before them.

Caleb came over to his wife and quietly said, "Wow, quite the talk from Commander Gabe. The colonies are in safe hands from the Black Dragon Army as long as he's with us."

She responded, "The encounter with the child and her mother deeply affected him. Now he can inspire the others as well."

The other commanders said their goodbyes to Lana, Caleb, Dante, and Seth. It promised to be brief as they were overdue for an attack from the Black Dragon Army.

Commander Gabe was the last to say goodbye. "I will see you again soon." He paused and smiled at Lana. "Thank you for taking us to visit the colony. I know what you wished to accomplish with it, and that part of the purpose was realized. Nonetheless, what I gained personally cannot be measured, and I am grateful."

"Then the visit was worth every moment we spent with Emily and her mother."

"It was. I believe I'll spent more time in the colonies. I needed to be reminded of who I'm protecting, besides my own family. Speaking of, they are ready for me to come home, even if for a short time before the next attack. I'll await your call, along with the other commanders, until we are needed again, Lana."

"Until that time."

"He is changed from the person who arrived here a couple of days ago," said Seth smiling as he watched Commander Gabe leave.

CHAPTER NINETEEN

A full two weeks passed since they left the planet. Alika, Alena, and the girl settled in the place they would now call home.

They remained seated after eating breakfast, and the girl knew another change would be thrust upon her even before Alika spoke the words.

"Child, it's time you began the next phase. You will use much of the unorthodox training to accomplish it."

"I suspected as much."

"It's time you establish connections. You will need them, but you enter a different world than ever before, one that can change you terribly. You must find a way into this world without becoming a part of it, know of it, but not be known by it. In this way, you will use all your training. You must never forget who you are, or you will be lost to the depravity. It's dangerous in a whole new way. Seek out those who can help you, but only those you can work with and not lose what you hold dear in the process. You will find them, I promise."

"I understand, but I was forced to be a part of it already. I saw the ugliness of it with my father, and I won't let it do that to me. I promise, Alika."

"I don't doubt your resolve. Hold on to it tightly, child. You will need it."

"This next phase begins immediately?" She knew the answer, but she hesitated. They trained her for so long, and they said she was prepared for this next part. Although she was seventeen years old now, times like this left her feeling as if she were still the child from long ago, meeting Alika and Alena again for the first time.

"Yes, but you're never alone. You know this from the beginning," Alika said as if reading her thoughts. "You can always come back here as you need. This is your home now. Also, you know where the safe havens are, and I can be there for you if need be. Both you and Alena have committed them to memory," Alika paused, looking at her with a smile. "Also, there's the fact Alena will accompany you in your travels."

The girl's face lit up, and she looked from Alika to Alena. "Really, you're coming with me!" Her expression registered relief.

Alena laughed. "Yes." She didn't get further as the girl wrapped her in a hug.

Alika smiled and said, "We planned it from the beginning, child. I'm glad it brings you comfort."

"It does, Alika." She turned to Alena, "You're not just my teacher after all this time. You're my friend, the truest to be found. Surely, you know that by now. Are you certain you want to come? We're going to be put in dangerous situations. It must be your decision, Alena."

"It is my decision. You need a friend to watch your back, and I'm there. I know what I signed up for the first day I started training you." Alena hugged the girl again. "Let's get prepared to go."

～ℓℓ～

"Did you say yes?" asked Alena.

"Sorry, I did. I mean I said yes, it's here," the girl answered, looking back at Alena.

"Anything else you think we need?"

"No, I'd say we're set."

"Ready for a new adventure?"

"If you say so, Alena." She laughed.

"We'll settle for ready to go then now that everything is loaded on your ship." Alena grinned.

"My ship? You're kidding, right? All this time, I worked on my own ship, and you didn't tell me. You two are seriously sneaky."

Alena's eyes twinkled. "Well, you know it inside and out. I bet you could fix it with your eyes closed."

Alika cleared his throat. "Neither one of you test out the theory, please."

"We'll try to avoid doing so, Alika," agreed the girl.

The ship was more than adequate. The original framework was strong, and they had made countless modifications to strengthen it. It consisted of two small quarters connected by a small bathroom. The girl wondered about the two quarters, but it made sense now. It also contained another small room, which could serve as an extra quarter if necessary. The ship had a deceptively small open area with seating and table which was situated behind the cockpit control chairs. The ship also boasted a spaciously hidden cargo hold. Inside it appeared average, but the clever design concealed state-of-the-art technology. They had done much of the modified communications between Draco and the Dark Lord from the ship. The ship also boasted a built-in system to change the appearance of the vessel itself to the beholder. It included a combination of holographic, cloaking, and structural technology. They also incorporated advanced encryption technology on the communication and data pad devices on the ship. That was only the beginning of what the ship could do.

"I assume you're acquainted with your identities, child?" asked Alika.

"Of course. Took care of that first. Such wonderful storytellers," she teased, looking at Alena and Alika.

"Ready?" the girl asked Alena. Alena nodded.

Alena hugged Alika. "I'll watch over her, I promise. We'll be back soon."

The girl's eyes misted over. She felt unprepared again, but so much could be lost further if they delayed.

Alika hugged and released her. He smiled at her and gazed into her eyes. "You're ready. You know you are. Do not fear what is ahead. You are equipped for the path you chose. Remember who you are and cling to that truth. Now go, child."

The girl and Alena left. His eyes briefly followed their ship and went inside. He found himself sitting in front of a familiar manuscript, gaining comfort as he often did.

CHAPTER TWENTY

The initial days were strange for the girl and Alena as they grew accustomed to the task before them. It was harder for the girl as she would be the one mostly going out and making the connections, the one they would deal with most of the time, not Alena. Yet, Alena would always be there on the ship, monitoring the girl's movements and seeing and hearing what she did. The exception was the first couple of weeks when they went out together to determine how best for the girl to do the task without harm coming to her. They both understood as the work continued, it could take them only so far. It would always be dangerous. For the girl, an extra dangerous element existed, the necessity of keeping her identity under wraps. Although the cover she chose fit perfectly, since no one used their true name or identity in this business. Both Alena and the girl retained their sunspear with them but concealed the weapons well on their person for obvious reasons. In contrast, they kept the more traditional handheld photon blasters prominently displayed that could be effortlessly reached.

At the end of each day, Alena and the girl compiled the information. They began to see the players in the business and how they interacted. The girl had always commanded an excellent memory, and she memorized the connections. She would need it in her head. One of the big questions remained. Who were these connections she could deal with and wouldn't find herself dodging fire from a photon blaster? She felt confident they would locate them, but it proved painstakingly slow with a galaxy collectively shaking in fear. Once she found that first connection, she must ensure the first transaction went as planned to inspire confidence. Alena, Alika, and she understood that part because it was the only way to gain friends in the world she had entered.

Three months into the work, the girl entered a place advertised as a diner but something closer to a bar. It was a common scene in the colonies and where most business got done. She ordered something light to eat and took only water with it. After all, she didn't come for lunch but for information as had become routine. She was intent on finding the person with loose lips for the day. Suddenly, she felt drawn to turn and look behind her. A man sat alone in a booth, and she didn't recognize him as someone they knew in the business yet.

"Who?" whispered the girl. That is all she said, and Alena went to work as the girl turned back in her seat.

"There's no record of him. I checked other databases and nothing either," answered Alena.

"Go to him," said the voice she knew.

The girl smiled. "Now we're getting somewhere." She rose and walked up to the man. She slid into the booth opposite to him and met his eyes. "You look like someone I should meet."

The man held her gaze. "I'll be the judge of that."

"You can put the blaster away. I'm just here for a meet and greet."

He studied her. "You're bold. I'll give you that, and for now, I will hear you out." He shifted, relaxing his hold on the blaster, but it stayed in his hand. "I don't recall seeing you around, and that doesn't often happen for me. Do you have a name?"

"Many. It's necessary in this line of business, but you know that."

"True. So, you understand if I'm not forthcoming with mine at this stage either."

"Absolutely."

"Why did you come over to me?"

"I anticipate I will need things in the future, and I believe you can assist me with them."

"You said you didn't know me, though. It's a dangerous business. A minute ago, I aimed a blaster at you, ready to fire."

"A necessary precaution, which I do many times as well. As for the other, I don't know you. Although I have a good feeling about you, I trust it to guide me in these meetings. It provides help for me many times."

The man scrutinized her again, and he understood the meaning behind her last words. He shifted again, and the girl perceived he put his blaster away wholly now. "Perhaps we can do business. I work by the usual ground rules like anyone in this business, but I adhere to additional ones if we're to work together. They will not be an issue with you from what I judge so far."

"You'll find your instincts continue to serve you. As a token of my goodwill, let me take care of something for you. I want you to see you can trust me. Words are one thing, but action is proof in this business."

"You speak truth beyond your years. I thought to ask to see your work, but you beat me to it. All right, take a look at this." He handed a data pad to her. She read the data pad and handed it back to him. "It's causing an issue with being able to do business as I wished, and I contemplated several solutions. None I'm satisfied with for various reasons."

Her mind spun into action. "I can see where this causes you a considerable number of issues. I'm guessing the solutions which came to my mind at first are the same as yours, and I can see the problems inherent with them too." She leaned back in the booth, and her eyes reflected one deep in thought. "Can I see your data pad again?"

He handed it back over, watching her curiously.

She angled it so only the two of them could see it. "I figure, with your solutions, this is the central issue of why all them are disagreeable to you."

"Yes."

She continued to study it. A word surfaced. *Bypass.* She smiled. "We need to find a solution where it no longer goes through this issue."

"I don't see how, but if you know a way, let's hear it." He listened, fascinated now.

In a few moments, they leaned over the data pad, and she gained his undivided attention as she explained her solution.

"I believe it will work. I don't know why it didn't occur to me. Perhaps because I don't possess the expertise to do it at the present, but I'm figuring you do."

"Yes, and I will if you would like."

"Your price?"

"We covered that. Your trust for the future."

"Agreed. How long?"

"Give me three days. Tell me where you want to meet, and we'll do so. Then I'll complete the rest of the task."

They decided the particulars for the next meeting. They exchanged communication codes; ones only good for this task.

"Do I get a name now that we are doing business?"

"Chris."

"In that case, I'll be Christopher to you. Well played." The man chuckled.

The name of the diner was Chris's Hideout.

⁓ ℓℓ ⁓

"Well done," said Alena when the girl arrived back.

"It went smoothly." She took her time coming back as she expected the same careful practice from Christopher. She didn't want him identifying her ship this soon. "We better get to work on this. I only gave us three days to obtain what we need and complete this job. We need Christopher's trust. Once we gain his, the others will come. I know it somehow. There's a reason we can't find him in any of the databases."

Alena agreed. "I'm sure you're right. We'll deliver as promised. It was no accident you met him today."

⁓ ℓℓ ⁓

Three days later, they arrived back, and Christopher sat in a secluded booth again at the appointed place.

He looked at her expectantly. "Well?"

She pulled out a small device from a protective casing. "Please scan it. I expect nothing less. I wouldn't bring anything on my ship without doing so."

He seemed surprised but nodded. "You're right. Glad to see you expected that." He pulled out a device of his own and ran it over every inch of the device. After then doing his own visual examination, he appeared satisfied. He secured the device she gave him and turned to her. "Are we ready?"

"Lead the way."

She walked into Christopher's ship and set to work.

"I assume you would prefer me to use your equipment to install this rather than mine."

"Yes, no offense. In this business, you should be paranoid, right?"

"No offense taken. Yes, It's a healthy part of the profile as it keeps you alive from what I observe." She continued to work as Christopher handed her his data pad.

Christopher watched her as she immediately dove into the task. She literally worked inside what controlled his ship. She gave him no reason to distrust her, but he couldn't let her be unsupervised on his ship with his data pad. He'd just met her. He felt sure they worked on the same side, something tough to find in this line of business.

For her part, the girl knew the second she walked onto the ship, her every move would be monitored. She had no issue with it. An hour later, she completed installing and integrating the device into Christopher's ship. She tested it with Christopher to ensure it worked as he wished, and it did.

"Impressive. Are you sure you don't want payment?"

"I received my payment as agreed. The only other thing is I'd like the opportunity to work with others in the business who share your additional ground rules. Perhaps, you could help with that possibility."

"I believe that can be arranged, but you understand I can't hand you a list."

"Of course not. That would sign everyone's death certificate. I know I like breathing another day, and I've seen others share that desire. Anyway, all the names would be fake, so it wouldn't get me anywhere, right?"

"True. You are a pleasure doing business with, Chris. I guess we need to agree on a way for you to reach me the next time."

"No. I'll be able to reach you if need be."

"If someone else said that to me, I'd start looking for something planted on the ship. I must say, though, after the first encounter with you, I believe you'll locate me on your own. Until next time, Chris."

"Yes, until next time, Christopher." She smiled and walked out of the ship.

The man sat and leaned back in the cockpit chair. He watched her go and said out loud, "There is more than meets the eye with you, Chris." Her youth and beauty surprised him in this business. They seemed a dangerous combination for her in this line of work with the way most others handled their affairs. He hoped she would be careful, but for some reason, it seemed unnecessary to worry, and that puzzled him. Despite her youthful appearance, she didn't act like one with the experience of a mere youth. Every interaction echoed what he said to her, that she spoke and carried herself as one beyond her years. Somehow, he had no doubts she could take care of herself if need be. He continued in his musings, intrigued by this one who called herself Chris. He settled on saying, "Mysterious, but I like her."

⁓⁓⁓

Alena and the girl were right. The connection with Christopher provided the opening the girl needed. Connections began to be made with those the girl could work with in the future. They also continued to find those they needed to avoid, but useful information as well in this business. Five months passed. Every couple of weeks, they returned home to see Alika and update him.

CHAPTER TWENTY-ONE

"You okay?" asked Alena.

"Yeah. Actually, no, I'm tired for some reason. It's a couple of days sooner than normal, but I need to head home today. I'm sorry," said the girl.

"Hey, it's fine. This is unusual for you, so we need to listen. We should be completely present during this, or we can end up putting one or both of us in danger."

"Thanks for understanding, Alena. I'm glad one of us does."

They arrived home in about ten minutes as there was a portal a few minutes away from their current location.

Alika smiled as he came out to meet them. "This is a pleasant surprise. Is everything okay as I didn't expect you this early?"

"I believe so." Alena hesitated and glanced in the direction of the girl. "She felt tired but didn't know why. She wanted to go ahead and come back early. I thought it best to do so."

"Strange for her, but I'm glad you went ahead and returned."

The girl walked up and hugged him. "Alika."

Alika hugged her back. "Why don't you lie down before dinner? It sounds like you hit a limit, and your body is pushing back."

"Perhaps. I'll try to rest for a while." She sounded doubtful but went inside and headed for her room.

Alena peered at Alika. "What do you think?"

"I honestly don't know." His eyes followed the girl for another moment, puzzled.

Alena went to the girl's room to tell her dinner was ready, expecting her to be asleep. Rather, she found the girl sitting at a desk looking over information on the data pad.

"What happened to sleeping?"

"I tried, but I couldn't sleep. So here I am." She got up. "I'm assuming dinner is waiting?"

"Yes, come on."

They ate and reviewed the almost two weeks of happenings with Alika as they routinely did. Initially, they held off doing so, but the girl assured them she felt fine to do the standard review. The girl hoped when she laid down for bed, she would sleep as usual. Later, she indeed went straight to sleep.

—ele—

The sun began setting, and it seemed like an ordinary evening at first. The boy was outside. He appeared to be around eight or nine years old, maybe younger. He bent down, exploring something on the ground, or he searched for something. Perhaps something he played with earlier. Someone approached him, but it didn't bother him. The little boy knew every inch of this place with his eyes closed. Ah, this must be his home. He looked up smiling, knowing it could only be a few individuals. They probably came to tell him to go inside for the night. He saw the person, but his face went from smiling to disbelief to horror. He screamed, putting his hands up in defense, but he could do nothing.

The girl screamed with the boy. Then someone spoke to her, trying to arouse her from her terrifying slumber, "Child, child, awaken, it's only a nightmare."

Her eyes opened wide, and she recognized Alika's voice calling to her. Alena sat by her side as well. The girl's whole body shook. Alena got up and brought her something to drink. When the girl became calm enough, she sipped it.

"I know why I needed to come here a couple of days early."

"Agreed," said Alika, giving the girl the time she needed.

The girl spoke wearily, "I saw a vision from the past of a young boy, eight or nine years old, outside in his yard playing, right around the sunset hour. Someone approached him. He assumed it was a family member. There's no doubt in my mind of that part. He thought that until the very moment ..." she stopped, and her voice shook. She collected herself and continued. "He turns, and a woman approaches him. She wields a long dagger, and she ..." the girl couldn't finish. "He tried, but it was useless. He put his hands up and screamed before she ..." A sob escaped her, and tears streamed down her face. "What mother murders her own son?"

Alika and Alena stared at the girl in silence. Alika said what she thought, "They don't, child."

"You're right." The girl knew that, but she could still hear the boy's scream in her head and see the dagger shedding the child's blood. If it had been her father and her, the scene would make sense. He wouldn't give a second thought of ending her life. Yet, the child in this scene gazed up in disbelief at what he saw. Another explanation existed for the horrific scene that terrorized her sleep, but she didn't know what it might be.

"There is more," she continued. "I saw a figure behind the woman watching it. It was an Elder, Alika. The Elder helped her do this. How can this be?"

Alena and Alika both shook their head, and Alika answered, "It is not as it shows at first. It cannot be."

Alena nodded in agreement. "Remember with your mother how you saw our actions toward you. There is something you're missing from what you saw, or things are not as they appear on the surface. Walk back through it with us, and together we'll find the answer."

The girl did, describing it to them. The boy thought it was his mother. This time she watched the scene and did not turn away from any of it, no matter the horror she felt. Then she glimpsed it. For a second, she thought she imagined it. No, she hadn't, so briefly, it flashed in the woman's eyes after she struck the blow. The true form revealed itself. She gazed at Alena and Alika with a mixture of sadness and anger, "No, his mother wouldn't do such a thing, but we know who would." She felt sick to her stomach.

Calming herself again, she regained her composure and continued through the rest of the scene. It seemed like an Elder. He wore the clothing of one, even down to the exact markings on the bottom of the cloak. Unfortunately, the way he stood and lowered his head made it impossible to see his face to identify him. Then it hit her. "I am such a fool. Clothed like an Elder ..."

"Doesn't make one an Elder," said Alena. "Though, in the past, an Elder would keep the cloak protected since it signals the person is an Elder."

"I think we would find an Elder mysteriously disappeared or passed away during the same time this event occurred," said the girl.

"I believe you would be right," said Alika. "The cloaks used to be destroyed or accounted for, or both depending upon the situation, but I can see one being overlooked under the right circumstances."

"Of course, if an Elder mysteriously disappeared, the ones responsible for this whole thing would take the cloak from the Elder before they ended his life. They would kill an Elder without hesitation if they would take the life of a child," said the girl.

"Do you know the child?" asked Alena.

"Yes, I do." Fresh tears streamed down her face. "His name is Collin. He is the son of Abigail and Ethan. Their oldest son is Dante."

There was silence.

CHAPTER TWENTY-TWO

The girl continued as if reading their thoughts. "Ethan goes by a different name now, the Black Dragon Commander. Nevertheless, Ethan is his true name. Many of the visions I saw of him were Ethan and his family before becoming the Black Dragon Commander. I believe the reason I saw that part of his life is connected to why I saw this vision tonight."

The girl turned to Alika. "Did this happen when you became an Elder? I can't imagine this being explained away. There must be a reason I'm seeing this now."

Alena sat quietly, her eyes downcast. Undoubtedly, she remembered, or she heard the story already.

Alika sighed, and his eyes turned sad as he recalled it. "I had not been an Elder for long when it occurred, and the tragedy would mark the beginning of the dark times. The child was found murdered, and such horror for the child's family. There are no words, nothing to ease such pain. It got worse when evidence appeared to show an Elder responsible for the deed. Ethan became convinced of an entire Elder plot at the core of his son's murder. The Elders tried to investigate the matter, but Ethan had already decided what happened. We never understood how he could jump so swiftly to such a conclusion. Ethan believed the Elders betrayed him and destroyed his family. He turned against literally everything he had been taught, from the beginning by the Elders and his training as a sunspear-bearer. Although he still uses the sunspear on rare occasions, as we found out. Soon after that, he launched his mission to defeat the Elders. We realized he did not work alone. He found an ally in one who called himself the Dark Lord. Then it became apparent who whispered the words against us to convince him of the course he took."

"In his grief, the darkness found an entrance to him. It is a harsh snare, Alika."

Alika reached over and squeezed her hand delicately. "It is, child. Many pay for the snare which entraps him," Alika continued, "Once he began on the course, his intent was clear. The Elders stepped in and took Dante before his father could leave with him. If they failed, Dante's existence would be as a servant of the Dark Lord too. Instead, Dante continued his training with the Elders as you do. Dante is one of the strongest trained by the Elders to this day and serves the colonies well. However, Ethan never forgave the Elders for that either, and as far as he's concerned the Elders destroyed his family."

"I believe, sadly, you're right, and Ethan does see it that way. I'm grateful the Elders stepped in and saved Dante from such a horrible fate." She stopped and wondered aloud, "What happened to Dante's mother? She would be able to say she didn't kill Collin and at least try to convince them of her innocence."

"No one knows. At first, Ethan became convinced she fled in her guilt. Later he voiced the possibility the Elders murdered her as they did Collin. Ethan believed anything as long as it pointed back to the Elders being at the center of the plot. Of course, we surmised whoever was responsible for slaughtering Ethan's son probably murdered Abigail as well. Ethan wouldn't hear of it though, because he gained footage of what happened. He saw it and heard the whisper in his ear urging him what to believe. He never questioned other possibilities of what he saw, what he was told. Instead, he allowed his grief to take over and blind him to the truth."

"And that's what it did. You're right about Abigail too. They would kill her. The truth is lost to the grave with her."

"No," said a whisper. The girl saw another image. She didn't understand all of it but enough.

Alena and Alika watched her, knowing something had changed again.

The girl gaped at both of them in disbelief. "Abigail still lives."

Alena and Alika shared her shock for several moments.

Alena spoke first, "How?"

The girl spoke deliberately, her head spinning as if not believing her own words, "They took her and still have her. It's a chamber of some kind. She surrounded by things ... hooked up to some of them, like part of a larger set-up. An experiment ... No, not that really." The girl's frustration mounted as she searched for the words. "I don't know how to describe what I saw. It was strange. The image was brief."

Alika said, "The days are getting darker with something in the works from the Dark Lord. Could the Black Dragon Commander be keeping her alive for something as part of the operation? The darkness is strong, which binds him now."

The sick realization hit the girl. "No. For all the darkness, which twists Ethan's being, that's not it. This is purely the Dark Lord's brutality. He took her prisoner and keeps her. She does play a part in his operation. Her spirit struggled against it for all this time and continues to do so. I could sense it. As the Black Dragon Commander, Ethan is carrying out the operation, but this is the part he knows nothing about. He still believes his wife dead by the hand of the Elders. With each step Ethan completes in the operation, he is minute by minute killing his wife. He has no idea what he's doing." Tears streamed down her face anew. Ethan hurt so many people, including his own family as the Black Dragon Commander, but he was deceived into doing it. He didn't deserve this. Abigail laid struggling against this darkness for all this time and made to suffer. She didn't deserve this. Then there was Dante. He believed his mother dead, endured his brother being murdered, and he fought against his own father. Dante didn't deserve this. Her heart broke for them as the tears continued to stream down her face.

They all sat there in stunned silence again.

Alena asked the obvious question, "What do we do now?"

Alika answered, "I don't know, but there is a reason we obtained this knowledge. Ideas come to mind, but dangerous doesn't begin to be the word for it."

The girl stared out, seemingly lost in another world. "The battles go back and forth, with more destruction and lives lost, and it will only worsen. The Dark Lord forged his advantage, because he gained the heart of one by perverting the truth in the cruelest way possible. Everyone will continue to pay dearly for his treachery. "

Alena said to the girl, "I hear a decision in there."

"We can tip the balance. We grasp the knowledge and means to break the Dark Lord's hold on Ethan. Abigail is the only way to convince anyone of the truth. Besides, she has struggled too long alone against the darkness they plan for her. We must get her back before time runs out."

"Even if we can get her back," Alika hesitated, "how will you survive the encounter long enough to convince Ethan of all this?"

"I wouldn't." She took a deep breath. "Someone else must do that part."

"You're certain?" asked Alena.

"Yes, he's the only one who can get through to Ethan." She tried not to show the concern she felt for him. It was strange, but her visions centered on him the last few months. She knew him now, and her thoughts kept going back to him.

There was silence again. They all felt concerned as well.

"Where is she being held? How do we get her back?" asked Alena after a few minutes.

"I don't know, and I don't know." The girl sighed with displeasure at her own answer.

Alika gave her a stare that said he was rethinking his entire speech months earlier about her being ready.

The girl met his eyes to show she read his thoughts. "Yes, you're the one who said I would be equipped with everything I needed for the path I chose."

"I did." Alika wasn't sure about hearing his own words now. "Are you sure this is the path we must go?"

"It is. I'm certain."

He returned her steady gaze. "All right, child, we will press on with this course of action. We need to figure out where she's being held."

CHAPTER TWENTY-THREE

Lana, Caleb, Dante, and Seth continued searching for the final piece that would unlock the mystery after watching the commanders leave earlier in the day. The search proved fruitless. Even though evening arrived, and Lana felt exhausted, she couldn't sleep. She got up and ended up knocking on Seth's door.

The door opened for her.

"Lana, this is unexpected but never unwelcome. Are you okay?"

"Yes, well, I guess, Seth. I can't sleep. I'm sorry for the late hour."

"I see. Come in, and I'll get tea for us. Let's talk."

"I should be tired out of my mind."

"But it won't stop. You're running through all the scenarios."

"I wonder if we're doing the right thing. I feel the urgency to stop them, but the other part of me says it's our own destruction rushing in without the intel. Then I'm worried we're letting ourselves be destroyed because we're allowing them to go in this next time."

"And you're the one who made the decision, and so you feel responsible."

"Yes, what if I'm wrong, Seth?" She met Seth's eyes, and her eyes filled with uncertainty.

"Lana, you can't be. You always seek guidance from the Ancient One as you were taught from the beginning. You review any other information available to you. Based on that, you make the best decision you can. We can ask no more of you as it's all we can ask of ourselves."

"You're right, Seth. Sometimes it's not the decision that is bad, but I'm not happy with the options before me. I wish there were one where we already figured out their plan and arrived at how to stop them."

"You're hoping for the option we all wish laid before us, but we don't have it yet."

There was silence.

"Lana, you're a true leader and will always be." Seth reached over and took her hand. "It can be a lonely place, though, dear."

"It is, Seth."

"It may feel as so, but you're never alone. You were taught the lesson from the beginning as all are, especially those taught by the Elders to bear the sunspear. There is a reason we're constantly reminded of the lesson as it sounds like a simple truth on the surface, but it's one of the hardest ones to grasp at certain points in our life. Yet, the truth remains that you're not alone."

"Feel lonely, but not alone. Seth, I feel it more sometimes in this role, though."

"I know, but I don't believe it will always be that way." His face showed puzzlement after the words emerged.

"In what way?" Lana asked.

"I'm not sure." He sat in thought but shrugged. "You're doing well. They would be proud of you and how you lead everyone."

"I miss them, but they taught me well before the massacre swept them from me."

"We all learned a great deal from them in the time we had them." Seth observed Lana, and her eyes drooped now. "Why don't you try to sleep? I believe you will find success now."

Lana yawned. "I think you're right." She let herself out and returned to her and Caleb's room. She admitted curiosity about Seth's comment. He made comments like that at times and would find out later what they meant. He said it would come to him, like a foreshadowing of something. It was a strange gift from the Ancient One. Sometimes more helpful than others.

Seth sat back and wondered. However, he learned a long time ago that meaning would become clear. A yawn escaped him, and he decided to take his own advice.

CHAPTER TWENTY-FOUR

The next day came. They finished the last of the ship repairs the previous evening. Seth looked over information with Caleb when it arrived.

Lana walked briskly into the room. "We're getting a report of a possible attack. I already contacted the others accordingly."

At Lana's announcement, Caleb, Seth, and Dante were already on their feet and rushing toward the ship hangar.

❦

Dante arrived at the planet's surface, and Commander Ryan and his squadron greeted him.

Dante asked, "What do you see?"

Commander Ryan answered, "Less than a hundred troops coming. Isn't that low?"

"No, it's the pattern, but listen for a few tanks or those large artillery robots," Dante replied.

Commander Ryan groaned. "Great, I remember you telling me about those. You're not concerned, though, so I'll relax, Dante."

"They sound scary, but so far, they're predictable."

"We'll follow the plan, and you lead, Dante."

❦

Skyward, Commander Caleb led his group against the squadron of Black Dragon ships.

"Same scene in the sky, everyone. Have your pilots go for the squadron ships as long as possible. Don't engage the command ship. We'll attempt to do that as long as we can."

Seth led the small squadron on the undercover operation. They dressed plainly as not to draw any attention, appearing more like building security. They were armed but carefully concealed.

"Okay, Seth. Similar industries, three of them on the colony. The footage from the planet spotted a small group of Black Dragon soldiers headed toward the one called Neurochemical Labs," reported Lana from the command post.

"We'll make it there before them, Lana."

Seth turned to the group. "Remember, we are to be eyes and ears only. We are not here to stop them or be seen by them."

The group nodded back to Seth in understanding. They arrived at the Neurochemical Labs and reviewed the setup of the building Lana sent them.

"We must hurry. The Black Dragon squadron will be here any moment. Go to your assigned place in either the warehouse or the lab part of the facility to observe. Do not come out until the Black Dragon squadron leaves the grounds." As the last word left Seth's mouth, the group hurried away.

The Black Dragon soldiers approached the warehouse as during the other attacks. The guard at the watch post took one look and momentarily contemplated standing his ground. Tracking the situation on his data pad, Seth observed one of his troops move forward in position slightly. He deduced what the troop considered doing, but his troop couldn't be allowed to follow through. Seth continued to watch the data pad with one eye and the guard with the other. He could tell his troop still pondered intervening, so he sent a gentle message through the data pad to him. They couldn't risk it. Hopefully, the guard would see he couldn't fight the Black Dragon troops and leave as most others did.

To their relief, the guard comprehended the odds before him and decided his life was worth more value than protecting whatever the facility held. He backed away and fled as the Black Dragon soldiers got within several yards of him.

The Black Dragon soldiers entered the warehouse first.

One of the Black Dragon soldiers barked, "We need that one, that one…" He continued pointing to boxes, calling out different numbers and using a device to scan them.

Another Black Dragon soldier placed the boxes on a cart and left.

What seemed like only moments later, a Black Dragon soldier brought in a fully loaded cart into the warehouse. The soldier began unloading the boxes from the cart and putting them back in the same places where the boxes had been they had just loaded on the cart.

The Black Dragon soldiers completed the task in no time and set off to the lab next door.

⁓ele⁓

Miles away, Dante and Ryan led the battle against the Black Dragon ground troops. Dante heard the familiar sound. He called to Ryan and made a motion, as Ryan hurried alongside him.

"This is what you were talking about, Dante?"

"Yep, right on time. A few of the tanks as usual. Cover me, and I'll go take care of them."

"Will do. Be careful."

"Always."

Dante headed for one of the tanks and fought his way inside, taking care of the two troops controlling it. He aimed a shot at one of the tanks, and it burst into flames. After getting a second shot off for the other tank, he felt it. Something was wrong. He sensed too much activity right outside the tank, and Ryan confirmed it a moment later.

"Dante, your tank is surrounded, and they're coming in close to you. We can't get over to help you yet. Get out of there now!" Ryan's voice rang out in a panic on his data pad.

Dante knew Ryan wasn't exaggerating. The last tank would fire to blow this one up, but an ambush awaited him the instant he emerged from the tank. He aimed the final shot toward the last tank and hoped he shot sooner. Throwing several firestones from the top of the tank toward his welcoming party, he jumped out at the same instant. He landed hard on the ground as the last tank got its shot off before his shot hit it. Excruciating, fiery pain, sliced through his shoulder and ripped down his back, but he forced himself to block it out. The explosion from the firestones and the tank also threw the Black Dragon Army troops surrounding the tank off balance briefly, just enough for Dante's escape. He turned on his back, groaning in agony, but raised his sunspear in time to meet a Black Dragon blade. Dante found his mark and took care of the troop. He got up with a struggle, but forced himself to concentrate on the task at hand. His sunspear managed to find its mark in a couple of others that thought they had him surrounded. Luckily, Ryan and the others pushed forward to help him. He had cut it too close, and Ryan's approach was a most welcome sight. He felt incredibly tired all at once, and his sunspear weighed a ton.

Ryan reached him and stared at a place on his back. "Dante, I thought I told you to be careful!"

CHAPTER TWENTY-FIVE

The sky lit up as the air battle raged. Caleb and the commanders and the squadron were, by all appearances, winning. They incurred minor damage to their own ships. The Black Dragon ships appeared to sustain substantial damage, but Caleb and the commanders knew this was nothing more than a distraction for something else. They battled as in the previous attacks, since it must appear as before to the Dark Lord.

⁂

Seth continued watching on the screen as the Black Dragon men entered the lab facility. They followed the same process collecting materials as they had at the warehouse, and then carts appeared back in with the materials. They put the materials back from where they had taken them. It didn't make sense.

One of the Black Dragon men entered one of the lab rooms. A lone lab assistant remained in the room, despite the lockdown order. When he saw the Black Dragon soldier, he fired his weapon rather than running or hiding. He proved no match for the Black Dragon soldier. The Black Dragon soldier stopped, stunned momentarily, coming closer to the lab assistant, and fired his weapon simultaneously. The assistant dodged unsuccessfully, and the shot hit him in the leg. He fired again in defense, crawling backward on the ground in desperation as the Black Dragon soldier moved to finish the job with his sword. Without warning, a figure jumped in front of the blade and knocked it from the Black Dragon soldier's hand. The figure shot his weapon, and the Black Dragon soldier fell. He started to finish the Black Dragon soldier off, but he heard his data pad go off loudly, "Don't do it. Scan his tag and data pad. Hide in the closet next door with the injured lab man and don't move again."

Seth watched in horror, helpless as the scene unfolded. The one rule and one of his men breached it. Then the man stopped before striking the final blow to the Black Dragon soldier. He quickly bent down over the Black Dragon soldier before dragging the injured lab assistant from the room. The Black Dragon soldier would awaken in minutes. The weapon only short-circuited the soldier temporarily, and the Black Dragon would be alerted now.

Awakening, the Black Dragon soldier glanced around and rose. He arrived here to secure something. A beep from his data pad would be the squadron commander questioning why he was not back with the package. He better hurry and secure it. Then he remembered the interruption by the security guard, but he didn't see the person anymore. He scanned his data pad:

We had a couple of people who attempted to be heroes at the lab. They were eliminated and disposed. Now finish up, soldier.

He remembered now. He needed to hurry and finish securing the items.

Meanwhile, the Black Dragon leader stood outside the lab, waiting impatiently for the last package. A message appeared on his data pad, and he sneered, "I guess that is the last time we have any colonists play the hero. Foolish ones to think they could overpower one of my soldiers. Handy having an incinerator on location for easy disposal."

Seth saw a message on his data pad minutes later: *We're okay, waiting for them to leave as instructed.*

The message originated from his troop member, who violated the rule. It appeared the Black Dragon squadron did not discover them after all. Seth was puzzled but answered back: *Okay, stay there.*

Seth watched as the Black Dragon men continued to retreat. His group would be able to go back and watch precisely what the Black Dragon men seized.

The last one left, and Seth received another message on his data pad: *The Black Dragon report for today will be a couple of people at the lab tried to be heroes and failed. They were easily overcome, and their bodies disposed of. That is what the Black Dragon soldier recalls as well.*

Seth smiled, puzzled and curious to find out how Lana performed the trick. There was no end to her talents.

⁓ℓℓℓ ⁓

Ryan said, "Caleb, the few leftover troops ran to an area away from the fighting a few minutes ago. I'd look for the transport ship soon."

"Right on time, Ryan. It just appeared. Everything stayed predictable today."

"Yeah, right, Caleb," he finished the communication and turned to Dante, "Not everything, huh, Dante."

Dante gave him a look that mirrored a mixture of unhappiness and pain.

One of the men from Ryan's squadron approached. "Commander Ryan, here is what you asked to be brought to you."

"Great, thanks."

"Okay, Dante. We've got to do something about your nasty burn, injury, whatever you did before you pass out on me. I don't enjoy seeing the inside of your back exposed. I don't know how you kept fighting. This will do until we get back to Lana. I'd say this will hurt, but I don't understand how you're standing that. Ready?"

Dante nodded.

"Would you put the sunspear down or at least keep your hand far from it while I put this stuff on?"

Dante laughed despite the pain. "Sure, Ryan, I promise I won't chop off any part of you while you treat me."

"Okay, but I see you fight with that sunspear, so it's a legitimate request. Here goes." He sprayed from the bottle, and the medicine soaked into Dante's skin.

Dante tried to hold back, but he jumped and bit his lip to keep the yell of pain from escaping. After a few deep breaths, he turned to Ryan. "Thanks, Ryan."

"What are friends for? Remember, that's only to hold you over until we get you back to base."

Dante groaned. The real treatment was to come.

Ryan smiled and his tone turned serious this time, "We got this, and we'll head back as soon as possible to get you treated. Sit. Take it easy. That's an order, buddy."

Dante didn't disagree this time. He'd be doing the same if it was Ryan.

"Is he okay?" asked Lana.

"Yeah. I treated him with the spray on-site. It's beyond me how he kept fighting. It's an ugly bloody gash down his shoulder and back. I'm sure it contains pieces of the tank in it when it blew too. He's tough, but we need to get him treated now."

"Done. I'll get a ship there and have him off the planet. The Dark Lord's squadron should leave through the portal soon now that they have the transport ship."

⸺ℓℓℓ ⸺

A few minutes later, Caleb reported, "Lana, the Black Dragon Army is through the portal."

"Good, coordinate with Seth what help he wants on the ground. Also, take control of Commander Ryan's squadron. Commander Ryan is coming back here with Dante," stated Lana.

Caleb caught the last part of her statement. "Something happened."

"Yes and no. It's under control. Dante took a hit, but he'll be fine, I promise. He's coming back here to be treated, but Commander Ryan insisted on accompanying him."

Caleb felt better. Lana sounded sure.

"Okay, we'll see you soon," replied Seth. Everyone was accounted for, including his squadron member who intervened in the lab. The lab assistant was transported to the nearby treatment facility for his injury.

"Commanders." Seth nodded as they approached, but his eyes questioned Caleb.

"Commander Ryan got held up with Dante. Dante took a nasty hit, but he'll be fine." Caleb saw the concern fill Seth's eyes. "Really, the words are from Lana, so he'll be fine."

"All right, let's get to work."

CHAPTER TWENTY-SIX

"Yes, there are pieces of metal in the wound. Seriously, cousin."

"I told him to be careful, Lana."

"He was never good at taking orders."

"Funny, you two."

"Seriously, cousin, I'm glad you're okay. They're getting started. We'll talk after they're done." She started to hug him but decided that with his injuries, a hand squeeze would suffice.

They carefully sprayed a liquid gas substance to Dante's injuries, and the area went numb. They pulled out a device to cautiously extract the metal pieces from the wound. It was akin to using a magnet on a person. Thankfully, it methodically removed the pieces of metal from the wounds rather than snatching them out like a magnet would. Another mist sprayed out a substance to clean out the wound. An instrument scanned the injury, and an affirmative beep sounded. Another spray came with medicine. The wound began to heal and his skin to regenerate.

Lana and Ryan came back into the room.

"Better, cuz?"

"Much better."

"Buddy, it sure looks better. You can't be getting holes blown in your back. You scared me."

"Come on, Ryan, let's go join the others, now."

"You're kidding me, right?"

"We're seeing what the Black Dragon Army left behind. There's no danger now. We can be helpful," He looked at Ryan. "You're not to blame. It didn't matter who was with me. I'm fine." He turned to Lana. "I promise, all good now. The ground troops caught on to our game, and I realized it at the same time Ryan did. It just came too close today."

Lana didn't say anything for a minute. She could try to keep him here, but it would be no use. She sighed, "Okay, but be careful. Oh, never mind. I'm don't know why I'm even saying it after today." She rolled her eyes at her cousin. "The two of you try to take care of each other, whatever that looks like, and go help the others. Commander Ryan, at least make him wear one of these protective shirts for a few hours while he's out since he just received treatment on the wound."

Ryan handed it over to Dante. "Seth is going to kill me after this."

"Ryan, would you stop beating yourself up over what happened? I'll tell Seth," Dante assured Ryan as he carefully put the protective shirt on under his regular shirt.

"Like Seth is going to believe either one of us."

"Good point."

Lana watched both, holding back her laughter as they left.

⁓ ℓℓℓ ⁓

Seth summarized what his group witnessed with the supplies and showed them on the data pad.

"They loaded the boxes, scanned them, left, came back, and unloaded them again," said Caleb.

"I told you it doesn't make sense," said Seth.

"What doesn't make sense?" asked Commander Ryan.

Seth and the others turned around to see Commander Ryan and Dante approaching.

"Shouldn't he be resting or something?" Caleb asked, looking at the two. "Don't bother answering me. If Lana couldn't stop him, there's no hope for the rest of us."

"You're right," said Commander Ryan.

"I'm right here. Geez," said Dante.

"We're glad you're okay, Dante. We were concerned," said Commander Gabe.

"Thank you, Commander Gabe. I'm glad someone is happy to see me." He pretended to be offended. "So, what's the big mystery we're trying to solve?"

Seth smiled. "I'm glad you're recovering, Dante." He did a recap for them.

Dante was thoughtful. "Did we check the boxes yet?"

"We were about to do so," said Seth.

"Can I see the data pad for a minute, Seth?" asked Commander Ryan. Seth handed it over. Commander Ryan studied the recording of the Black Dragon's movements in the facility, with Dante doing the same beside him. "Do we have any footage of outside with the boxes before the carts enter the building?"

"Yes, I'm sure we do on one of the data pads," said Seth.

"We need to see the whole route of the transport. On second thought, it may be unnecessary once we check the boxes," said Commander Ryan.

"I think I see where he's going with it," Commander Conrad said.

"Like we're not seeing the same boxes," Caleb said.

"Only one way to know for sure," replied Dante.

They entered the warehouse. Seth checked the data pad. "This was one of the boxes."

Commander Austin reviewed his data pad. "According to the information, here are the contents." He bent down next to Dante, intent on inspecting the box.

Dante focused on the box side. "The side of the box matches what's supposed to be here."

Commander Aegeus said, "I thought we would find something different, but it looks like the same box."

"We didn't open it yet." Dante ignited his sunspear barely and used the tip to open the box. He pulled out its contents.

"It appears right," said Commander Cephas.

Dante lifted one of the items from the box. "I guess." Dante moved it to his other hand and back again. Then he brought it closer to his face to examine it and used his fingernail to rake a line across the surface.

"What is it, Dante?" asked Seth.

Dante shook his head. "No, it's not right." He pulled his data pad out and scanned the item. He turned the data pad around.

"Mystery explained. This type of equipment would never be made from this material, which means what was in here the Black Dragon Army confiscated," stated Commander Ryan.

"And replaced what they took with these boxes. Nobody would know until the boxes got to where they were shipped. If those on the receiving end caught it, they either assume it was a defective item or someone tried to cheat them by making it out of inferior material. With this type of business, it happens," said Caleb.

"I'm guessing we find the same swap took place with the lab materials," responded Commander Austin.

"Chemicals, dangerous crazy chemicals for months acquired by the Dark Lord. Troubling, indeed," murmured Seth.

"We need a list of what they got today, fast. Compare it with last time. See how similar it is," replied Caleb.

"Once we've done so, we should enlist the help of a lab employee. They can give us insight into what use the chemicals could be the Black Dragon is obtaining," Seth said.

"First we check the lab to confirm our theory holds true," said Caleb.

"Slow it down, Dante," Commander Ryan said as he helped Dante up. "You were stubborn and insisted on coming, but you just got treated."

Seth reminded Dante. "Yes, don't overdo it. Give the treatment time to work. Obviously, it was quite a hit." He smiled at Commander Ryan and turned back to Dante. "I'm glad Commander Ryan could be there to get you treated promptly."

They all walked toward the lab.

"See, I told you. Seth is fine about earlier. I'm fine. Stop worrying," said Dante to Ryan as they stayed a little behind everyone.

"You keep believing for the both of us, Dante," said Commander Ryan with a laugh.

Commander Caleb bent down this time and read the side of the box. "I have no idea what this chemical is, but it displays several warnings on it. Terrific. We definitely need one of the lab people here."

A couple of minutes later, Seth brought the head of the lab to them. "We need this box opened to see the contents of it."

The lab person peered at him, confused. "It's marked on the side of the box."

"We believe there is a mix-up on the contents of some boxes. It's important. We need you to open it, test it, and confirm the contents," said Seth.

"Yes, of course. I'll get gloves and equipment depending on the contents. You should leave the room as a safety precaution since we're dealing with chemicals," said the lab person.

"Understood. We expect what is actually in the box is far less dangerous than what's marked, but we're uncertain," said Seth.

The lab person set to work while they watched from outside the room. He opened the box and poured out a small amount of the substance in a lab container. It didn't react. He poured another substance into the container. His face reflected puzzlement. He inserted a testing stick into the container and stuck it in a machine. After viewing the display results, he smelled the container. He removed his protective mask and motioned for the group to join him in the lab, which they did.

The lab person shook his head. "You were right. This is no dangerous chemical. The worst would be a nauseous stomach if you mistakenly took a drink of it. It's dyed blue to look like this particular chemical. I don't understand how this could happen. We make most of the chemicals here." The lab person stared down, lost for words.

Seth said, "This discovery must stay with you. I assure you this didn't come from your lab. We'll need to take some boxes from the lab and the warehouse. We know which boxes are incorrect. You can redo them if needed. None of this happened today. Do you understand?"

"I do. I'm guessing this involves today's situation with the Black Dragon men I learned were on the premises. None of it can be good." He sighed. "Do what you need. The list of the boxes would be helpful, though. We'll redo the boxes, and I'll delete any record of the list. There will be no indication they were redone."

"Thank you. We may require your assistance further. We need to find out how the chemicals are normally used that were taken. Your knowledge would make the process go faster."

"I'll be glad to help. With most chemicals, they're not bad in themselves. Even combined with other chemicals, they're still not harmful many times because they're for a specific purpose. However, some of these chemicals in the wrong hands, I don't want to think of the possibilities. If you put them together and your intentions are malicious, then it could be devastating. You must find those supplies."

No one said a word, but everyone shared the same thought. The attacks started gaining momentum over six months ago, and so the Black Dragon Army obtained six months' worth of chemicals.

Dante finally settled into his role of identifying the boxes from the warehouse and lab that needed to be taken while the others did the loading.

CHAPTER TWENTY-SEVEN

Lana met them as they came inside, and she continued sifting through the information from the data pads.

Commander Ryan went to talk further with Seth, and Dante followed him. Ryan still couldn't get what happened to Dante out of his mind, no matter what Dante said to him.

"Seth, I'm sorry about Dante. I feel bad about today."

"There is nothing to feel bad about, as I'm sure Dante assured you. I'm glad both of you are fine. Dante would have incurred the same injury no matter who fought alongside him."

"I told Ryan the same thing, but he thinks I'm just saying it."

"It's hard to believe you. You didn't see the chunk taken out of your back after the hit."

"I can understand your doubts, Ryan, but it's time to move on from the incident. I know what close friends the two of you are, so that's probably a large part of it." Seth smiled. "Dante is recovering, though. I admit I'm curious about what happened. It could change the strategy for the future attacks when disarming the tanks."

"Yes, it will. I disarmed them in a similar way too many times, and so it cost me today. Ryan and I realized it at the same instant. Any later..."

"And we won't go there. It's what I suspected. We'll go through the more detailed version in a bit. For now, I'm glad you're okay. Please take time to recover as instructed. I need to see Lana for a moment. I'll be back."

"Seth, everything worked out after all. I was worried."

"Thanks to you, Lana. You helped a great deal today. I thought they discovered us for sure."

"You and your team did everything. We obtained the information we needed thanks to your operation. There was Dante, but he is relatively fine, as you can see."

"No, I referred to the incident at the lab between the lab employee and the Black Dragon soldier and our soldier. Thanks to your assistance, our presence remained hidden."

"Seth, what are you talking about? I heard something about one of their personnel hurt today, and they sent him for treatment. Was there something more with him?"

"You have no idea what I'm saying? I was sure the message originated from you."

Lana gave him a clueless look.

Seth got his data pad out. "Troop member Anthony, I need you here with your data pad now." He turned back to Lana. "He was the one involved in the incident. One of the lab employees didn't go into lockdown, and a Black Dragon troop walked into the lab to retrieve one of the boxes. The employee tried to shoot him. It didn't work. The Black Dragon troop shot him in the leg and moved to finish him. Our man left position to rescue the man, surprised the Black Dragon troop, and started to kill him. Our man stopped before doing so and got the lab person to safety in lockdown, but not before The Black Dragon troop spotted him."

"The one thing which couldn't happen." Lana moaned, but then she turned to him, puzzled. "You said we weren't discovered, though."

"No, fortunately we weren't." Seth sighed. "As much as I wanted to reprimand him for disobeying orders, I couldn't. He's sworn to protect, and he couldn't watch a fellow colonist slaughtered in front of him. I wouldn't expect him to do so."

"Me either. It's why he's a Freedom Fighter. I don't think any of us could have that on our conscience. So how did we escape detection?"

"I'm here, sir," said Troop Anthony coming up about that time.

"Troop Anthony, you mentioned a message you got right after you stunned the Black Dragon troop."

"Of course, sir, the first one you sent me."

"I only sent you one message."

"Sir, I got two."

"I need to see them, please."

Anthony tried to show them to Seth. "Sir, I don't understand. I received two messages from you, I promise. There's only one showing now."

"I believe you. The one you see is the one I sent you. Can you tell me what the other one said?"

"Yes, I remember most of it. It said, not to finish him. Scan the tag and data pad. For me and the lab person to hide in a closet in the next room and not move again."

"I see. You did so, and when you sent the message to me, you stayed put as told. Then I messaged back to you."

"Yes, sir."

"That's all for now. Thanks, Anthony, for your help," Seth said, turning back to Lana. "Then I had a message on my data pad, which I assumed came from you. I planned on showing it to you, but I'm certain it won't be there now." Seth checked his data pad, and as he guessed, it was gone.

"Seth, what did the message say?"

"It said, 'The Black Dragon report for today will be a couple of people at the lab tried to be heroes and failed. They were easily overcome, and their bodies disposed of. That is what the Black Dragon soldier recalls as well."

Lana stared at him and shook her head slowly. "I didn't send it, Seth."

"And I thought you had learned a new trick."

"So, who did, Seth?"

"I don't know, but it saved us from being discovered today."

"Someone we can't identify, but they kept our operation safe. I'm not sure what I should feel. Do we try communicating with them?"

"I think so. Perhaps they'll answer if they're still monitoring." He typed on the data pad: *Do you belong to the Black Dragon?*

They waited, and a message popped up: *You have no friends inside the Black Dragon. You knew already.*

Seth typed again: *You will not make yourself known, though.*

Another message appeared: *It must be so. I'm glad your enterprise proved successful, and I could be helpful. Also, I'm relieved everyone ended up being okay. Some close calls on a couple of fronts. Communicating further is not safe, so goodbye.*

Seth and Lana stared at each other. "You want to try one more message?" Lana asked.

"We won't get a response. The message is clear," said Seth. He typed: *Thank you.*

There was no response. "My guess is these messages will disappear." At that instant, Seth watched as his data pad blinked, and the entire conversation deleted from the screen. "They're making certain not to leave any tracks."

"They're monitoring our operation, and they can access our information. I feel uncomfortable. In any other circumstances, I would start changing our security systems."

"But you aren't jumping to do so. I understand. They accessed our systems and hacked into the Black Dragon systems too. Granted, some access for the Black Dragon probably derived from scanning the data pad and badge from the soldier, but still, it took work to pull off what they did today. They used all their access to help save our operation and trick the Black Dragon troops. Changing our security would be useless. Whoever they are, they're excellent at what they do, and they're striving to help us."

"Agreed. They monitored the whole operation, though. You saw the comment about everyone being okay and close calls."

"Yes, the wording is clear it goes beyond the incident with the lab assistant. Our unknown friend knows what happened on the ground with Dante as well."

Dante walked up with Caleb and Ryan. "What's going on? I heard my name, and this is the longest moment of talking with Lana."

Seth and Lana looked at each other. Lana turned to the others. "We're finished."

Caleb studied her face, unconvinced. "Something is up."

"Lana, I can start the others through the data if you want to talk to them."

"That would be great, Seth."

Seth walked off to work with the other commanders.

Lana set out explaining the discovery from the day.

"We have a friend somewhere who doesn't want to be known or found, but we owe this person a big thanks for keeping our operation from being discovered?" said Caleb.

"And they can hack into systems, manipulate them, and they decided to randomly help us?" said Ryan.

"And they monitored the whole attack and were concerned about our safety?" said Dante.

"That sums it up," said Lana.

"Beyond strange. I'm nervous too, but I agree with you and Seth. There's no time to concentrate on it. We hope we made a true friend," said Caleb.

"They could be working both sides, but it's a lot of trouble to set us up. I think your instincts are right, Lana," said Ryan.

"The communication sounds like there's something with their situation which makes this the only way they can help us. Like they have a good reason to keep their aid to us from being discovered. I don't feel we should fear them." Dante said, pondering it.

"I'm still having a hard time with the knowledge a stranger is monitoring everything even if they appear to be on our side," said Lana. "Let's go help the others."

CHAPTER TWENTY-EIGHT

"Let's say we could somehow get that far into their records. I don't see us locating where she's being held in them," said the girl.

"She ties into the operation somehow," said Alena.

"But she's the one part the Black Dragon Commander knows nothing about, so they can't keep her with the rest of the operation. The chance of discovery would be too high," said the girl.

"You think she is somewhere else entirely," said Alika.

"She must be," said the girl.

"Maybe it's a good thing since she won't be in the center of it," said Alena.

"She will be carefully secured, though. Also, it wouldn't be any troops the Black Dragon Commander maintains authority over. This is all the Dark Lord's operation," said the girl.

"She could be in the Dark Lord's ship," said Alena, but sounding doubtful as soon as she said it.

"Too close, too great of a chance to be discovered by the Black Dragon Commander," said the girl. "The Dark Lord and the Black Dragon Commander are frequently on the same ship and bases of operation. The area I saw was the inside of a building or a facility, I think."

"The Dark Lord would want someone he could trust to run this operation. Only two people come to mind. One is already eliminated," said Alika.

Alena realized at the same time.

"Yes," said the girl. "She's overseeing it."

"Do you think the Dark Lord gave her a Black Dragon command to keep the operation secure?" asked Alena.

"He would without hesitation as he's done many times with other tasks. Except there's special discretion needed with this ongoing operation. The Black Dragon Commander can't ever know about it, which would make it difficult for a squadron of Black Dragon troops to assist," said the girl.

"You believe he hired mercenaries or a special force to secure Abigail, don't you?" said Alika.

The girl sighed. "I do. Then the Dark Lord puts her in charge of this part of the operation."

"Makes sense. A whole Black Dragon squadron on an ongoing mission that the Black Dragon Commander knows nothing about wouldn't work. He'd question the scenario pretty fast," said Alena.

"In conclusion, it's going to be harder to free Abigail than we thought," said Alika.

"You said it. I didn't. We know who holds the key to where Abigail is located, so we start there," said the girl.

"That doesn't help us," said Alena. "She's not volunteering to tell us where she's holding Abigail. Any encounter with her isn't ending well."

"She'll tell us without knowing it," said the girl.

"How do you figure that?" Alena groaned. "Really?"

"She's bound to go there regularly to supervise it. The Dark Lord would insist on it," said the girl.

"You would need to get close to the center of everything to pinpoint her ship and to follow it," Alika said, looking at her, not liking where the path took him.

"I know, but once we learn which ship is hers, we can figure out where she's going. It'll be somewhere she goes consistently. We established one place is where she visits the Dark Lord. Those will probably be in the center of all the activity, and so they can be eliminated. There will be somewhere else, and it will be away from the operation, the Black Dragon Commander knows. That location will be where they're keeping Abigail," said the girl.

"How do get that close without ending up dead?" asked Alena.

"Ideas are forming, none, either of you'll like. I'm open for suggestions, a better idea," said the girl.

"Darkness," said Alika.

The girl and Alena both turned to him.

"My hunch is she comes to the Dark Lord for evening visits. The night is easier to go unnoticed and keep her visits discreet with him," said Alika.

The girl agreed. "You're probably right. Night would also be easier to sneak our ship past to watch, and there'll be less activity making it more likely to spot her ship."

"There will also be a greater chance to spot a ship which doesn't belong," Alena hesitated, "Like ours."

"Then, we'll make sure we blend in with the company around us for the evening," said the girl with a smile.

"The word in space is they're working on something, and they're always doing a lot of shipping. They don't take sleep breaks." Alena said. "We may need to make modifications to the ship's programming."

"We might pull this off in one piece."

They both shook their head at the girl.

"Okay, can one of you pretend to be optimistic with me?"

It was late afternoon of the next day as the three of them analyzed the results. They decided on three different modifications to the ship's holographic and structural program and made the final adjustments. They already had a couple of programs, including ships that imitated the Black Dragon, but this needed to be spot on for the operation.

"Impressive work," said Alika nodding with satisfaction.

"I admit I feel better about this operation," said Alena. "Do we have the other items ready to send out undetected?"

"Yes, I prepared those while you did the modifications on the ship," said the girl.

"I'll monitor the two of you as usual."

"Alena, we better head out to start surveillance. The faster we get a feel for the night activity where the Black Dragon crowd hangs out, the sooner we pinpoint which ship is hers."

—ele—

"This is an ideal spot. We can see everything, but not close enough to draw unwanted attention," said the girl.

"I like your choice of the ship for the evening. Nice touch," said Alena.

"Yeah, I thought the standard security or surveillance ship for the Black Dragon would work. Wouldn't want a ship sneaking up on your operation, right?"

"I'm guessing that took serious clearance," Alena grinned back at her.

"What can I say? As the operation progresses, they need extra security. At least that's what the system read."

"Are you cold?" asked Alena as she noticed the girl rubbing her arms a few times.

"No, I forgot how much I detest the darkness. I remember with my father, or when one of them entered the doorway, how you could sense the darkness radiate from them. I can feel it permeating the air here," said the girl.

Alena said, "I can too, and I'm not nearly as sensitive to that like you are. At least we know we're in the right place for this. The Dark Lord is in..."

The girl zeroed in on what appeared to be a command ship in the back of the others. "Yeah, I'm certain he's in that ship too, where he spends most of his time."

They watched the ships go in and out. A pattern emerged to the flow for most of them, maybe dropping supplies off as they were quick trips in and out of an area. After a couple of nights, they had a list of suspicious vessels that only frequented the command ship.

—ele—

After the third straight night of returning to Alika incredibly early each morning and sleeping a few hours, together, they examined the results again.

Alika pored over the list. "You think it's one of these?"

Alena answered, "Yes, but there's something about each one which put it on the list."

"Yeah, we hope a new perspective makes the difference," the girl said to Alika.

Alika stretched back in his chair after reviewing the footage with them. "I see why you're having an issue narrowing it down. We need another way to distinguish her ship along with this information."

"By now we should know it with all the trouble she has caused," said Alena.

"But we do!" exclaimed the girl looking at both of them, "One of those times when she dealt with us."

It all came back to them at the same time.

"Do you think she used her own ship?" asked Alena.

"I'd say there's a strong possibility," said Alika.

"Only a few guards accompanied her. It was one of those tasks the Dark Lord or the Black Dragon Commander sent her to supervise, to ensure it was done correctly, as she put it." The girl couldn't hide the bitterness in her voice as the sting of the woman's words came back anew from that day. "So, I agree it could be her ship."

The two gave her a moment before pursuing it further.

"Do we still have the footage?" asked Alena.

"Yes, and I'm on it," said the girl as she scanned through the data pad and projected it on the wall. The girl went back to the last day she saw her mother alive. Once her mother started her training with Alika and Alena, they installed an additional surveillance system and continued to make it better after her mother's murder. She sat there for several seconds and took a deep breath before she could open the footage. They found the ship.

"There should be something to distinguish it. Even the Dark Lord must know what's in his inventory," said Alena.

"Like a name or a tag number," said the girl searching the image.

"Actually, the opposite. It doesn't show a tag number or anything. I'm seeking another way to identify it," said Alena as she continued to turn the picture of the ship over at every angle as well. "Wait."

"She couldn't resist." The girl shook her head.

Embedded on the ship's underside in tiny print read the words. "Black Beauty."

"I wonder if the Dark Lord knows she did that," said Alika.

"I bet we find a match now," said Alena.

"See, Alika, we simply needed to bounce it off of you," said the girl.

Alika laughed and said, "Glad I could be of assistance."

"We have everything ready?" Alena asked.

"Yes, at least on paper, but I'm not confident enough until we double-check. We'll take the rest of this evening and tomorrow before we move into position to tag her ship." Something on her data pad made her frown.

"What is it?" asked Alika.

In response, the girl projected it for them.

"They waited for this," said Alena.

"So hopefully, it goes as planned. We'll return to our planning for tomorrow evening's operation, but we should monitor this today. They need it to go well, and they may save us work with what they gain from it," said the girl as her fingers played across the screen as she talked.

"It appears we are connected to everyone now," said Alika.

Alena murmured, "I don't like that one over there."

"Me either, but we're not the only one. Seth sees him," said the girl.

"He called him down," said Alika.

"This time," said the girl, worried it would be repeated before the operation ended. Her mind was already working.

They continued to watch and found their fear confirmed.

"Not good," Alena's voice rose in alarm.

"He's going to intervene," said Alika, with a sigh.

"And he did," said the girl, and in a flash, she spoke a command out to the man's data pad. He heard it loud and clear through his communication system before it was too late. "He followed the instructions, though."

"The soldier will be awake in minutes. Alena, we need the commander on site to think these two got put through the incinerator. I'm sending a couple of messages now, to induce some amnesia," said the girl as she worked lightning fast on the data pad as Alena matched her pace.

They continued monitoring until it was clear there would be no more need for their intervention.

"That was close," said Alena, shaking her head.

The girl leaned back in her chair. "That one troop almost ruined it, but he had to stop it. He would never get that image out of his mind, be able to forgive himself if he had let it happen."

Alika sighed. "We all know that, including Seth. It's the heart of a true Freedom Fighter in the man. They chose their team well." He paused. "Thanks to your quick thinking, they accomplished their objective today without Seth's troop having to make that difficult choice."

"I'm glad that ended up being the case. They acquired a lot of data to go through. It's going to take considerable time. What they saw today is puzzling," said the girl continuing to read the data pad.

"Did they find something?" asked Alena as the girl frowned at the display.

"No, not yet," she answered as she finished scanning the display. "Dante took a nasty hit when disabling the tanks during the battle. Enough that he had to be taken back and treated for the injury."

"They need him," said Alena.

"With his training, strange he took a hit disabling them," said Alika.

"Along with the fact he has done it countless times." The girl finished for him, nodding. "I think he did it the same way too many times and didn't realize it. He's smart, among the other things we know about him. He knows why things went wrong today for him. It won't happen again."

Alena watched her and could tell she tried to appear unconcerned, but it wasn't working. Alena said in a gentle voice, "I'm sure he'll be fine."

The girl attempted to smile back and said, "I'm sure you're right." She stared down at her hand. Some lessons stayed with you long after the wound disappeared.

They were making preparations for the following evening when the message came. The girl glanced at Alena and Alika, and she typed and sent back a message on her data pad. The second message arrived, and she sent the final dispatch.

"They realize someone obtained access to their systems as well as great access to the other side. They're nervous," said Alika.

"Who wouldn't be? We'd be crazy if the situation became reversed. However, we used it to help them," said Alena.

"Which is why they settled on letting us continue to access everything. They know how differently things turned out today because of our involvement. Also, bigger issues lie before them to consider, so their choice is to let this current arrangement be," said the girl smiling.

CHAPTER TWENTY-NINE

"There's the ship," said Alena. It went straight for the command ship but in through a small back entrance, as it did the previous evenings.

"Right on time. She should follow her nightly pattern, and the ship will come out that same access point. We don't know how long her visit will go, so we better be ready," said the girl.

They released two black saucer-like devices into the cold dark night. Alena and the girl each controlled one. They needed to get both of them over to the command ship unseen before Black Beauty's ship reemerged. Then at least one had to get onto her ship when it departed later. Two devices were ready for deployment in case one didn't make it through this mission. They watched as both devices were in position near the command ship and breathed a sigh of relief.

"They're doing sweeps," said Alena.

"I know. The devices shouldn't be detected, but we'll keep redirecting the sweeps until we get a device implanted. Usually, her ship emerges in about an hour or so. The sooner, the better," said the girl.

They both stared out, watching the doorway as they talked.

"Did you see any more of the data from the sites earlier?" asked Alena.

"A bit more. They figured out the boxes are being swapped out. So, the boxes which were in the warehouse and the lab are now in the possession of the Black Dragon Army. The other boxes being brought in the warehouse and lab were fakes."

"Months of this."

"Yeah, the mood I picked up on was despondent after it started to sink in over there too."

"Do they know what the boxes contained?"

"They're still putting the list together. From a few of the boxes I saw listed, it was scary considering where the items are now. The consensus was anything and everything dangerous, including weaponry, machinery, items to build all those things, and of course, all kinds of dangerous chemicals put together which could do things one doesn't want to fathom. I stopped looking at it to get back to this. Even if they do find out the items taken, I don't know if it helps them figure out what's being built or planned. Alika is monitoring it while watching our operation. I mean, I received the vision with Abigail, and it still didn't help us figure out what part she plays in the Dark Lord's operation."

"We just know she has a part in it somehow, and we need to get her out."

"Exactly. It could become clearer. We'll see, but I'm not counting on it."

"Is Dante really, okay? I have a feeling you checked."

"He's fine, as you said. He ended up back on the planet helping them when they discovered the whole box swap, despite attempts to tell him to stay at the treatment center." She purposely failed to address the second part of the question and its implications.

"He sounds stubborn, in a good way, of course. He reminds me of someone else I know."

The girl grinned, still watching for the cloaked woman's ship to emerge. "He does, among his other excellent qualities. As for the other, I don't know who you're referring to."

"I'm sure you wouldn't."

"Alena, there it is."

Alena nodded.

They both quickly moved their devices into position to attach one of them to Black Beauty's ship unnoticed before it hit the portal and left.

"They spotted mine," Alena said.

The girl nodded and continued working to get her device attached.

Alena used her device as a distraction now, maneuvering it away from the intended target.

"Almost got it, but she's close to the portal."

Alena continued, but it became more difficult. They were attempting to haul in her device.

"It found the target, and the tracker is deployed on the underside." The girl finally let out a breath. A readout confirmed it had attached and began sending a signal to them. The saucer itself disappeared from sight and made its way back to Alika.

"That's a relief because they want a closer look at mine," said Alena. The Black Dragon ship had trapped her device to haul it in. They never got the chance, because it exploded when Alena set off the self-destruct.

"They know something is up now, and they're checking."

Alena nodded and moved their ship toward the opposite portal.

The action didn't go unnoticed. "Black Dragon ship, where do you think you're going?"

The girl indicated for Alena to continue the movement toward the portal while she handled communications with the Black Dragon officer.

"We received a report of suspicious activity near this area and have instructions to proceed with investigating as part of security."

"I don't see any such report, and I certainly don't see a command to investigate such a thing."

"I apologize, sir. I'm sending the information to you I received. We certainly want to investigate the correct area where we observed the suspicious activity. If the report is wrong about the area to investigate, we can redirect, sir." The girl received something on her data pad from Alika. It was nice and official-looking. She sent it on to the Black Dragon leader.

"I don't care what you have. I didn't receive any information of the sort." He stopped abruptly. Without a doubt, he suddenly got the report, and his confusion became evident. "Black Dragon ship, you need to stop so we can clear this up."

"Sir, I would, but the scanners show a ship in the area of the suspicious activity, and they're on the move. They'll be out of range soon. We need to investigate now."

"What is your clearance again, Black Dragon ship?"

"Sir, I'm sending it."

The girl nodded at Alena. The gig was up, but they were close to the portal, thanks to Alena continuing to move the ship during the exchange between the Black Dragon officer.

Alena punched it and raced the ship to the portal.

"We'll make it. You get us out of here, and I'll give them some damage to remember us." The girl furiously returned fire.

"Stand down, Black Drag ... whoever you are, now." The Black Dragon officer roared in fury. "After that Black Dragon ship!" He slammed his fist down on the view screen. His crew turned, looking baffled. They were attacking one of their own ships, but they followed the command.

"Basal region!" Alena yelled as they entered the portal.

"We're through," Alena announced as she took a deep breath.

"Let me make the switch." The girl hit a button on the control panel. She almost forgot.

"Yeah, it wouldn't be good having the planet thinking there's a Black Dragon attack."

"Extremely impressive replica of a Freedom Fighter ship, though. They didn't track us, Alena."

"I'll make a couple more stops in case."

"Agreed. I can think of other places that would be happy with a Freedom Fighter ship in their atmosphere."

Once they made their detours, the two returned to Alika.

"It's transmitting. Well done, and I'm glad you're both safe. We'll figure out where our target is traveling, and check for any repairs needed on the ship. First, sleep."

CHAPTER THIRTY

"She's busy," said the girl as they traced the ship's movements projected in front of them, courtesy of the tracking device. It was the second day with the device charting her ship's course. "It's a shame we can't leave it on the ship, but it's too dangerous."

Alika nodded. "Once this operation is completed, we'll ensure the device extinguishes itself as planned."

Alena said, "The longer it stays on, the greater the chance of discovery. I don't desire to outrun the Black Dragon troops any more than necessary."

"That makes two of us." said the girl as she followed the ship's journey. "We decided where these stops were," she said as she pointed. "They were also all near the center of this activity. They could be it, but we're thinking not. We know what this evening visit is, of course."

"We're left with these trips. Did she make any visits to the same places both days?" asked Alena.

"She did on some of them. What is at these places we're looking?" wondered Alika.

"I'm checking the first five places she went," said the girl. "Alena, can you check the next five?"

"Already doing it."

"The first, third, or fifth place on your list look promising," Alika said, speaking to the girl, "and the first or second place on your list," he continued, turning to Alena. "On the other hand, I see merits for the others as well."

Alena and the girl nodded.

"Let's check them, starting with the one we think most likely and down the list to the least likely," said Alena as she turned to the girl. "Do you think from the vision and with what else we pieced together, you'll be able to spot the right location quickly?"

"I do. Then we return here and formulate a plan to get Abigail out once we see what we're up against."

"Take note of the last time she went to the location if it's repeated trips. Maybe she'll be consistent with going at the same time for those places. You don't want to get into any unnecessary entanglements with her."

—еее—

The next day Alena and the girl set out on their trip across the galaxy. They were on their second stop from the list.

"This has possibilities. The scanners are picking up a building," said Alena.

"We need to keep our distance." The girl hesitated. "It's busy. I'm thinking too busy. What's that?"

Alena scanned closer and peered back at the girl. "Black Dragon soldier for sure. Could we be wrong?"

"No, the theory is solid. He can't be using Black Dragon troops for the operation with Abigail. I wonder what's going on here?"

"Exploring this won't help us find her." Alena reminded the girl.

"No unnecessary entanglements. This could qualify quickly. Let's go before we're spotted." The girl looked at Alena reassuringly. "I'm sure she's not being held here."

They continued onto the fourth place on the list.

"A building is coming on the scanner," said Alena.

"Now there's a building, surrounded by nothing. It's huge, Alena."

"It's secure too." Alena's scanning caught plenty of security guarding the building. She zoomed in closer to one of the security guards outside. "He's not a Black Dragon soldier, which supports the whole outside contractor theory. I'm sure the security for the building is state of the art too. "

"There's a covered area over there," said the girl.

Alena brought it into focus. "You're thinking the wall moves with extra ships ready to greet unwanted visitors."

A familiar sensation came over her, like a built-in alarm starting. "We can't stay much longer. They'll be monitoring the sky. Can you spot a ship outside or a name on the building or anything? We need something to work with to fake clearances, for hacking."

"I got a couple of things that should work. Lots of footage," said Alena.

"It will do because we must go, now, Alena." The alarm blared inside her.

"We're gone," said Alena. The panic in the girl's voice could not be ignored this time.

Alika greeted them as they landed. "It sounded like you found the location and avoided any entanglements."

"We did, but I'm certain we were about to be spotted."

"I think you're right. I heard chatter about a sweep in your area about to commence. I started to alert you, but you left at the same time."

"Hopefully, we gained enough information to do this," said Alena.

"We'll make it work," said the girl.

It was slow going. The ship's holographic system would require another modification. The process involved using an image from the footage or accessing the system to create a plausible reason for the ship to be in the area. The place clearly did not want anyone noticing one of their ships, so it took all three of them. Once they finally did so, Alena worked on the modifications to the ship. The girl tried hacking into the system to fabricate clearances and obtain the building's layout. She hoped to narrow down where Abigail could be in the building to begin devising her rescue. Alika assisted her, examining the footage and scans doing the same.

"Alika, I managed to gain us some access, but it's not nearly what we're used to having. I tried. Once we're in the building, one of the badges or data pads will be priceless. I probably could get more access with a lot more time at it, but honestly, I can't say it would be much more. Yet, time is not on our side."

"I know your skills from years of training you, child. So, I believe you when you say this is all that can be done with the time available. We'll go with the access you secured, and the task will be accomplished."

"Now you must be the optimistic one."

"One of us has to be."

Alena came in after finishing the modification, and they began discussing a plan. Nonetheless, every plan contained many things to go wrong, partly since the girl couldn't acquire the access she ordinarily secured. Also, the troops protecting the building appeared well-trained and intent that no one could figure out what project took place inside the building. The girl was unhappy at the option on the table.

"Are you sure, Alena? It's too dangerous."

"And the other options aren't?"

The girl couldn't answer her. Alena was right, so the next statement from Alena didn't surprise her.

"It's because the other options put the danger more on you, and this one puts it on me. We need to consider using it if it helps us get Abigail back."

"I share your concern, child, but Alena's point is valid."

"You're right, Alena. This will be dangerous for all of us, so we use any advantage we can. Let's explore every option before we settle on one."

"This may not go as planned once the two of you get there. You'll probably end up doing more that your share of improvising to retrieve Abigail, a skill both of you are adept at doing."

— ❧ —

It was the following evening. They spent the previous day deciding on a plan and gathering all the needed supplies. Today, they made final preparations. This operation presented more challenges than previous ones, a reality not lost any of them. So many places for it to go wrong, too many unknowns, and being absolutely outnumbered. They tried not to think about it.

Alika went outside. The girl stared out across the lake near her room, entranced by the moonlight glimmering off the water.

"Child, we can take more time to prepare."

"More time would make no difference." She continued to stare out, her blue eyes calm despite the task ahead.

"You understand you and Alena are essentially getting out a coma patient from the grasp of an entire security force, a well-trained one, I might add. Have you thought of the possibility it's time to involve others?"

"I knew how bad it sounded, but now ... Yes, I considered additional help."

"We've already established communication with them, and they believe we're helping them. It could be time for their assistance."

"Not yet. This is my part of the task. My help can only be from you and Alena as it has been."

Suddenly, they heard a familiar whisper from the direction of the lake, "She's right. Do not fear. You're never alone, and you will not be in this endeavor."

Then they heard Alena's gentle voice behind them, "And it looks like a diamond on top of the water." She had approached unnoticed to check on them, and from her expression, she heard the whisper too.

Alika and the girl saw it simultaneously as the whisper redirected their gaze to the lake. It was there, the image of a shining, beautiful diamond above the water, reflecting the moonlight and penetrating the surrounding darkness. Tears fell freely down the girl's cheeks, and she dropped to her knees on the grass, staring out. Alena and Alika sat down beside her.

"I am prepared for tomorrow now, whatever it brings."

"It appears you do have everyone you need for this task, child."

"Perhaps you just did the most valuable preparation you could for tomorrow," Alena said as she helped the girl up and gave her a hug.

They took one last look at the moonlit jewel before going inside for the evening.

CHAPTER THIRTY-ONE

Alika gave the two a hug as they prepared to leave the next day.

"We'll return soon," said Alena.

"Of course, you will. Dinner will be ready, and I expect the two of you back for it."

The girl smiled at Alika's attempt to appear unconcerned. "We'll be back safely, I promise. Just going to pick up someone, and we'll be back before you know it, right?"

"You two go before we come to our senses and call this operation off."

The two disappeared into the ship and headed for the portal. Alika went inside. He would take control of the vessel soon while Alena and the girl moved through the facility. They didn't do it often, but this by far would be one of the more complicated scenarios.

"This will work," said Alena. The ship landed far enough away from the facility's surveillance, but close enough, it shouldn't take them more than ten minutes to get there.

"Let's head for the back-rear entrance," said the girl.

They carefully made their way, and two guards met them at the door.

"We're here to take over your shift," said the girl.

"It's not over yet," said the security guard looking at the other guard. "We got no such orders."

"I assure you it's correct," said Alena.

"Where are your badges?" asked one of the guards.

"Oh, man, it got tucked under the top of the uniform on the way here. Hate when that happens," said the girl, shaking her head.

The guards started to put their hands on their weapons but never got the chance. The girl and Alena drew their small blaster, and aimed it in the guards' stomach. It went off without a sound, and the guards collapsed to the ground. The girl and Alena replaced their blasters. They quickly confiscated the guards' badges and scanned them with their data pads. They found the guards' devices and scanned those as well. Alena dealt with the camera temporarily. Alika would start working now, which included a permanent solution for the camera at this door. In an instant, it showed the guards standing at their post as before and no sign of the previous altercation.

"We're now official. We'll see how long it works." The girl checked her data pad. She hoped for a layout of the facility before they stepped in. Alena glanced around, keeping alert for them.

"Nothing as far as the room, but we know where the troops are now," said the girl.

"We're not going in blind. That's progress. Suggestions?"

"A room that we can get more access with the least security."

"Let's go."

They walked in easily with their new badges. Doors opened with no problem.

"I can't figure out which one it is yet. It's not exactly marked prisoner room. Although, I located the camera or surveillance room." Alika's voice came through to Alena and the girl.

Alena and the girl looked at each other. That could work.

"It's on the same level you're both on, Room 203. There's quite a bit of security there, though."

"I believe they're encountering glitches and require two techs to troubleshoot it. Why don't you get the process started for them, so we can get busy resolving their system malfunction?" said the girl.

"I see the order coming through now. They'll be impatient to see it fixed, so you two should hurry."

Alena and the girl entered the room. The room buzzed with activity, as Alika indicated. They walked over to begin work, but an imposing figure immediately stopped their progress.

"You're the two sent to fix this, I presume?" said the guard in charge and intent on reminding everyone in earshot.

"Yes, sir," said Alena.

"It worked fine, and suddenly, it started going haywire. We can't have any issues with our boss."

"Sir, we'll take care of it promptly," said the girl.

They started to work, and within a few minutes, all signs of the breakdown disappeared.

"It appears fixed, but are you certain that's the case?"

"We believe so, but we're doublechecking the system and scanning that the equipment is working in the rooms," said the girl.

"Do so. Our superior will not tolerate mistakes," said the guard looking at them sternly.

They nodded and continued through the rooms. Then they found the room where Abigail laid. The two displayed no reaction but scanned the room like the others. However, as soon as Alika saw it, he gathered all the additional data they sent. The two scanned a few more rooms after it as to arouse no suspicions. Also, it could be helpful to know of the rooms surrounding their target. Either way, a complete layout of the building found its way to their data pad while they fixed the system. They checked the doors outside as well and were pleased to see they all still appeared carefully guarded. Alika's camera manipulation would guarantee Abigail's room appeared calm as well, no matter what actually occurred. The rooms and hallways close by would do the same.

"We finished scanning everything. There should be no further issues," said Alena.

The guard nodded to them, dismissing them both.

"The room is on the top floor at the end of the hall. There are a lot of floors to get her down."

Alena and the girl nodded at Alika's words. Their hearts had sunk as soon as they saw that part.

They headed to the room behind where Abigail lay imprisoned. A sizable number of guards worked inside the room from the layout they obtained. Outside only two kept watch, and Alena and the girl approached them.

"The building computer system encountered glitches earlier, and so we need to check this door," said the girl, appearing to reach for it.

"We didn't hear anything about a computer glitch. We'll have to confirm that." The security guard never had the opportunity to do so.

The girl and Alena injected both in the neck, and the two guards slid down the wall, grabbing for their weapons unsuccessfully.

"Ready?" asked the girl.

Alena nodded. They would only have the element of surprise for a few moments, and they intended to do a great deal with that time.

The door slid open, and Alena struggled but slung the two unconscious guards inside the room far enough for the girl to close the door behind them. Alika jammed the communications inside the room. The girl blasted back, and the room became noisy fast. Few places existed in the room for cover.

"They're worried about a firefight in this room," Alena said in a raised voice over the blaster fire.

"It can work for us, though," responded the girl.

Although the guards didn't know what was going on with the captured patient, they were aware that they could be in a tremendous amount of trouble if they hit something by mistake.

"You think so?"

The girl nodded, and they ran for cover behind the metal capsule-shaped contraption holding Abigail and shot from the position. Their blasters found their mark much more effortlessly. The security guards tried to take shots, but their efforts to avoid hitting any of the equipment which held Abigail or Abigail herself was their downfall. It forced them to come in too close, making them easy targets for the girl and Alena. The two cleared the room.

They came from behind the capsule and opened it. Abigail laid in a perfect hibernation state. Attached to her were standard instruments to monitor someone and provide all necessary elements except for one bag. It resembled a large IV but was full of a black substance. Its tubes led to the giant crystal mechanism the girl saw in her vision. She stared at it and shivered. Alena took a couple of pictures of the mechanism for them to examine later.

"This bag gets unhooked." The girl did, but she pulled out a syringe, obtained a sample of the substance, and placed it in a tiny metal cylinder container, which automatically locked airtight. She handed it to Alena. The whole process took mere seconds. Alena unpacked the cart they brought for Abigail. With a push of a button, it sprang to the size of a small makeshift rolling stretcher. Unfortunately, their efforts to move Abigail from the capsule and onto the stretcher came to an abrupt end.

"What's that noise?" asked the girl.

"It came from the wall," said Alena puzzled.

It did indeed. They stepped back in alarm. Suddenly, a new squadron of men rushed through a second entrance in the room. The girl quickly closed Abigail's capsule in time for her and Alena to dive behind it again.

"There's a hidden door there. Are you kidding me?" shouted the frustrated girl, firing back furiously again.

"Clearly not on the blueprints," hollered Alena back, returning the blasts as well.

This time the battle was going much better for the facility security to the two's dismay. "They'll keep coming through the doorway. They're alerted now," said Alena.

"Okay. We must get her out of here," said the girl, clearly unhappy.

The girl continued to fire her blaster as Alena moved away from her. She felt hopelessly overwhelmed, because she was now. The blaster shots ceased, and a group of the security men surrounded her, with their blasters all pointed at her. Their ranks parted to reveal a cloaked lady the girl knew all too well.

CHAPTER THIRTY-TWO

"You do realize I changed my plans today due to all the trouble you caused." The cloaked figure glared at her.

"The situation is under control," said the ranking security guard to the cloaked figure.

"Really? This is your idea of having it under control? Would the Dark Lord agree this is under control?"

"Sir, we can't find the other one. They were both here," said one of the other guards to the ranking security guard.

"Two individuals undermined this entire operation," said the cloaked figure, visibly angrier. "And you lost the second one in the time I helped you secure this one."

"Ma'am, the other one ..."

"Enough. Such incompetence. It will not go unpunished. My master is far less forgiving than I. Find the other one and bring the intruder back to me now. Perhaps try the other door. I'm sure they messed with them." She turned her attention to the girl. "Correct?"

The girl watched her stone-faced, trying to hold back her fear.

"I will loosen your tongue soon enough."

The cloaked figure turned back to the security guards and spoke in a voice of controlled fury, "I said go find the other one this instant. Do it such as your life depends on it because it does. I'll try to remember and take it into account when I decide your punishment."

"What about this one? Shall we finish the prisoner?"

"There is no we in this. This one will suffer, and it will give me great pleasure to carry it out. I will take care of this one myself. I said go, and I will not say it again."

The cloaked figure knelt and leaned into the girl's face. "I will make the walls vibrate with your pain, and you will beg for death." The girl shivered, and any remaining security guards ran from the room to find the other intruder as they didn't want to be there to watch the cloaked figure torture her prisoner. They feared they would be next.

A minute passed.

"You were convincing," said the girl, still shaking a little.

"They're gone now," said Alena as she removed the cloak and sounded and appeared as herself again.

The girl went over to the undocumented door and found a way to temporally block it, while Alena got the cart again. They lifted Abigail from the capsule and placed her on the stretcher.

"How do we get her down now? They are combing every corner of this place for us," said Alena.

"Now they are." The girl shook her head, but smiled under her helmet and knew Alena was doing the same under hers. Alena's ploy had saved their skin. "The only thing above us is rooftop, right?"

"Yes, but ... no, you're not," pleaded Alena.

"Are there stairs to the rooftop? It appeared to be a straight rooftop," said the girl as if she hadn't heard Alena.

"The stairway to the rooftop is the other end of the hall from you on the right," said Alika.

"Perfect. We need personnel off this hallway. Send something saying the companion of the prisoner made it to one of the lower levels. Divert them down there."

"This won't work long for you."

"You're right, but it'll be enough. I hope."

Thirty seconds later, the data pad lit up with an alert that all personnel needed to be looking for a suspicious person in the lower hallways. Another minute and the scan revealed the empty hall outside.

"Get the ship on the rooftop for our pickup."

"The ship will be waiting."

Alena eyed her like she was crazy but prepared to move with Abigail.

The two put a sheet over Abigail, just in case, and wheeled her out. They opened and shut the door behind them and the entrance to the rooftop. They alternated rolling and lifting the cart up the stairs and on the rooftop. Their ship arrived from Alika, and the door opened.

"Get in now, and pull Abigail inside the ship," instructed the girl.

Alena did and tugged one end of the stretcher as the girl pushed the other end into the ship.

Just as the girl got the rest of the stretcher and Abigail into the ship, blaster fire at her feet took her off balance. It was followed by more shots, the sounds of running feet, and shouts from multiple guards. She knew what it meant, and the voice inside her told her what had to happen.

"Go now!" yelled the girl as she turned to face those on the rooftop coming toward the ship.

"I can't leave you!" Alena didn't get further as the door of the ship shut, and the vessel lifted from the rooftop. Alika was still in control of the ship.

"Enough of this." The girl pocketed her blaster. The blaster shots came at her too fast, too many, and no cover could be found on the rooftop. She needed the better weapon for this, and it was time she used it. She ripped out her sunspear, and it whirled in her hand, finding its target repeatedly. Except the guards streamed onto the rooftop from all directions now. More than one way abounded to reach the rooftop, and the guards made use of all the access points. They surrounded their prey, and their number increased even as she struck them down. Then there was the tiny, troubling detail she stood on a rooftop fighting a more desperate battle as the seconds passed by.

Alena managed to secure the stretcher in the ship in her chaotic state and frantically worked at the controls trying to maneuver back to aid the girl to no avail. The ship headed toward the portal, leaving the girl behind.

The girl found herself dangerously close to the rooftop's edge.

Then she heard the voice, "Fall. I got you." She had forgotten about the cable she brought, but she felt unsure it would hook onto the roof. The instructions seemed strange, but she knew what she heard. Yanking the cable out with one hand, she continued to use her other to ward off the blasters using the sunspear. She threw the cable out, felt the hook attach to the edge of the roof, and pocketed her sunspear as she jumped. She thought she attached it, but it didn't catch right, or maybe the rooftop was weakened by the blaster fire. Either way, the side of her body slammed hard against the wall of the building. Stabbing pain shot through the side of her body that hit and scraped on the wall. She heard a pop at her shoulder and a crack near her rib cage. For a split second, she thought she passed out as the waves of agony vibrated through every nerve of her body. Pieces of the building's roof began to shower down from the top, and finally, the cable came loose altogether. With a sinking feeling, the girl realized the ground rushed to meet her, and no one would catch her after all. She calmed herself with the assurance Abigail got away safe, at least. Alena and Alika would get Abigail back where she belonged. Perhaps Abigail would awaken soon, and Dante could rescue his father from the Dark Lord. How she would have liked to see it, but it would be enough that Abigail no longer suffered under the Dark Lord's device. The girl found comfort in these thoughts as she surrendered to the death which awaited her.

"No!" screamed Alena as she watched the girl plummeting to the ground, and the ship went through to the other side of the portal. She fell to the ship's floor, sobbing.

CHAPTER THIRTY-THREE

The ship landed perfectly as if with many other trips. Alena opened the door and ran out.

Alika rushed to meet her and his face went pale. "Where is she?"

Alena shook her head. She couldn't manage to form the word. Alika brushed past her and burst into the ship. He saw Abigail, but the girl unaccounted for as he suspected. Alena came back aboard the ship and slumped in the chair, her head in her hands staring out.

Alika sat in the chair next to her and waited.

She gazed into Alika's eyes. "She told me to get Abigail safe and go. She shut the door to the ship and held them off, so we could get away. I did everything to go back for her, but the ship wouldn't do it. I tried to let you know I had to go back, but the ship just went through the portal."

Tears glistened in Alika's eyes. "We go back now. She's strong. Perhaps they only captured her. There's hope we can get her back."

"No, you don't understand. We can't." She started crying again. "She's dead. She fell from the rooftop, Alika."

His body turned cold, and his eyes glazed over at Alena in disbelief. "No, it can't be, Alena." But he knew the truth from Alena's face. A sob erupted from him.

"The last thing ... I saw as I went through the portal, her falling ... from the ... rooftop. I did nothing to help her, Alika." Her words poured out between her sobs.

"Oh, Alena," Alika murmured, having no words to offer Alena in her grief as he mustered none for himself. He reached over and put his arm around her shoulder.

"I broke every promise I ever made to her."

"We both did, Alena. You tried to go back, so you didn't abandon her as you feel now."

"It happened so fast. I couldn't communicate to you for some reason that I needed control of the ship again to go back."

So overtaken by his grief, Alika didn't grasp Alena's words. Now it dawned on him. "Alena, I realized you were attempting to go back, and I no longer controlled the ship. The ship was yours to command."

She stared at him, realizing what he meant. "There's only one other person with the ability to lock us out."

"No, even with her abilities, she did not possess the time and with the situation, it would be impossible."

"She was sent to rescue Abigail to be sacrificed herself. No, Alika, I can't accept it." She shook her head, and her eyes swam with tears again.

Then Alika realized something else. "The ship door closing too. Alena, that means she isn't the one who shut it."

Alena stared at Alika again as she whispered, "No, no, it can't be, Alika. It's not possible." Her eyes pleaded with Alika as another sob erupted from her.

He spoke as one trying to believe his own words. "He did what we could not do. She knew from the moment on the rooftop."

They both found themselves looking through the window of the ship. They could see the lake outside where they sat the night before with the girl.

Alena bitterly voiced their shared thought as they continued to gaze at the lake. "We were never alone, right? So, where does today leave us?" She wept harder as she put her head in her hands and leaned against Alika.

Alika shook his head and spoke softly, "I don't know, Alena." He tried to comfort her even as his own grief overtook him again.

⁓ⲉⲗⲉ⁓

I'm dead, thought the girl. I never felt the pain from hitting the ground. Strange. All the pain from the wall impact still coursed through her body, but her frame lifted now. Then she realized it. She remained on the planet. Someone or something held her in their grasp. She looked up to behold the biggest eagle she had ever seen in her life. Even with its size, her weight should pull them both to the ground. Yet it held her in its grasp and flew with her effortlessly as if she weighed nothing more than a feather. Its grip hurt now, but it was her fault. Everywhere it grasped on the one side stung thanks to her meeting with the side of the building. The eagle peered down at her with understanding, and the girl was convinced she even saw sympathy. The eagle flew away from the building, the blaster fire, and all the fray. They reached the forest surrounding the building, and it flew lower. It skillfully avoided the trees, making certain the guards did not see where the two ended up in the forest. Finally, when either the eagle felt he carried the girl far enough or sensed she could endure no more, he gingerly settled her on the ground. She laid on the ground, exhausted and in pain from her injuries, but alive. The eagle perched on a nearby boulder and waited for her.

Despite her desperate state, she couldn't stay out here long. She would be tempted to succumb to a sleep that would be a dangerous mistake in her current condition. However, her options were limited, and a great deal of this was her own doing. She needed a way to get off the planet, and the only ships she knew to access sat carefully guarded in the facility's hangar. They were anything but accessible with her current situation. Maybe stealing a command ship would be harder, but even it seemed a real possibility over getting one of the facility's ships. There was little chance of her tricks working, even on a good day now. She thought about waiting until evening, and she could use the darkness for cover.

Nonetheless, the help of the darkness would be eliminated by the one threat. That one threat alone snatched away any advantage of the night's concealment—the cloaked lady. The girl shivered. The dark agent probably arrived or would do so shortly after the day's events. Oddly enough, the girl would still consider a plan back to the facility, but she couldn't because of the one denominator in her situation, which was entirely her doing. In her currently injured condition, she wouldn't be able to secure a ship from the facility. It was a suicide trip. She felt angry with herself. She remembered the words on the rooftop "Fall. I got you."

If she did as instructed and trusted, her body wouldn't be in this state. Thanks to her adding unneeded parts to the instructions, probably half of her side had become a part of the building. She felt dizzy, nauseous, and her head hurt. She rubbed at her head, and her hand came back with streaks of blood. Probably a concussion from all the rock hitting her head when she fell. She did something to her shoulder and maybe bruised a couple of ribs too. There had to be another way to get off the planet, but she would only be able to go so far in this condition. It came down to one thing. She was utterly empty; she had no idea how to get out of her current situation.

The girl stared out into space, and for a moment, she stood back at the lake, seeing the diamond shining in the moonlight, clinging to a whispered promise. "I am not alone, but I have no idea what to do next. I need help, please."

The voice said, "Get up and walk, child."

The girl started to ask where to go, what to do, but she stopped with her questions. She simply needed to follow instructions this time. She rose, and the eagle stirred. He nodded at her. She understood and followed it. The eagle alternated between flying from branch to branch within sight of her and walking on the ground ahead of her. They provided a peculiar pairing at first, but she grew accustomed to it. They walked for about thirty minutes when she needed to rest for about five minutes. Nausea overcame her, and the bird perched patiently while she threw up and recovered enough to continue. They set off again and stopped after about the same time, and she rested. They had only gone for about fifteen minutes longer when the eagle stopped, and so did the girl. The eagle stared at something on the girl, and she followed its focus. She knelt, and the eagle came closer to touch its head to her data scanner. She pulled her scanner out, and the eagle nodded ahead.

"I need to scan ahead." She did so, and to her surprise, it indicated a ship. There were individuals around it, but not many. A spark of hope flickered inside at the first real chance of finding her way off of the planet. "Unusual to be out here. Maybe they're en route to smuggle something. This area appears remote once you're past the facility. Looks like I found my ride."

The girl found new energy as she approached the area, and somehow the trek became nothing more than five minutes, She couldn't take a chance on their leaving.

The girl crept close to the clearing and observed from behind the trees. Straight ahead revealed a ship with several boxes outside. Four men came in and out of the ship, loading the rest of the boxes into it. The girl scanned again, and it confirmed only the four men. She could find a way to overpower the four of them even in her state. She felt a nudge and realized it originated from the eagle, indicating their time together had come to an end. She nodded and mouthed thank you. Strangely, she didn't feel silly talking to this eagle, and it nodded back. The eagle started to fly off, and the girl still assumed it left for the day. Instead, the bird flew in front of the men and settled on top of the cockpit of the ship, capturing the men's attention.

One of the men shook his head and said, "I'm going inside now."

The other three men stayed to watch the eagle. The eagle flew from the cockpit to a small tree in front of the them, directing their gaze there. It ushered them from the entrance of the ship.

The girl smiled. She only needed to deal with the one man on the ship. Her feathered friend gave her time to prepare for the other three men. Getting her blaster in position, she sneaked into the ship. The man sat at the cockpit, leaned back in the chair. He watched the other three men laugh and point at the eagle as it flew from tree to tree in front of them. He heard someone approach behind him and thought at first it was one of his friends. Puzzlement came over his face, because he realized all three of his friends remained outside entertained by the eagle.

The man turned around and attempted to reach for his weapon, but too late. The girl grabbed his arm to successfully stop the motion, and she quietly shot her blaster pressed against his back. He slid to the ground unconscious. She forced herself to ignore a spike of pain, which tried to gain her attention anew.

The girl used her data pad to acquire access of the ship's control portal. She quickly discovered where the ship was headed because it determined her next move. She kept one eye on outside, hoping the distraction lasted for a little longer. She dragged the man to the back of the ship, found his data pad, scanned it, and held onto it for the moment. Taking a deep breath, she willed the dizziness to stop so she could finish this. She crouched down in the back of the ship and resolved to get this group flying again.

The message read: *Come on, guys. I'm sick of watching you goof around with the eagle. Let's get on with this.*

"Looks like someone is ready to go. Geez," said one of the guys outside as he ambled toward the ship.

"That had to be the biggest eagle I've ever seen in my life," said one of the other men as he followed behind with the last guy at his heels.

"We're here," said the man, walking in with the other two men. The door shut behind. "Mike, you're in such a hurry."

He never managed another word as two blaster shots bolted through the air. He fell, and so did the second man almost in the same split-second from the shots. The third guy turned in the general direction and reached for his blaster but didn't get a shot off before another shot rang out and nailed him.

She came with two handheld blasters for this operation, and now, she was grateful for both. The girl let out a deep breath and inched out of her hiding place. She painstakingly heaved each of the three men to join their friend in the back, but it felt like shoving a mountain into place. She stumbled several times during the process, fighting alternating waves of nausea and pain. The men laid simply stunned, so there was no time to waste. With the setting she used though, they should be out for at least a few hours, more than enough time for what she needed. She'd leave the planet and finish this shipment delivery. From her earlier chat with the ship's computer, she gathered where to take the shipment. She and Alena visited there before in their travels. It wasn't Black Dragon territory, and that's all she needed to know. A person could encounter a fair amount of shady business dealings there, but it was a place where one could be persuaded to look the other way for the right price. She anticipated no issue as long as the ship made the delivery. Also, from the itinerary, the men allowed themselves plenty of time before the shipment delivery time, no doubt to engage in more leisurely activities on the planet. Instead, they would settle in for a long nap.

However, she wouldn't relax until she saw Alena and Alika again. She lifted off and trusted she would reach the portal. The eagle sat on the treetop watching her and gave her a reassuring nod. The scanners showed no ships near her position, but she raced toward the portal, sure there would be a firestorm trailing her the next second. To her relief, there was none. Finally, she cleared the portal and headed for the planet to deliver the shipment.

Then she did something she wanted to do all day since she survived her rooftop plunge but knew she couldn't do until now. She sent a message.

CHAPTER THIRTY-FOUR

Alena and Alika eventually left the ship and transported Abigail off it as well. They transferred her to the chamber, made ready, and hooked up the necessary things to her. Alena handed Alika the cylinder tube containing the sample of material the girl obtained. He placed it in a safe compartment to deal with later. They managed to do the required things, but they could muster nothing further. Abigail laid in the room safe and getting what she needed to remain stable. They sat there, neither one saying a word, trying to fathom the day's events and lost in their grief.

Suddenly, their data pads lit up at the same time, and a unique signal went off for a split-second in the room. It was a signal worked out only between Alika, Alena, and the girl when they arrived at their new home. Alena and Alika looked at each other and snatched up their data pads. It came through a special communication and encryption code known only to them as did the message now on their data pad:

I'm alive. Yes, it's really me. I'm not squished at the bottom of the building. Going to need a ride back once I deliver this shipment. Maybe I can make dinner tonight if you hurry.

Alena and Alika both jumped up, tears flowing again, but they didn't mind the tears this time.

"Alika, I don't know how."

"But it's definitely her."

"Where is she? There's something attached. I got it. I'm leaving now to get her." Alena read the data pad and ran to the ship at the same time.

"Bring her home, Alena."

"I will, I promise."

The girl approached the planet and landed. She experienced no problems since the ship was expected.

Her data pad flashed with a message: *Alena is on her way, child. Hold on, please.*

The girl checked behind her, and the men continued to be out for the count. She took nothing for granted after today's events. She set to work creating fake clearances for Alena to land but found Alika beat her to it, so she quickly moved to erasing the day's events from the ship's cameras. The men would awaken and have quite a story, but there would be no footage to account for it. She also returned the man's data pad to him.

Another message blinked on her data pad: *I'm here.*

The girl looked outside the window and started crying despite herself. There stood Alena, and the ship parked right outside. The girl opened the door. Alena ran in and covered the girl in an embrace.

"Let's get you home."

"Do you have ...?"

"Yes." Alena pulled out a cloak. The girl was injured, and they didn't want to arouse any suspicion.

Alena and the girl walked out of the ship, and it shut behind them. They boarded their ship, lifted off, and headed for the portal.

"Go to one of the safe havens first, just in case."

"You're in a lot of pain."

"Please, it's not worth the risk."

"All right, one detour."

They took the one detour to satisfy the girl, went through the portal again, and this time they opened on the other side for home.

"We're here."

All of the day's events finally caught up to her. The pain she held back to necessitate her escape suddenly reached out and grabbed her with a fierce vengeance as they landed. It felt like coming to the end of one of those horrific rides she heard about somewhere in her childhood.

The girl started to get up but almost fell over. Her head spun, and countless waves of nausea washed over her. She fought it and willed herself not to throw up on the ship.

Alena quickly grabbed her and steadied her. The girl had used her reservoir of strength for the day.

They walked off the ship, and the girl tried vainly not to lean on Alena. Alika would think she was dying walking out in this shape. It didn't make sense. She summoned enough focus and strength to get off the planet. Yet, right now, walking down the ramp felt like more effort than what she could possibly exert. Then she understood. The momentum she found to escape had indeed been beyond her, and now He carried her back home to them, enough for that task only.

She reached the end of the ramp, and Alika embraced her. She fell into his arms as she could no longer stand.

"We thought we lost you, child. You're home now," whispered Alika, his voice cracking.

The girl only wept in response.

Alika and Alena tried to help the girl inside, but she fell to her knees, coughing. The nausea she experienced on the ship finally overwhelmed her. Alika and Alena stayed with her and waited until the girl signaled she could move again.

The girl nodded and laboriously got up. They all went into the house.

"Lie down, child."

Alika prepared to treat her as Alena helped the girl onto the bed and assisted in unpacking all her gear. Alena laid the girl's data pad and weapons, including her sunspear, on the table.

"What about ..." asked the girl weakly.

"Not another word. It's probably taken care of or will be," said Alika looking at the girl and then Alena.

"The cloaked woman's ship, the device."

"You're relentless. I'm watching." He reviewed the data pad and motioned Alena closer.

"She's heading for a portal, Alika. We should know any minute." They waited. "Yes, there she goes where we thought. We're good."

Alika nodded his agreement and pushed a button. Suddenly, the signal from the device tracking the ship's movement disappeared. The device would be disintegrating now and would blow away like dust in the wind, leaving no sign of it by the time she landed.

"It's done as agreed. I took care of various other things too, such as erasing the cameras on the planet with any signs of you and Alena. Your next question, I'm sure. No more questions. It's time to evaluate and treat your injuries."

She couldn't resist one more question. "Abigail got here safe, right?"

His expression softened. "Yes, child. She's in the other room we set up for her. Now, no more questions until we examine you."

Alena handed Alika the medical scanner. He started at the girl's head. "That would be a concussion. You managed to put a whole new meaning to rocks in your head. Pieces from the roof hit hard enough to dig into the top and side of it. Your shoulder is dislocated, and there are two broken ribs. A little closer and maybe a punctured lung. My compliments on avoiding that part. A couple of the blaster shots got a piece of you as well. You're awfully bruised and banged up. Being thrown like a rag doll against a building will do that to you. Then there is the whole side of your body you tore off on the building. You're also severely dehydrated. However, you're alive, and you managed to escape, though I have no idea how."

"Where do we start?" asked Alena.

"Getting the shoulder back in place," said Alika and then addressed the girl, "I'm sorry, but this is going to hurt much more for an instant, dear."

"I know. Just do it."

Alena held the girl steady as Alika grasped the girl's arm and put it back into place. The girl screamed in agony, and it took all of Alena's strength to restrain her.

The girl breathed deep and closed her eyes. Alika and Alena thought she passed out, but she opened her eyes after a minute.

"Keep going. I'll be okay."

"Something to deaden the pain before we do the next part," said Alika. He sprayed a substance on the top, side, and back of the girl's head. He brought a device over that slowly pulled the rock pieces from her head.

"Could I get this off me? It sounds strange, but half of the building stuck to me, among other more unpleasant things."

"You're weak, but it would be easier to clean and treat the wounds. If we alleviate the nausea from the concussion, it will help."

"I'll make sure she's fine while she gets cleaned up, Alika."

Alika handed the girl a tablet. "First, take this. Dissolve it under your tongue to help take away the queasiness."

After taking it, the girl slowly got into a moving chair mechanism. Alena guided her to what appeared to be a walk-in shower. The girl and the chair continued into the shower. The chair lowered with the girl in it until she sat in the tub. Slowly sliding out of the chair, she settled in the tub. She undressed and signaled for Alena to remove the chair along with the pile of clothes. Alena did so and turned the handheld sprayer on for her. It spewed out a gentle water and soap combination. Finally, when the girl washed all the debris, dried blood, and everything else she tried hard to forget off her, the spray switched to simply water. It appeared the day's chaos was cleansed from the girl.

"Are you still, okay?"

"Yes, Alena."

"Do you feel up to the medical combination spray too? Alika is asking. It would be easier now, but we don't want to overdo it in your weakened condition."

That explained it. She heard Alena and Alika conversing when she rinsed the last bit of the debris from herself. It made sense to do the medical combination spray now. "Yes, I'll be fine for it."

The girl closed her eyes. The spray wouldn't hurt them, but it was slightly scented, so she never cared for it in her eyes. It cleaned out the wounds and consisted of a healing element too. The slight fragrance derived from the oil, which contained the healing properties. Also, none of the elements burned or hurt when they came in contact with the injuries.

"It covered you, so it's time to get you out. I'm sending the chair in with a towel and robe. Let me know when you're ready to come out."

The girl did so, and several minutes later, she emerged from the shower wrapped in the robe still sitting in the chair.

Alena moved the girl to another bed closer to more medical equipment. The girl could guess what the next order of business would be in dealing with her injuries, and she didn't look forward to it.

"The two broken ribs," said Alika as he pulled out the scanner again. "You'll need to be out for this."

"How long will I be under?"

"The length of time it takes to put two ribs back together."

"So, not for long, right?"

"You're not going anywhere in your condition, so stop acting otherwise."

"How about Abigail? Is she still, okay?"

"He checked on her when I helped you with the shower. He's doing this now, so stop with your questions."

The girl never got another question out as Alika inserted the anesthesia, and she fell asleep. When she awoke, it was evening. She started to sit up but was stopped by her own body and Alika and Alena looking down at her. She groaned. "How long?"

"Only for a couple of hours after the repair. My medical judgment tells me it should be a few hours at least to allow you to rest. However, if I listened to my better judgment, I would not hear the end of it from you. You'll be sore for a bit from this repair. Of course, that doesn't count all the other injuries, which will take time to heal. We applied more of the healing element to a few places once we saw the extent of them."

"Like where you left one whole side of your body on the building. That one will hurt for a while. Your head too."

"Everything went okay with my ribs, I gather."

"Yes, child. I made a small incision and used the medical laser. I fused both ribs back together with Alena's help. It was a clean break on both, so there were no pieces to remove. That was the good part of it. We went back over the incision, and so there's no sign of it."

The girl tried to sit up, but it hurt.

"You must rest, child."

"I'm fine."

"There's nothing to do which cannot wait. Besides, we're curious as to what happened after you fell from the building."

"Yes, we believed you were dead until we received your message."

"I as well when the cable broke, and the ground rushed into view. When I fought the guards, a voice commanded me to fall, that I would be caught. I should have done exactly as instructed. The last few hours would be different, much less painful. You saw the rest. The cable fell, half the rooftop tumbled down on me, and I hit the side of it. I saw the ground coming toward me, and I couldn't figure out how I heard the voice wrong. I guess that was the last thing Alena saw when the ship passed through the portal."

Alena and Alika both nodded, waiting.

"You know in the manuscripts where it talks about flying like an eagle?"

The two of them looked at her, puzzled, but then a look of realization came on them.

"It's as close as I'll come here. It had to be the biggest eagle ever. The eagle caught me before I hit, carried me into the forest, and set me down like it was nothing. It even guided me to the ship in the forest and helped as a distraction at one point, so I gained control of the ship."

"Amazing," said Alena.

"It was. I hated worrying you. I wanted to contact you as soon as I survived the fall."

"But you didn't." Alika sighed. "We understood why later."

"My first instinct urged me to do so, but the voice prompted me to wait. I knew if I contacted you immediately, you'd come after me, and we'd all be stuck on the planet, captured or dead. I'm sorry for what I put you through in the interim."

"You know we didn't leave you on the planet, right?" asked Alena with tears glistening in her eyes.

"I would never think such a thing, not for a moment," said the girl surprised, but from Alena's expression, the thought weighed on her. "Oh, Alena, no, I knew as soon as the ship door shut itself." Despite the pain of her injuries, she forced herself to sit up and hug Alena. "You and Alika stood by me in my darkest moments. Neither of you would ever abandon me."

As she laid back, the girl teased, "Anyway, you provided the fastest service at the hangar when I called for a ride home. Not to mention the excellent medical services I have received. Even with being such a lousy patient, but there'll be no improvement in that area. I've always tested my medical personnel."

Alika and Alena laughed. The girl started to laugh but stopped immediately from the pain in her ribs.

"We're glad you returned to us, child," said Alika with a smile.

"And I made it home by dinner," said the girl with a twinkle in her eye.

"She is getting back to her normal self." Alena laughed.

"Were you able to make any sense of the sample I retrieved, Alika?"

"No, you kept our minds occupied with other matters today, but the sample is in one of the safe compartments."

"Maybe I could look at it."

"No, you cannot."

"What about getting Abigail to them?"

"We must work that out. It's not a simple drop-off, child. Also, the time draws near for them to deal with another attack."

"We should monitor what's happening. They may get an alert of an attack, and we'll miss it. What if they need our help? Where's my data pad?" asked the girl, looking like she might jump out of bed.

"It's different now. There's a piece out of the equation," Alena said as she lightly nudged the girl back in bed.

"Alena's right. Think about it. Abigail is no longer in the Dark Lord's grasp. She was a part of the operation, but we still don't know how she tied into it. How will it affect the attacks on the colonies, on that part of the operation?"

The girl settled back down, clearly deep in thought. "You're right. Surely the Dark Lord knows he lost Abigail now. However, this is the part the Black Dragon Commander knows nothing about and can't find out about from the Dark Lord, or else the truth would be revealed. From that point of view, it could be the attacks continue as there's no other choice, so the Black Dragon Commander won't question it."

"The Dark Lord may hope he can retrieve Abigail in time to complete the operation and the Black Dragon Commander continue the operation," Alena said. "Much of it depends on what part Abigail plays in the operation."

"Maybe he comes up with an alternate way of accomplishing the same purpose without Abigail," said Alika.

"Possibly. The Dark Lord is cruel. Abigail may be the perfect choice in his eyes, the ultimate way to feel he destroyed Ethan's world without his realizing it. I'm not sure he settles for someone else, or if so who it would be." The girl said.

They sat pondering but knew they were only guessing.

"What do we do?" the girl asked, eager to do something.

"Wait." Alika restrained his laughter at the girl's disappointed expression. "We don't want to bring Abigail to them in the midst of an attack. We know the most days without an attack, so we wait the time plus another day to be sure. If there's no attack, we'll know that her no longer being a prisoner did make the Dark Lord change his plans. If there's an attack, we wait until after they deal with the attack, and then we immediately get Abigail to them. They'll need time to deal with this revelation and what it means to them before the next attack. It'll change a great many things."

"So, we really must wait," said the girl like a deflated balloon.

"It's not as bad as it sounds," said Alena. "You need to recover. There are tasks to be done, such as uncovering the nature of the sample. We need to sift through the information Dante and his companions collected from the last attack."

"Alena's right. Like I said, turning Abigail over to them is an operation on its own. This will be the first time one of us makes ourselves known to them, and considering what we reveal to them, I'm not sure how they will react."

"Put that way. there's quite a bit to keep us busy."

"Dinner first, since you went to all the trouble to be here for it tonight," said Alika as he gave the girl a hug.

The girl insisted on coming to the table for dinner. Alena helped her dress more comfortably for sitting at the table. The girl convinced both of them to unhook the hydration bag from her. She ate a broth mixture tonight since her stomach still felt topsy-turvy from the craziness of the day's events.

They finished eating, and Alika suggested to the girl, "Why don't you get rest now?"

"I want to see Abigail before I go to bed."

"All right, but then rest."

Alena and Alika went with the girl to see Abigail. The girl sat in a chair at Abigail's bedside.

"I wonder why she hasn't awoken."

"I don't know, child."

"I hoped when I came home, she'd be awake." She closed her eyes briefly and took Abigail's hand. "At least the darkness no longer makes her suffer as it once did. I can tell for sure."

"She'll sleep in one of our rooms during the night where it's safe," said Alena as if reading the girl's next thoughts.

"Good. A few more minutes, and I'll get to bed."

Alika touched her on the arm softly and said, "We'll be back to check on you and make good on that." They both walked just outside the room.

The girl looked at Abigail's sleeping form and spoke softly to her, "Abigail, I'm sorry it took us so long to come to you, to help you. You're safe now. We'll get you back to Dante, I promise. He thinks you're dead, as does Ethan, but they'll know the truth, and it'll change everything. You didn't fight in vain all this time, Abigail. Dante will be able to do this, you'll see." She felt sleepy. "Please, Abigail, won't you wake up?" The girl laid her head next to Abigail's head, her hand grasping Abigail's hand. "Mother's love ... Ethan ... Dante ..."

Alena and Alika walked back into the room quietly. They heard the girl's words, her plea to Abigail. They discovered the girl asleep at Abigail's bedside.

"Alika, there's the extra bed in my room. Why don't we put her in there? She sometimes sleeps there, and she'd feel better tomorrow to wake up in the same room with Abigail and me after today."

"I agree. I can lift her and put her into bed. She won't feel it for once in her life." He lifted the girl, considering her injuries, and Alena helped him with getting the girl into the bed. Alena went and put the girl's data pad and sunspear on the table in the room as well. The girl would look for it as soon as she woke.

They moved Abigail's bed into Alena's room for the night.

Alika and Alena returned to Alena's room, sat at a nearby table, and looked at the sleeping girl. They found it impossible to comprehend what she had survived today.

"I can't remember the last time I needed to carry her to bed."

"You'll hear about it tomorrow. I still remember when we started training her."

"Some sessions wore her out completely, even as she denied it the entire time up to the point when her eyes closed in sleep. Certain things will not change about her."

"I guess not. Alika, she'll miss Abigail when Abigail is gone."

"That's a certainty. Abigail reminds the child of her mother in many ways."

"I thought the same listening to her tonight," said Alena, but the next moment her eyes turned mischievous. "There's another resemblance around here."

"And that is?"

"Our lousy patient as she called herself and another recent patient in another camp."

"Yes, they both are resistant to receiving treatment and following doctor's orders. Then eager to go off again to add to their injuries."

"Stubborn is the word you're searching for, Alika. That's the word I told her when I brought it up one evening."

"And I assume you didn't get far with your observation."

Alena shook her head and laughed.

CHAPTER THIRTY-FIVE

The Dark Lord sat waiting. Right on schedule, his evening companion entered the room. Tonight, she'd be here for longer. There was more business than usual to discuss before the normal leisure of her visit.

"I expect you're prepared to give me an update about the incident at the facility today."

"We are still trying to recover our prisoner, and there are no signs of the two individuals who accomplished the rescue effort."

"Who are these two individuals that executed such a bold mission?"

"We don't know, and there's no record of them at the facility. They wiped clean all evidence of their presence on the cameras, so we're depending entirely on the recall of the guards in the building."

"The two did not just vanish."

"From the guards' report, one got away on a ship with our prisoner through the portal. The other stayed behind to fight and fell from the rooftop. The one was presumed dead initially, but later reports indicate the individual ended up rescued at the last moment and carried to safety deep into the woods. We haven't located the individual so far, but the person sustained multiple injuries from the rooftop tumble when the person hit the side of the building. It could be the individual died of injuries in the woods."

"You sound unsure of the conclusion."

"Considering what the two individuals accomplished before they were cornered, I'm doubtful of the individual's demise. They got through a significant amount of security and took out numerous troops to get our prisoner free. The one individual single-handedly took care of multiple troops on the rooftop before she fell. Her life was spared from certain death by a large eagle." The woman hesitated, staring at the Dark Lord. "She wielded a sunspear."

"A woman wielding a sunspear. Are you sure?"

"The reports all agree on that point. For most of the encounter, they succeeded in keeping their appearance hidden. They stayed disguised as a part of the security and kept their helmets on as well. Towards the end, it no longer worked when the rescue fell apart on the rooftop. It became apparent the spear-bearer was a woman. Her gear did not fare well in her descent from the roof, and it revealed a woman's form and features. She used the sunspear for the first time when battling on the roof. She used a blaster the rest of the time. It's possible the companion is as well, though that one did not ever draw a sunspear."

"So, it was not Dante. There's his cousin who bears a sunspear, but we've kept all of them busy lately. Besides, Dante would never allow her to go in alone and place herself in such danger. Neither would her husband."

"I agree."

"Two strong unknowns working together, with at least one highly trained in the sunspear, possibly both, and they possess our prisoner."

"They did not enlist the help of Dante and the others."

"Very strange."

"It is."

The Dark Lord beckoned her closer, and his eyes did not show their usual warmth toward her. "There is another problem. You and I are the only immediate ones who knew the location of our prisoner. I'm trying to figure out how they pinpointed my prisoner's whereabouts. Please enlighten me."

There was no way to hide it from the Dark Lord, so she told him as much as she dared. "They probably discovered it through me during these visits, but I'm only guessing. Several nights ago, an incident occurred with suspicious activity when I left a visit with you. I thought nothing of it. We nearly captured one device during the incident, but it blew up before it could be examined. My assumption is another device existed. I checked my ship this afternoon when I landed and found nothing. Undoubtedly, the incidents were related."

The Dark Lord's face calmed. The explanation made sense. "That sounds like a correct theory. They're good at what they do. I can appreciate it." He sneered. "I am puzzled as to why they're not openly helping the Freedom Fighters. What are they planning with their prisoner?"

"What are you going to do?"

"For now, operations continue for our Black Dragon Commander. He must not wonder what is amiss. I don't know that it will take many more attacks before he acquires everything he needs. I meant to get an update from him. As for our prisoner, she was perfect for my masterpiece, and I'm quite sad she escaped my grip so close to the end of our operation. I planned on using her for so long. My storybook ending for Dante's family is ruined. Perhaps we can get her back. If not, maybe there is another with a fighting spirit like her. There is Dante's cousin, but I don't see she would be any easier to obtain. There is this one who managed to rescue our prisoner, and we think survived. She would certainly be interesting. Yes, she would do excellently."

"What if we can't get one of them?"

"My heart is set on carrying it out with our prisoner or one like her. It works far better doing it that way. Nevertheless, if we don't secure a worthy prisoner to sacrifice for our operation, I'll find another solution. I always do," The Dark Lord said with a cruel laugh. "Continue to prepare everything as so. Listen to see if you discover our prisoner's whereabouts, as I'm curious about what the two are planning on doing with her. It won't be as spectacular of an ending as I had intended for her. Try to discover more about the two that rescued her. Keep up with your other errands as well. They're needed, so the whole operation stays on task. My commander is stretched thin with all his duties."

"It will be done, my Dark Lord."

"Enough of business tonight. I do not wish to dwell on today's events any longer. I am in a foul mood from them. Go make my evening drink and sit with me. Let us hope you find me in a better state of mind before the evening ends."

CHAPTER THIRTY-SIX

Lana sat back, trying to feel a sense of accomplishment but failing miserably. They had compared the list of taken items from the latest attack with compiled lists from previous attacks. The verdict, a massively unhelpful list and a room full of frustration.

"Hey, it's okay, Lana, we've been stuck before. We'll find a way to break through it." Caleb sensed her frustration, and he leaned over and kissed her.

Her face softened as she gazed up at him. "I need a reminder sometimes."

"That's what I'm here for." Then he turned to the others. "Let's look at this from another angle. I don't see us figuring out what they're doing with the supplies by the next attack. We need to decide what we want to accomplish the next time."

"Caleb's right. We discovered what they're taking, and nothing good can come from it. We can't let them take anything further. Unfortunately, once we stop them from doing so, they know we're on to them," Dante said.

Seth agreed. "It does present an unwelcome option. We could try to stop them at the beginning, which I'm not sure is possible. They seem to get behind the line quickly, ahead of the attack. The other option is to wait until they reach the facility and eliminate them before they enter the facility."

Ryan brought up what crossed everyone's mind now. "The next time, it could get ugly for the colony once the Black Dragon realizes we figured out the real purpose of the attacks. Dante is right. We can't let them stockpile supplies to create whatever."

Dante wondered out loud, "If only there's a way to know exactly which boxes they're coming for ahead of time."

"We don't even know which planet they'll hit next," Commander Conrad said.

"And there's which facility," Commander Austin added.

Seth agreed, "They took similar items, but not the same ones every time, so there's no way to arrange it. Too many unknowns. I understand Dante's sentiment, and it's been echoed several times. We're all searching for a way to stop them from obtaining more supplies, but without them realizing we discovered what they're doing. I don't see the solution, either."

"Ryan and I will handle the ground forces again. We'll come up with a different plan after my last encounter with the tanks. Seth's group should be larger since we're talking about stopping the Dark Lord from getting the supplies, unless we come up with an alternative."

Lana looked at Dante. "You're still wondering if there's another way to do both, aren't you?"

"Yeah, but I'm stuck too."

Caleb smiled. "I admire your persistence, but I don't see it happening, Dante."

"Well, they tricked us with the whole box swap thing. There should be a way to return the favor. I'm not saying it'll work every time, but maybe a couple of times." Inside, Dante wished for the expertise of their unknown friend.

Commander Gabe looked at Seth and said, "I see where Dante is going with his idea. There is the time period where the cart is coming out with the actual supplies, and the fake ones are going in. Maybe something could be arranged in that interval."

"But can we do it without alerting or taking out at least a couple of the Black Dragon men?" asked Caleb.

"Perhaps, there's no way to avoid that part. Maybe a distraction and during the time make the switch," said Seth.

Dante continued, "And they think they leave with the real thing. Even if it only works for a couple of attacks, it gives us time to figure out what they plan with the supplies."

Commander Aegeus said, "If it doesn't work, go to the backup plan."

"Exactly. Just take them down, so they don't leave with the real supplies," Seth said.

"Caleb, why don't you get Seth teamed up, so he can make it happen? Dante and Ryan also need to work out a new strategy to deal with the ground forces and the tanks. Then you know who is left to work with in the air," said Lana.

Caleb replied, "I agree. Lana, we can always come back to trying to figure out what they're doing with the supplies after we plan how to handle the next attack."

⁓ ✺ ⁓

"Weird. No problems, though, and it occurred at night. Maybe the scanners picked it up wrong. Okay, let me know," said Ryan.

"Everything okay?" asked Dante.

"I guess. One of the region's planets is reporting something strange that happened during the evening about a week or so ago. It appeared a single Black Dragon ship entered the atmosphere, but when they checked again, it showed one of our ships."

"Easy to clear up. Just question the ship."

"Only the ship didn't stick around. They said it left immediately back through the portal, so they didn't get the chance. All I can guess is a mix-up with the scanners."

"Maybe. It's unusual."

"Huh, something else. When they reviewed it, the scanners didn't pick it up. Almost as if the incident never happened."

"Sounds familiar, Ryan."

"Yeah, it's their signature."

"They don't want to make themselves known. Maybe they're using their ship to accomplish their work. That kind of ship takes serious expertise, although our unknown friend showed far-reaching talent at the last attack. Again, they may not be related. We better get back to work with the other."

"It's a theory. Either way, our part of the attack has to go smoother next time. You can't come back with another chunk out of you."

Evening came, and the group packed up for the night.

Caleb and Lana retired to their room, and Caleb came up behind her. She sat on the couch, staring at the data pad, and he watched her stuck on the same page. He reached down and began sliding the data pad from her hands.

"What are you doing, Caleb?"

Caleb finished removing the data pad from her hands, placed it on the table, and sat next to her. He gazed over at her and slid his arm around her waist. "Saving you from yourself, sweetheart. You need to rest."

"I can't figure it out, and it's driving me crazy."

"No, WE can't figure it out yet, but we will." He got up and gently pulled her up from the couch. He smiled and brought her close. "You're not in this alone, ever. I'll always be here by your side. Okay?"

Lana smiled up at her husband. She got so wrapped up in this, but she needed to hear those words from him. "Okay."

"You're going to stop thinking tonight about boxes, chemicals, and the rest. You're coming to bed, and I'll be your guide, so there's no chance you lose your way. You're prone to that, I see."

She started to say something, but he reached down and gave her a gentle kiss. He took her hand. "Come on. It's time you came to bed, Lana."

He eased her down in bed and wrapped her up in his arms. She curled up next to him contently.

"Okay, Caleb, this is much better than analyzing a list."

"It is. You should listen to me more often. I have great ideas sometimes. Another one came to me." He leaned down and kissed her once and again and again.

Lana forgot all about the day's events as she surrendered to her husband for the night.

CHAPTER THIRTY-SEVEN

"These items from the warehouse are everywhere," said Ryan.

The group was back to staring at the supply lists from the warehouse and lab after finalizing their plans to meet the next attack.

"Which is why this didn't help as we had hoped," said Commander Cephas.

"Yeah, with these supplies, there are so many possibilities of what you could do with them," said Caleb.

"And then there are the chemicals added," said Seth.

"It's like what the lab guy pointed out. Certain chemicals can be dangerous, but in this case, who gained them is the concern. The Dark Lord will find a way to make them into something troubling, despite their normal use, "Dante said.

"We're back in a rut, going in this circle," said Lana.

Caleb smiled and said to his wife, "You're right. Any more out-of-the-box ideas or field trips to figure it out?"

"Nothing comes to mind to help us." Lana laughed.

"You did well the last time, so it's someone else's turn." He reached over and kissed her.

"I wish we could get information as to what they planned with the supplies," said Dante.

"You really are wishing, now, Dante," said Commander Gabe.

"Yeah, I suppose you're right," said Dante, sighing. Although, Caleb, Lana, Seth, and Ryan knew what Dante meant. Their unknown friend displayed an uncanny ability to manipulate information systems but only chose to help them the one time. Dante and Ryan needed to tell the other three about the incident in Ryan's region, so they did at lunch.

Caleb was puzzled. "Strange, but the scanners are usually right if it's a Black Dragon ship. The colonies' sensors are tuned to pick up one of those for sure."

"But if they tried to infiltrate the Black Dragon ranks for a reason, it would make sense," said Seth.

"As would the fact our people ended up seeing a Freedom Fighter ship a few moments later leaving," pointed out Lana.

"Because that wouldn't alarm a planet in our regions," finished Ryan.

Dante wondered aloud, "Sometimes operations don't go as planned. We've experienced it on occasion. Maybe they needed to get out quicker than they wished."

"So, they had to appear as the Black Dragon ship to escape in time. Then they switched the ship to something friendly," said Ryan.

"It must be the same person," said Lana.

"What are they doing?" pondered Caleb.

"I can't guess, but I want them to work with us openly. I wouldn't be surprised if they didn't have intel which would be helpful or could get it," said Dante.

"I'm still getting over the ship. I'm familiar with that type of system and would love to put it on even one of our ships, but it takes building it from the ground up for it to work right. It also involves massive time and expertise. Once you do it, I've heard you can make the modifications as needed, but the initial building and creating is something else entirely." Caleb paused. "I'm with Dante. I'd be eager for whoever it is to help us to a larger extent."

Dante glanced at Seth with the obvious question. Seth shook his head and said, "They won't answer any messages. They made it clear they'll initiate further contact, but they are monitoring our operations. Perhaps if they felt their help would provide an overwhelming solution, we'd receive another communication. It is only a theory, of course."

They finished lunch and continued sorting through more material for less than an hour when an aide came briskly walking in toward Lana.

Lana nodded to the others. "A Black Dragon fleet showed up at one of our planets. It's time to move."

"We'll be back soon," said Caleb giving Lana a hug and kiss before he left.

"You'd better be," murmured Lana smiling.

"Dante, I don't want to see you in medical today," teased Lana.

"I'll follow orders, promise, cousin."

"Ryan, are we ready?" asked Dante.

"Yes, remember the small group will help you with the tanks. Let them. We should be good. I hope Seth's group works out as well," said Ryan.

"Yeah, that makes two of us."

The two spied the troops headed their way, and the tanks would soon follow. They would mow down as many of their opponents as possible before the tanks arrived.

Dante pulled out his sunspear and went to work on the Black Dragon men coming toward him. Ryan and his squadron did the same with their swords and blasters. Dante heard the first rumblings and motioned to Ryan, who came alongside him.

"They're over that way," Dante pointed to the left of them. "so I'll head there with the group to start knocking them out."

"We're right behind you," answered Ryan.

Dante signaled to a group of about twenty troops to break off from the rest of the squadron and follow him to fight their way toward the tanks.

Once he reached the first tank, he used his sunspear to disable the moving mechanism for the tank, stopping it to a crawl. Then he jumped on top of the tank and with his sunspear chopped off the tank shaft. The troops covered him taking care of any Black Dragon soldiers trying to surround him while also watching the other tanks' actions.

He moved to the second tank and shot a cable out, successfully winding it around the tank shaft—the other half of the cable attached around a nearby tree.

The Black Dragon men in both tanks emerged to figure out what happened, but it didn't matter. Plenty of Ryan's squadron swarmed on them and eliminated them once they climbed out of the tank.

Dante got to the third tank but kept a watchful eye on the movements of the fourth tank, particularly after the last attack. He started climbing onto the third tank when he glimpsed the shaft of the fourth tank move.

"Dante, the fourth tank has taken notice of you."

"I saw it, Ryan." He pulled back from the third tank and waved for the group to follow him. "We'll switch it. Keep an eye on the third tank for me."

Dante and the group reached the fourth tank. He made a quick visual note of the third tank, and he saw its focus back on Ryan and his squadron. Dante hurried to get the fourth tank out of play before the third tank thundered past Ryan's group.

"You're good, Dante. The third tank is occupied here."

"Got it. Tell any of your team to move away from tank four." Dante retrieved two things from his bag, a spray substance and a small device. He sprayed the sticky substance near the fuel line on the tank and placed the device on the tank. "Clear tank four now! Disengage combat and clear the area now!" yelled Dante as he ran from the tank.

Fifteen seconds later, the tank exploded into a ball of fire.

"Nice explosion, Dante."

"I thought so too, Ryan. This last one is closer to the line than I wanted. I'll stop it from getting closer, draw them out, and disable it from inside."

"We'll cover you."

Dante spoke to the small group, "I'm going inside to disable it, so ensure there's no Black Dragon welcoming party when I come out." The group nodded in acknowledgement of his instructions.

Dante climbed onto the third tank and created an opening on the top with his sunspear. He fingered the light crackers in his hands, waiting for the right moment to spring his distraction. The Black Dragon men in the tank started to look up, but too late. Dante threw the light crackers inside and followed after them with his sunspear raised. Dante easily brought the three surprised Black Dragon troops down with his sunspear. Lastly, he destroyed the tank's control panel with a few swipes of his sunspear.

"Ryan, tank three is done."

"I'm outside the tank, Dante. Come on out. I'm told you didn't want any unpleasant surprises."

Dante scrambled out of the tank, and Ryan greeted him with a grin.

"Yes, I must keep the promise to my cousin. I can't get in trouble with her anymore."

"You? That would be both of us. As for the second tank, that's a neat trick, but it could possibly be used again if they got it loose."

"Yeah, I thought so too. We'll take care of it."

Dante, Ryan, and the squadron headed for the second tank. Dante entered the tank, and his sunspear rendered it inoperable as well. The squadron finished off the last few retreating Black Dragon soldiers, and Ryan and Dante made ready to return to Lana.

CHAPTER THIRTY-EIGHT

Meanwhile, Seth, Commander Gabe, and a portion of his squadron found their way to Technological Solutions, the target for the small Black Dragon group. This time with the added troops, Seth and Commander Gabe confirmed everyone in the building followed the lockdown. They could not afford another distraction from one of the colonists like the previous attack.

The Black Dragon men approached the site, and the guard ran as soon as he spotted them. They proceeded straight to the warehouse as the previous times. They brought the empty cart into the warehouse and loaded the boxes onto the cart, scanning the boxes as they did. They took the fully loaded cart just to the door. Then they brought the cart into the factory with the counterfeit boxes.

They had not unloaded the first box when a commotion from outside caught their attention. They ran outside to check the source of the noise, and the ones outside followed behind them as well. The disturbance originated from behind the building. Several men on speed gliders armed with blasters challenged the Black Dragon men despite the lockdown orders. The Black Dragon men mistakenly identified them as security for the warehouse by their dress. The security force stood its ground for only a few moments and quickly determined they would not win this fight. They sped off from the warehouse.

The Black Dragon men returned to their places. After taking their data pads off the boxes where they left them when they were interrupted, they unloaded the packages to the warehouse. They took the other cart of boxes away for transport and headed for the lab.

Seth looked down at his data pad. He didn't know if they would get any additional help, but it wouldn't hurt to try. He had scanned a few of the Black

Dragon data pads in case. A scanned data pad went a long way with their unknown friend's skills, and they could get access to Seth's data pad if they wished. Seth had provided them all the tools if they chose to help. He felt uncertain with two similar distractions in the same place successfully tricking the Black Dragon troops.

Suddenly Seth saw a message on his data pad: *Impressively done. Not sure about two times. Will you have anyone behind the warehouse again?*

Seth sent back: *No.*

Instantly a response showed: *Keep it that way and be sure no one is in the path from the lab to there as well. You may not require your security detail again. Can you tell them to wait?*

Yes.

Be ready. You won't have much time if they can all be led somewhere else.

Understood. Then Seth quickly communicated to his team a possible change of plans and to stand down on the second distraction.

The Black Dragon men walked into the lab, bringing in the empty cart, filling it with the boxes, and moving the cart right outside. They brought the counterfeit cart inside the lab.

Suddenly, the Black Dragon troop in charge stopped everyone. "Apparently, the security team didn't learn their lesson. They returned to the warehouse, and we can surround them. We can't risk the items being damaged in transport, so we'll take care of these pests now."

The Black Dragon men left and headed back to the warehouse, but they saw no one when they went to the back of the building.

The Black Dragon in charge communicated on his data pad: *There's no sign of them behind the warehouse. What do you wish us to do?*

We are checking. The message read on the data pad. Moments later, another message appeared. *Their courage left them once they saw your approach. They realized they would be signing their death sentence. Give them no more thought. Complete your task at the lab.*

The Black Dragon troop in charge laughed. "A pity. I wished to sharpen my blade with them today. We'll wrap up this operation."

The Black Dragon troops headed back to the lab and completed their work. They transported the lab supplies to the ship.

Seth, Commander Gabe, and the squadron watched them go.

"It worked, but I'm not sure entirely how, Seth."

"It's time we spoke with you and the other commanders about something once we return. It must stay only with the commanders. Commander Ryan already knows since he's second in command. Of course, Dante, Lana, and Commander Caleb also are aware of the information. We acquired an advantage recently, but we aren't in control of it."

"I'm intrigued. It certainly helped us today. They left with nothing from this colony, and they don't realize it yet."

⁓ℓℓ ⁓

"Lana, they're leaving through the portal as usual." Caleb's group had finished their usual firefight with the Black Dragon fleet.

"Good. Looks like everyone is headed back as planned this time. No reports of any visits to medical today."

"Your cousin can follow orders."

"For one day at least. I'll see you in a few."

"We're headed back now, sweetheart."

Lana sat, satisfied with the information coming through so far, but she would get the whole story soon. Caleb and the commanders who handled the air attack arrived back first, followed by Dante and Ryan, and lastly, Seth and Commander Gabe.

After welcoming her husband back, Lana went straight to Seth.

"Well?"

"Successful. Even better than hoped. We got help again today."

"Really?"

"It's time we spoke with the rest of the commanders and shared with them. We'll try a message before we gather them."

Seth sent a message while Lana watched: *Thank you for your help today. I hoped you would assist if you could.*

They waited. Suddenly, after almost a minute, a message appeared: *You're right. There are limitations as to how I can intervene at a moment's notice since I don't know your plans. Obviously, it wouldn't be safe for you to disclose such detail here. We understand the danger of doing the same thing too many times. They'll catch on. The other factor depends on the nature of what we're doing, as we may be unable to break from our operations to assist you. I'm glad I could aid you again today.*

"Lana, this is the longest message we've gotten."

"And it's carefully crafted."

Seth sent another message: *Maybe we'll get the chance to meet you in person to thank you.*

No message appeared, and Lana looked at Seth. "They may not like that one."

Seth started to answer, but a message appeared at that instant: *You never know when one of us will drop in on you.*

Seth peered up at Lana in surprise and said, "Or maybe our message suited them fine."

Seth wrote back: *We'll look forward to it.*

Long enough for today. You'll know if there's anything further. Goodbye. You know what comes next.

Seth and Lana read the message. Less than thirty seconds later, Seth's data pad blinked. The conversations from the day between him and the unknown friend disappeared from his data pad.

"Lana, we learned something else. The message used us a few times, so it's more than one person assisting us."

"Yes, but it sounds like a small group, maybe a couple of people."

"The way they said if they ran their own operation at the same time, they wouldn't be able to assist us makes me think the same. Also, from the incident with the Black Dragon ship, it bolsters our theory of a small operation that got too close for comfort. Certainly a situation where they couldn't divide their attention to help us."

"Do you think we'll see them soon?"

"I don't know, but they won't reveal any specifics on the data pad. We'll know it's them when they arrive, and they'll come for a specific reason. They've determined the perimeters of every interaction so far. I don't expect that to change."

Caleb walked up, along with Dante and Commander Ryan.

"What's going on?" asked Caleb, looking at Seth and Lana.

Lana replied, "It's time we spoke to the commanders about our unknown but helpful friend."

"Something happened?" asked Dante.

"Yes, help again," said Seth.

"I'm assuming the operation worked," Ryan said.

"Yes, but we don't need to keep the commanders in the dark any longer. Yet, we must be careful how we do this. Some commanders will be nervous since we don't know the identity of our help," said Seth.

"Understood. Seth, why don't you take the lead on it? You may be better at handling the disclosure to them in this case," said Lana.

Seth nodded, and they sat with the commanders and told them about their recent help. Seth left out specifics for the reasons Lana wished. He mentioned the incident at one of the planets in Commander Ryan's region appeared to be the same individuals and said it seemed the individuals' ship could be modified to assist them with their current operations. He made no mention of the latest communication regarding the possibility they may show up.

Seth finished when he saw another message come through on his data pad.

Lana said to him, "I thought no more messages today from them."

The others watched Seth, waiting for him to respond.

Seth said, "There's no way to trace it as it's from an unknown source. It's an attachment, but I'm sure it's from them." He opened the attachment. It revealed a list of all the boxes the Black Dragon scanned today and thought they confiscated from the warehouse and lab. "It's from them. They sorted through the data when I scanned the data pad and thought this would save us time. It will."

The commanders nodded in agreement. The more help they received, the more their misgivings wilted away.

Everyone worked together for about an hour, comparing the information from today with the things taken from the last couple of attacks. It went rapidly with the list from today done for them.

***

Seth, Lana, Caleb, Dante, and Ryan sat together and talked apart for a little at dinner as the rest finished eating. Seth and Lana told them about the communication Seth received when he arrived back at the fortress.

"More than one for sure, huh?" said Ryan.

"Well, think about some of our operations. One person trying to do all of it. Even on a smaller scale, there are going to be operations...." said Caleb.

"It'd be impossible," finished Dante.

"And don't forget the ship," said Caleb.

"No, we can't forget the ship," said Ryan, laughing.

"And they could drop in on us. That sounds promising," said Dante.

"We'll see," said Lana. "Don't get your hopes up."

CHAPTER THIRTY-NINE

"I guess we're almost ready," said the girl.

"Are you recovered enough?" asked Alika.

"Even if she wasn't, there's no way we'd keep her from coming." Alena laughed.

"I'm fine, thank you," said the girl to Alika and smiled at Alena. "It's strange leaving the place without one of us here, but we'll be monitoring it. With our system, nobody is coming in. It should be fine."

Alena reassured her. "It will be. It's not much different from the safe havens. You're probably feeling unsure after what you went through with the rescue."

"I suppose." Her voice could not hide a sadness, and her face reflected the same.

"There's something else," said Alika waiting.

"There are a couple of things I hoped would happen before we did this, such as figuring out the black substance we obtained and the whole setup they connected to Abigail," said the girl as she slowly walked over to Abigail's bedside.

Alena and Alika walked over with her.

Alika touched the girl's shoulder and said, "And you hoped Abigail would be awake, didn't you?'

"I did wish so very much," she whispered as she took Abigail's hand. "I don't understand what still holds her." She turned to Alika and Alena. "Will Dante get his mother back, or will she remain forever in this sleep?"

"Child, you did your part, and it almost cost your life. We can't control when she'll awaken," said Alika.

The girl sighed and said, "You're right. It's up to Dante to complete the rest of the task."

"You have a lot of faith in Dante," said Alika eyeing the girl.

"I have no faith in Dante," said the girl as Alika and Alena both stared at her in surprise, "any more than I have faith in myself when I go for an operation. However, I know the One who entrusts Dante with the task, and He will be beside Dante for it. He'll give Dante the means and wisdom to carry it through." The girl tried to convince herself of the words and bury the concern she felt for Dante. She looked down toward her ribs, continuing to heal. "The process is not always good, so I do hope Dante listens to instructions better than I did."

"You two do share similarities in that regard," said Alena remembering her conversation with Alika when the girl slept.

"We need to stop because our bodies can't take too much more of it," laughed the girl, and it only hurt some this time. "It's time we dropped in on them today. We should be catching them before lunch."

"Let us get Abigail and everything she needs into the ship. Everything else is already in the ship?" Alika asked.

"It is." The girl looked over at Alena and received a confirming nod.

The three headed for the ship, loading Abigail on the ship with them.

"I confirmed security is set," said the girl as the ship lifted off. "Are you ready for this, Alika?"

"I am, dear," said Alika smiling at the girl. He wore his Elder clothing and carried his staff. He appeared official today, and he would need to for this meeting.

"Crossing the portal now. We're about to be overhead and let them know we've arrived," said the girl.

CHAPTER FORTY

Lana sat with Caleb, Dante, and Seth working, and the other commanders did the same at another table. Ryan alternated between the two groups to study the data with both. They ate breakfast about an hour ago as mid-morning approached.

A call from the communications center directed Seth's attention to his data pad.

"Yes?"

"Sir, there's a communication for you."

Seth waited, and his data pad flashed *Confidential*. "Give me a moment." He pulled himself aside from the group. Lana, Dante, and Caleb looked at him curiously but resumed working.

"I can speak now."

"Yes, sir. I'm sorry to interrupt. A ship just arrived requesting permission to land. They put out the signal of peace and say they'll only speak with you further. They also said no one else is to be aware of their arrival at this time besides Lana. Normally we'd send ships out to escort them to land, but we'll do as you wish in this situation."

Seth recovered from his initial shock and said, "No, don't send out the escort. They're friends. Relay back to them that I'm on my way to clear them for landing. Do nothing else. I'll speak with them further upon my arrival."

"Yes, sir."

Seth went over to Lana. "I need to speak with you."

Lana excused herself. "What is it?"

"They are here."

"You're serious?"

"Yes, they'll only speak with me, and they said no one else is to know they're here at this time besides you and me."

"I'm not sure about this, Seth."

"It'll be fine. They said at this time, so I'm certain that will change. I'll clear them for landing and send you a message soon."

"All right. Let me know."

Lana returned to the group as Seth walked from the room.

"Everything okay?" asked Caleb, studying Lana's face.

"Yeah, he left to take care of something. He'll be back as soon as he can," said Lana, hating to leave her husband in the dark.

"Okay, let's get back to work," said Caleb, knowing he wasn't getting the whole story but not pushing for further explanation.

❧

Seth arrived at the ship hangar's communication center. "I'll take over from here. Thank you."

"Yes, sir."

"This is Seth. I'm here as you requested to clear you for landing."

His data pad flashed a message: *We wish to land at the outermost hangar. Is there a small, private room we can meet near the hangar?*

"Yes, on both counts. You are cleared to land as you wish. I'll be there to meet you and take you to the room."

Thank you. Remember no other personnel at this time, and that means none on the way to the room as well.

"I picked up on that part. It'll be done."

Seth turned back to the troop. "You may return to your post. The ship is cleared to land at the specified hangar. I'll handle everything concerning this ship and those in it. They're my guests only. Do you understand?"

"Understood, sir," said the troop.

Seth arrived at the hangar as the ship landed. The ship door opened, and Seth could not hide his surprise as he caught sight of an Elder emerge from the ship. The door shut behind him as he strolled toward Seth.

"Right this way," Seth said.

The Elder nodded and followed Seth to the room.

They started to sit, but Alika stopped him. "You'll need to be assured I'm an Elder as I claim."

"I do not doubt."

"I believe you," Alika said with a smile. "Except when we discuss what brings me here, you may question my identity as an Elder. Please, indulge me."

Seth did as his guest wished. The two joined hands briefly with their staff crossed. A yellow light appeared at both staff's ends, then disappeared.

"Now we can sit, Seth."

"I thought others would join us."

"The other two are here, but they're remaining on the ship."

"They're Elders as well?"

"No, they're my students. You should send a message to Lana now. She's probably getting anxious for your safety."

"You know us well for never having met us." He quickly sent a message to Lana and returned his attention to the Elder. "Do you have a name besides Elder?" asked Seth laughing.

"My name is Alika."

"You instruct two students? Training one is challenging enough. Who are the two?"

"It's one of those things I can't disclose now and possibly not at all. I taught both from an early age. Once the older spear-bearer reached about fifteen, we received the task of teaching the younger one. We've both taught the younger one since that time."

"How old is the younger student?"

"The same age or almost the same as your student, Dante. There's no point in trying to figure out the identities. Knowing who I am won't help you. At another time, it could provide a clue. After the dark times, Elders are spread everywhere, and it's no longer recorded. Moreover, no one remains who knew of the younger spear-bearer's training except for myself and the other student who helped in the training."

"You trained them well. I assume they provided the assistance we received along with yourself."

"I did little of that part, as you'll see. I leave the majority of those tasks to them. So, yes, they manage exceptionally well, many times in very formidable circumstances. It's time to discuss why we chose to come today." Alika sighed. "It will change everything for your group, above all for Dante."

CHAPTER FORTY-ONE

"Please, go on, Alika."

"When we began training the younger one, the student possessed the many strengths that mark a spear-bearer. Additionally, the younger one possessed an understanding of the teachings at a deeper level than most, and the gift of visions was the strongest I'd ever encountered. Initially, many of the visions involved my student, pieces of my student's past, and immediate events of my student's future. Later they involved other individuals, ones not in my student's circle of life. We wondered why, but it became clear recently. Less than a month ago, both students returned from one of their operations early. The younger one complained of tiredness, a general sense of not feeling well. During the night, the older student and I woke to the younger student's screams. The younger one received a vision from the past." Alika took a deep breath. "It showed the younger one the murder of Collin, Dante's younger brother."

"Why would your student see this?"

"To be shown the truth and end the bondage that has ensnared someone for too long and continues to even now, Seth."

"What else did the student see?"

"The younger saw a woman who appeared to be Dante's mother murder Collin with a long dagger. The child could do nothing, but scream as he was slain. The younger also saw what appeared to be an Elder watching the whole thing and ordering it to be done."

Seth shook his head at the reality of the information. "The vision matches the account by Dante's father. We said there's no way it could be true."

"We were right, Seth. I said it appeared so. After we calmed our student, we went back through the vision, piece by piece. The woman was not Dante's mother, but a woman disguised as Dante's mother. This woman still lives, and she serves the Dark Lord to this day. She leaves nothing but pain with every encounter she is a part."

Seth continued to listen, with a mixture of relief and sadness. He sensed from Alika this woman had created pain for either himself or one of his students.

Alika continued, "As for the Elder, the younger noticed the Elder kept his head bowed or concealed the whole time, so his identity could never be disclosed. He wore the clothing of an Elder, but the resemblance ended there. We're certain the cloak previously belonged to another Elder who died suddenly at the same time or went missing. It could be researched, but it'd be wasted time. There's no doubt in our minds. We, as Elders, always wondered how Ethan so quickly jumped to such conclusions. The Dark Lord crafted for him what he wanted Ethan to see that evening. The Dark Lord dressed as the Elder and watched as his lady companion did the bloody deed for him."

Seth sat back for a couple of minutes, not knowing what to say. Alika sat there, allowing Seth to process what he heard.

"Alika, we have discovered this now, but we could not convince Dante's father to consider other possibilities at the time of Collin's murder. Now he is under the Dark Lord's control. How is there hope of changing things?"

"Because we have a piece of the puzzle we lacked then. My student saw another vision immediately after the first vision of the child's murder. It involved another member of Dante's family."

"There's only Ethan or Abigail." Seth stopped. "But she's ..."

"No, she's alive."

Seth sat again in stunned silence, and Alika allowed him time.

"Alika, after all these years? How? I don't understand."

"The Dark Lord kept her prisoner, Seth."

"Oh, no," whispered Seth. "She can't possibly be alive. There's no way she would've survived."

"She did. He kept her in a coma-like, tortured state. It's unclear what the intent was for her. She hasn't awakened."

Seth heard Alika. The familiarity Alika had of her current status seemed strange. Seth didn't connect what Alika had said. "We must get her back, Alika. We'll work with you to do so," Seth's voice shook.

"You don't understand. There's no need to do so. My two spear-bearers already reclaimed her from the Dark Lord's facility. Abigail is in the ship now." While Seth watched in disbelief, Alika pulled out his data pad to reveal an image of Abigail peacefully lying on a rolling bed inside the ship, with the necessary medical equipment hooked to her.

Seth sat there for several minutes as he sorted the information and the range of emotions rushing through him. Memories from that horrible day in the past rushed forth again to combine with what Alika had shared. Seth had felt the events of that day years ago differently, much deeper than the other Elders because he really knew the family. He was the family's Elder, given the privilege of training their two children in the ways of the sunspear and helping keep them from harm. Never had he envisioned he would be protecting them from their own parents, but he could never believe Abigail guilty of such a terrible act. Then he immediately found himself forced to save Dante from his own father. It had been the only way to keep Dante safe, and yet it had torn his spirit to do it. Yes, today did change many things. Yet one terrible truth it did not. Collin was gone. An innocent child taken, one he had started training along with his brother, Dante. One he had failed to protect. He could still see Collin's bright smile, hear his laughter... Seth closed his eyes for a moment and shook his head. Alika waited patiently.

"I'm afraid to ask, but are there more revelations you're about to tell me?"

"No. The rest is what you would infer. I told you it would alter things for your group, but for Dante it goes far beyond that."

"I do see where this is going. Did your young student have any further visions?"

"Not direct visions, but rather impressions or guidance from those already received. Ethan knows nothing of this operation involving Abigail, as he believes she's dead. If he learned the truth and could be convinced, it would break the hold on him. So, securing Abigail is part of that purpose besides the fact she no longer should be suffering with whatever the Dark Lord planned. My two students owned the task of securing her from the Dark Lord, and they did so. However, the next task is not theirs to do. They did not hesitate to rescue Abigail, despite the danger and the odds. I know my students' heart and spirit. If they could, they would assist in this next task, but they cannot. No one can. It's meant for the one to accomplish when the time comes. Seth, there's only one person who can convince Ethan of the truth and break the hold of the Dark Lord."

"Oh my, it did go where I thought. No vision on how Dante is to accomplish it, I suppose."

"No, but my young student is certain Dante will be able to do it. The Ancient One gives him the task and will be beside him every step of it. My student is concerned for Dante in what he must do, but confident he can do it."

"Your younger student sounds like a sensitive spirit." Suddenly something occurred to Seth. All this time, Alika never said he or she, and Seth realized it now. Seth assumed the spear-bearers were males. He didn't know why. Lana is a spear-bearer. Although she usually stayed back and monitored, she could decimate a squadron in as little time as her cousin and husband did. Seth went ahead and asked as his curiosity mounted, "Alika, you won't give me the names of your spear-bearers, but you are careful in your speech. I believe both of them are women. Am I guessing right?"

Alika looked at Seth closely. "We spoke a bit about their training when I first arrived. One of my tasks with training them, particularly the younger one, was guaranteeing the one safe because of the training circumstances. I must keep that promise to my student and ensure we understand each other."

"Even though I don't have the story behind it, I understand you perfectly in the way you need me to. I would never put them in danger."

"All right, then you're correct, and both are women spear-bearers. It'll make it easier to speak when it's only us, but with the others ..."

"I understand."

"We also have something for your group to examine from the rescue. We tried but came up empty in our analysis of it. Perhaps a different set of eyes will uncover what we didn't." Alika got his data pad out as he spoke, and it lit up. "This is the outside of the facility where the Dark Lord kept Abigail. Here's a layout of the inside, minus at least one hidden door which my two students had the misfortune of discovering during the rescue. This is Abigail's room at the Dark Lord's facility and the setup they hooked up to her. Do you see this bag?"

"Yes, what is in it?"

"That's what we can't identify, despite our efforts. The younger one obtained a sample of it before they got Abigail out. The younger one told me to give you this sample of it. She's hoping one of us finds success. You're right when you said her spirit is sensitive. In the vision when she saw Abigail hooked up to all this, Abigail's spirit constantly struggled against the darkness. Once they rescued Abigail, the younger one no longer felt the struggle, but Abigail is not awake. When she started working with the sample, she still felt the darkness from it. So, she cautioned not to get it on you and not to spend a whole stretch of time working with it. Ideas came to my mind about the substance, all unpleasant possibilities."

"Yes, we're going the same places, especially when you consider where he receives his power."

"Yes, handle the sample with care," said Alika as he handed over the sealed metal cylinder to Seth.

"Do you have footage from the rescue?"

"Yes, WE do."

"But of course, they don't."

"Correct. The facility presented an obstacle for my younger student. It proved extremely secure. Not until they got to the entrance and dispatched the guards did they gain decent access. Since Ethan didn't know anything about the operation, it wasn't Black Dragon troops guarding the facility. The building was staffed by a special security force hired by the Dark Lord himself, and the cloaked woman came usually daily from what we gathered. Obviously, my students' voices and images will be disguised."

"Naturally."

Seth watched the footage. They reached the door. Suddenly the two men next to the door collapsed to the ground. The door opened. Seth deduced the two got their clearances and accesses situated as Alika indicated. A trip to the surveillance room followed. Then it got interesting—two more guards fell to the floor. Another door opened, and the two men got thrown inside the room. Seth registered flashes of lights everywhere, but they all aimed at one spot. Gradually it quieted down, and the image focused on Abigail in a capsule-looking mechanism with the bag hanging over her. The black bag was connected to a large device overhead, and someone unhooked the bag. Seth saw the capsule close quickly on Abigail, and flashes of light resumed, once again concentrating on the same spot. Without warning, he watched in horror as the troops closed in, gaining the advantage. It stopped altogether, and they surrounded their prey. He could see all the blasters pointed at the one spot. Seth turned to Alika, but he watched it calmly. Suddenly, the troops ran out the door in pursuit of someone.

"Stop it there, Alika. What happened? It looks like they shot one or both of your students."

"Oh, no, they didn't get my students. My students worked out a ploy ahead of time, and it worked beautifully. They got in the situation initially because of the hidden door."

"Quite the ploy. It's one of those things you'll disclose to me one day, but not today." Seth started the footage again. The next image reappeared of Abigail being switched from the capsule to a rolling stretcher. There were a series of doors opened and closed, and Seth realized Abigail was being taken upstairs. Finally, Abigail emerged on top of the roof with a ship in waiting. In the midst of loading Abigail inside, the flashes of light commenced on the rooftop. The ship door closed, but the flashes of light were still everywhere and appeared to originate from outside the ship. The footage stopped.

"I don't understand. They're in the ship, but it's as if they're still outside the ship dealing with blaster fire."

"The end of the rescue did not go as smoothly as planned."

"What happened? You did say both of your students are with you?"

"They both are, but the younger one almost didn't make it. As the older one placed Abigail into the ship, the whole building's security force rushed the rooftop. The younger told the other to go and get Abigail to safety. After the ship door shut, the ship headed for the portal. The older tried to turn back for the younger, but the ship would not do so. The younger got too close to the edge of the rooftop while fighting and fell. It's the last thing the older saw when she went through the portal."

"How did ...?" Seth didn't finish, his face in horror.

"The biggest eagle ever seen. She heard a voice on the rooftop telling her to fall, and she would be caught. However, she added a cable to those instructions. It didn't attach to the rooftop right, so her body met it hard in extremely painful ways. The eagle carried her to the woods. She located a smuggling ship there with four men. She overpowered them somehow in her condition, borrowed their ship, and contacted us to retrieve her. Yet, for those hours, we thought we lost her. We also both thought we left her. We realized later we didn't, that we could not control the ship as we thought. The Ancient One knew what must be done, and He would get her back to us. She understood on the rooftop when the blaster fire began."

Seth was silent. He couldn't imagine coming to such a realization and thinking your student dead at the same time. Alika cared deeply for his young student as Seth cared deeply for Dante.

"Do you need to have her seen about? How badly was she hurt?"

"Exceedingly," Alika whispered. He regained his composure after the incident replayed through his spirit. "However, I anticipated the missions they would both be doing from the beginning, so I am trained to treat most injuries. She came back to me with a concussion, pieces of rock from the rooftop embedded in her head, two broken ribs, a dislocated shoulder, and she got scraped up badly on her left side from the building. A couple of the blasters claimed a piece of her as well. We treated everything, extracted the rocks from her head, put everything in place, and repaired the ribs. She's recovering and insisted on coming today. There's nothing I could say or do to keep her away. We remarked to her on a couple of occasions that she and Dante are similar patients in that respect."

"I'm grateful she came through it. They both sound remarkable, Alika. I wish you would reconsider, so I could meet them today. I'm stunned the two of them rescued Abigail on their own as I watch the footage. Your younger one paid the price on a couple of levels, and I can't imagine the emotional toil for all of you."

"Yes, but she's strong in many ways beyond her years. The older was horribly shaken at almost losing one who is as a sister to her. Our concern now turns to Dante and the task before him. The younger is especially concerned for Dante's safety."

"Really?"

"Well, true," Alika smiled, reading Seth's thoughts, "but remember she knows him though he's not in her circle each day. Her visions are intense, vivid. The other people she saw in the visions involved mainly Dante and his family. Even with Dante's father, she sees Ethan, not the Black Dragon Commander. Her heart broke for Ethan, and the deception dealt him in his grief. For at least a couple of months now, she implied the visions centered on Dante. With Dante, she knows him and cares for him, although he's unaware of her."

"I didn't think of it that way. It must be strange for her. Dante has gained the deep concern of one he truly doesn't know exists."

"Indeed, he has. Seth, I don't envy the task before you. We're running operations to determine what the Black Dragon is doing and how Abigail's operation played into it. We haven't established how close the Black Dragon Commander is to completing his part of the operation, and we wondered if Abigail's rescue would affect the attacks. They continued, though. We're questioning if the Dark Lord can do the operation without Abigail, if he'll try to get her back, or capture a replacement for her. Abigail must be carefully guarded, and all your people, including Lana, Dante, and Caleb, must be careful. The one who serves the Dark Lord is a master at changing her appearance."

"Your students should practice the same caution if the Dark Lord is hunting for a substitute. It will be difficult to keep them safe with the dangerous missions I foresee in their future. I'm worried for them. I believe they had another close call recently with their ship disguised to look like a Black Dragon ship."

"So, they didn't get the ship changed over in time? They wondered. Yes, they had to outrun a Black Dragon ship after they got the tracking device onto the cloaked woman's ship to pinpoint Abigail's prison."

They sat in silence.

"Seth, it'll be obvious when it's time for Dante to complete the task before him. Do what you must to prepare him. It will be training unlike what you've ever done."

"You're right, but your young spear-bearer said the task is his and he'll have all he needs when the day comes. I'll do my part so that's the case."

"Well said. How would you like to do this? You can get Abigail now and speak with the others or vice versa. We'll remain until you're done. I can meet with all of you after you have spoken with them. I want to give you time with them first, primarily Dante. He'll need it once he hears this and sees his mother alive. It will be much for him to take at once."

"Let me speak with them first and then get Abigail. Based on everything you said, I must be sure where she'll be kept is secure before we transport her."

Alika nodded, and they walked to the ship.

"Let me know when you're ready, Seth. I'll assist in any way needed."

"Thank you. This will take time, but I'll be back."

Alika walked into the ship, and Seth headed back to the others, dreading the start of this conversation.

CHAPTER FORTY-TWO

Seth's entrance back into the room caught Lana's attention immediately, and Dante and Caleb followed her look. Seth held her eyes, and she excused herself.

"Seth, what is it?" Lana asked. His eyes reflected a range of emotions.

"It's lunchtime. Dismiss everyone for the remainder of the afternoon with the understanding we'll meet later, probably not until tomorrow, to discuss the current information. Explain the dismissal how you wish. We need you, Caleb, Dante, and Ryan only for this in a private room."

"Seth, are you all right?"

"It's difficult to answer now. Make sure Dante is seated between us." Seth spoke gently. "Please do as I instructed."

"Of course, Seth."

—⁓—

Dante, Caleb, and Ryan found themselves seated by Lana in a small room as Seth sat with them. They waited.

"I have no clue how to begin this. The messenger told me this information would change everything for us, especially for you, Dante," Seth gazed at Dante, his face full of emotion, "and it will."

"Seth, whatever it is, tell us. We'll figure it out."

"Our unknown friends landed."

A collective gasp followed from everyone except Lana.

"There are three in their party, an Elder and two that bear the sunspears. The Elder trained the two since they were young. He trained the first one alone, and then the younger one came to them for training. I met with the Elder, and he made it clear he's the only one we'll meet on this trip. He provided all the information we need and the purpose of their visit. The information involves a past event which has a direct bearing on the present circumstances. The younger student possesses the strong gift of visions from the Ancient One. The visions began centering around one family for some time." Seth held Dante's eyes. "Your family, Dante."

"Why would someone see visions of my family?"

"They wondered the same until the young spear-bearer witnessed a troubling vision from your past. The student saw the murder of your brother, Collin."

Dante went pale. The others were silent. Lana reached out her hand and touched her cousin on the back.

"Dante?" Seth said gently.

"Keep going."

"It initially showed what appeared to be your mother striking down Collin and an Elder commanding her to do so, which is exactly what your father believed happened." Dante started as if hit with a blaster, so Seth continued quickly. "On closer examination of the vision, that's not what happened. The woman was not your mother but a Dark Lord agent, a woman who worked and still does for the Dark Lord. She's able to disguise herself well, which is what she did that day. The one who appeared to be an Elder was only dressed as one, but definitely not an Elder, but the Dark Lord."

Dante stared out into space. He'd always been told an explanation existed, that his father couldn't be right about the events of that day. That somehow, the Dark Lord twisted the event and used it to gain his father's service. Now, Dante knew how the Dark Lord accomplished it. The Dark Lord stood by that night at his home and helped slaughter his brother. He didn't understand, couldn't comprehend the words.

"Dante?" Seth said again, and this time he touched Dante's arm.

"Why did the Dark Lord choose my family to destroy?" asked Dante, his eyes becoming moist.

"I don't have that answer, Dante," said Seth gently, his spirit burdened for his student.

"More?" Dante's voice asked softly, and his eyes filled with pain as he stared at Seth.

Seth nodded slowly.

Dante choked out, "Go on."

"The question became why would the student be shown this now. After all, the Elders tried to convince Ethan of other possibilities when Collin's murder occurred rather than the one he settled on. So even if he could be told the truth now, why would he believe it? The only one who would know the truth of what happened that day and could provide proof for him would be Abigail, your mother. The Elders long decided the Dark Lord murdered her along with having a hand in Collin's murder, but the Dark Lord convinced Ethan otherwise. Either way, Abigail could not be found. The answer came immediately in another vision." Seth took a deep breath and watched Dante closely. "It showed Abigail stills lives."

Dante's face went pale again, his hand shook, and the tremors continued through his whole body. His eyes swam with tears. Lana pulled her chair closer to him and wrapped her arm around his shoulder. Her face filled with shock.

Dante tried to speak, but the words jumbled. "Why would she stay away? Where is she?" He couldn't finish. His emotions overcame him.

Seth looked at Dante with tears in his eyes. "Dante, the Dark Lord took her prisoner and kept her in a sort of coma state, her spirit tortured, but she fought all this time."

Dante's eyes pleaded with Seth. "No, no, Seth. We have to get her back." The image of his mother under the Dark Lord's control all this time, struggling, enduring all of it ... it was too much.

Tears slid down Seth's face as his spirit broke for his student. "Dante, she's no longer in the Dark Lord's grasp. The two spear-bearers rescued her."

"She's ... you're sure?"

"I'm sure. However, she's still asleep, and our friends don't know how to awaken her. She's safe now."

Dante could process no more. He openly wept. Seth put his arm around his student's other shoulder. Caleb put his own arm around Lana's back as tears poured down her face for her cousin. Ryan moved his chair around to Dante and put his hand on Dante's back. "We're here, Dante."

Gradually a calm settled on Dante. "Where do they have her, Seth?"

"Resting comfortably on their ship. We will transport her shortly into a secure room here."

Dante stammered out, "She's here now. Have you seen her?"

"Yes and no. I saw a picture of her sleeping peacefully on the ship, but no, I didn't go to the ship to see her. Since our friends couldn't discover what the Dark Lord planned for Abigail, they are unsure if he still needs her to complete it or if he seeks a substitute to stand in her place. For that reason, we must make sure she's secure before we bring her into the building to prevent him from recapturing her. It also means everyone here must exercise caution when you're out, during an attack, or any other vulnerable situation, so you don't take her place."

Caleb finally spoke. The question spoke to strategy, and it gave Dante a moment to breathe. "Do our friends believe the Dark Lord would try to sneak here to get Abigail back? Surely he knows we'd expect such a thing."

Seth relaxed as it took the subject away momentarily from the last topic to cover. "The Dark Lord only knows someone rescued her, but he doesn't know who at this point. If he tries to secure her again, he may search for our friends first if he ever figures out who they are. From that perspective, they put themselves in more danger. We assume at some point the Dark Lord concludes our friends turned Abigail over to us, but the fear is not the Dark Lord coming. The concern is from the cloaked lady companion that undertakes many tasks for him and boasts a frightening ability to disguise herself. Also, she oversaw the operation involving Abigail, and she failed miserably. So recapturing Abigail would be this agent's means to redeem herself to the Dark Lord." Seth paused and gently pushed forward with the last difficult topic for Dante. He focused his attention back to him. "Obviously, Dante, there are no anxieties about a visit from your father as he knew nothing about the operation with Abigail. If he ever stumbled upon his wife and the imprisonment and torture done to her by the Dark Lord, the Dark Lord's hold on him would be broken. She is safe with us now, and so the truth can still be revealed. The deception can be uncovered to your father, but there is only one person he will listen to."

Dante's eyes registered understanding but a weariness from what he had processed today. "So, this is the endgame?"

Lana gazed up at Seth. "Are you sure?"

"Yes. The young spear-bearer saw they must rescue Abigail, and they did so, with one of them almost not making it back." Seth shook his head as he remembered. The others looked at him curiously as he continued, "The spear-bearer sees Dante is the only one who can survive an encounter with Ethan and convince him of the truth." Seth stared straight at Dante. "Dante, you can set your father free from the hold of the Dark Lord. It's a bondage which must be destroyed, one created in deception, and it can be broken by truth."

"How am I to do it, Seth?" asked Dante. It loomed such an enormous task, and he felt nothing left in him.

"I don't know yet, but the spear-bearer said the task is yours, Dante. Moreover, the Ancient One will be beside you for it, so you'll be able to accomplish it as long as you let Him be your guide."

CHAPTER FORTY-THREE

As Alika met with Seth, Alena and the girl tried looking through informa-tion as the girl insisted, but the girl couldn't focus.

"I don't know why you want to try to do this."

"Huh?"

"Exactly. Give it up."

"No, I'm listening." The girl touched Alena's arm. "I'm sorry, Alena. I'll try harder."

"We both know it won't work. Remember, you're the same one who got back to us in your half-dead state. A million things are running through your mind, and they all involve what we came here to tell Dante and his company," Alena paused, "and her." She looked over at Abigail and back at the girl.

The girl whispered, "You're right."

"You'll miss her. What's she like? You saw her with Dante, Ethan, and Collin."

"She's kind and gentle but strong at the same time. She followed the Ancient One, and He stood with her and still does. She loved her family with everything in her, which is why she continued to struggle against the darkness. She would sacrifice everything for them, as a mother..." the girl couldn't continue. Her emotions and images overwhelmed her.

"As a mother would for her child," Alena finished for the girl. She held the girl as she quietly cried in Alena's arms. Alena whispered to her, "I'm so sorry."

Alika returned and found Alena sadly looking at the girl, with her arm encircling the girl's shoulder. The girl sat staring out into space, with tears still glistening in her eyes. He'd expected an emotional day for everyone, but especially for Dante and the girl. Alika looked at Alena, and Alena looked from the girl to Abigail. No questions were needed.

"Well, Alika?" asked the girl as she wiped her tear-streamed face.

"Seth wishes to tell them first, get Abigail, and then I'll meet with them if needed."

"How was it?" asked Alena.

"As well as could be expected. Seth is visibly shaken understandably, but he doubts none of the information I relayed to him. You can watch it if you ever wish to when it's not so fresh for the two of you," Alika said, looking at them both, but he directed it to the girl.

"Did you give him the sample?" the girl asked.

"Yes, I did along with the precautions about its handling."

They looked out the cockpit of the ship, and something caught the girl's eye. "It's them."

"It's probably an easier route to get to the room to meet with Seth," said Alika.

"I guess," said the girl, still tracing their movements. Seth's face appeared burdened all at once. The girl read the worry in Lana's face. She felt a great sadness for them. Then, she found her eyes drawn to Dante. It was strange to finally see him. She'd watched him and his family so many times in her visions she felt as though she knew him, even if today was the first time she'd seen him in person. It felt like she'd spent months with him in a different time. She watched him disappear into the building with the others. The burden that would be placed upon him struck a fresh wave of sadness through her.

"It must be a weird feeling," said Alika, peering at her.

"I'm sorry. It shouldn't be," said the girl, suddenly feeling self-conscious. What was wrong with her?

"You personally know the past and present of someone, and you care for his family, his friends, and his well-being. All of this through your visions, and the person has no idea of your existence, certainly not the depth of your concern for him. I can only imagine how it feels, but I don't begin to understand," said Alika.

"He'll bear so much today, all at once. I worry about him. There's only so much one can handle." Her eyes reflected sadness. She understood that feeling.

"He's strong. It can be done. You know it to be so," said Alena.

"Alena and I felt the same worry before. Yet, our student found the path. He will do the same today, child," Alika said.

"I know. It hurts though," whispered the girl.

"It always does for those who walk the path and those who must watch them," Alika said as he clasped her hand.

The girl listened as Seth spoke to the group, but she didn't need to hear him. Somehow, she anticipated Dante's reaction and felt the turmoil of his emotions as they unfolded. She heard him ask why his family was chosen to be destroyed by the Dark Lord, and tears streamed down her face anew. It wasn't fair. It shouldn't have happened. His spirit began to break, and her spirit broke with him. I'm sorry, Dante. Then she heard him being told of his mother, and his spirit finally broke as he wept.

"Oh Dante, I'm so sorry." The girl found herself saying aloud this time, and she put her head in her hands. Alena and Alika sat on either side comforting her, with tears in their own eyes. The girl heard Dante being told the task before him and the question from Lana.

The girl looked at Alika and Alena, and choked out, "Maybe I saw... spoke wrong. Is there another way ... without Dante having to do this?"

"You know there's not, child," whispered Alika as tears slid down his face.

The girl collapsed from the chair to her knees, still weeping for Dante, feeling she had placed the weight of the planet upon his shoulders.

CHAPTER FORTY-FOUR

They sat in silence. Lana, Caleb, and Ryan waited on Seth and Dante to make the next move. Seth quietly watched and waited on Dante. Dante sat staring into space.

Finally, Dante turned to Seth. "What else?"

"That's all, Dante. I covered it all."

"You spoke with the Elder for awhile."

"There are no more startling revelations, Dante. The rest can be discussed later."

"We need to secure the room for my mother."

"Yes, when you're ready."

Dante nodded.

Seth looked at Caleb and Ryan. "I want input from the two of you on how to best secure her. This is your territory. I have footage on my data pad of what she was being kept in and her current state if it would be helpful."

"Maybe. I can't be sure," said Caleb, but he glanced at Dante hesitantly.

"It's fine. I know she's safe now," said Dante.

"Here is in the facility where the Dark Lord kept her a prisoner." The projection showed Abigail laying in the capsule, hooked up to all the equipment, including the bag with the black substance and the device leading up to it.

"What is all that?" Dante asked.

"They don't know. They retrieved a sample of the black substance in the bag and gave us a sample to see if we obtain better results with figuring it out." Seth went to another slide, showing Abigail in a bed in a different room, but the picture showed nothing distinctive about the room to give away the location. "This is the setup after they got her to their location. The room contains basic medical monitoring for her." Seth went to the last slide. "Finally, this is her on the ship." Seth checked in with Dante, "Still okay, Dante?"

"Yes, the Elder and two spear-bearers took good care of her. I'm thankful to them. What did you say their names are again?"

"I didn't. I'll let the Elder introduce himself, and he said he will not disclose the names of his spear-bearers. You can see Abigail needs medical monitoring, but we must maintain minimal access to her. Any ideas?"

"A few possibilities, but considering what we've seen from our friends, I'm wondering how they kept her safe," Caleb said.

Ryan agreed, "My first thought too. They seem to be excellent with this type of thing. Did that come up?"

"No, it didn't. I can ask, but what are your ideas in case they don't want to disclose, or we can't do it?" asked Seth.

"My mind went to a fingerprint access for the door to see her, at the least considering what we've heard," said Caleb.

"There are still situations where that security could be compromised, but this cloaked woman would have to get far in the building and knock out a few people first," said Ryan.

"Dante, what do you think? She's your mother, so we want your input," said Lana softly.

"I agree we ask the Elders and the other two for guidance, and if not, we go with our idea." He didn't understand the limited information about the two spear-bearers, but he left it alone. "I'm concerned about the access of the medical staff. Someone could sneak inside the room using that cover."

"Yes, I as well, but we'll work that out. If Abigail needs her own personal nurses, it'll be done. She'll be kept safe, Dante," said Seth. "I'll send a message to inform them I'm coming for Abigail and ask the Elder to return with me."

~ell~

Alika glimpsed the message on his data pad: *I'm ready now. Should it be only me, or may the others accompany me as far as the outside of the ship?*

Alika spoke to the girl, "It's time, child."

Seth scanned the answer: *They may come, but please only you approach the ship. I'll need to speak with you before the transport.*

The girl rose and walked over to Abigail's bedside. Alika and Alena followed her. The girl softly took Abigail's hand. Her fingers touched something on Abigail's finger. It was her wedding band. The girl hadn't noticed it until now. "Ironic. All this time and they allowed her to keep it. They took everything else from her."

Alena leaned over, and something sparkly caught her eyes. She gently pushed Abigail's hair to one side to reveal a necklace. "Look, this as well."

The girl peered over at Alika and Alena. "I can't think straight, but an idea came to me, and it left."

"I finished it for you, so it's okay," said Alika in thought. "Child, Abigail will be safe."

"I know." She gazed down at Abigail. "Abigail, you're finally home to Dante. Whatever holds you still, fight it. Please awaken, Abigail. Dante needs you." A sob erupted from her.

Alika's data pad beeped. He said to the girl, "They're here. I'll talk to Seth. Take the time you need with Abigail. Whenever you're ready, Alena will let me know. Then both of you go to the quarters, and I'll transport Abigail to them."

Alena nodded as she put her arm around the girl's shoulder. Alika left the ship, closing the door behind him.

⁓ello⁓

"Seth."

"Hello again, Alika. Is everything okay?"

"Yes." Alika motioned for Seth to move, so the rest of the group couldn't hear their conversation. "My young spear-bearer became quite attached to Dante and his entire family through the visions as we discussed. This has been difficult for her as I suspected it would since it is an emotional day for Dante. She's fond of Abigail and is saying her goodbyes. I told her we'd give her the time she needed, and the other spear-bearer will alert me when they're ready."

"She almost gave her life to bring Abigail back. Allowing her time with Abigail is the least we can do for her. Come meet the others, and when you receive the signal, we'll move Abigail."

Seth walked up to the group with Alika. "The students are ensuring Abigail is secure and medically ready for the transport. They'll alert us when that's been done. In the meantime, this is Alika."

Seth said to Alika. "This is Lana, and her husband, Commander Caleb." He turned to his right. "Our second in command and close friend, Commander Ryan." He turned to his left. "And this is Dante, Abigail's and Ethan's son."

Alika nodded to them kindly, but his eyes softened as they rested on Dante. His voice spoke gently, "Dante, I am sorry we've made your day so long and for the burden placed upon your young shoulders. It saddens me more than you know."

"It can't be helped. You and your students brought the information, and my mother is finally safe, thanks to them. The only one to blame is the Dark Lord for this."

⟋ℓℓ⟍

The girl kissed Abigail's forehead, tears still streaming down her face. "I'm so sorry, Abigail."

"You saved her life," Alena said, as she searched the girl's face.

"Why does it feel like I failed her again?"

"Oh, but you didn't, you mustn't believe so," Alena whispered.

The girl turned back to Abigail and took Abigail's hand, and brushed it to her own face. "Goodbye, Abigail." She put Abigail's hand back down and released it. She turned and buried her head in Alena's shoulder. Alena walked the girl into one of the rooms and signaled to Alika. Alena's tears fell in the girl's hair as her spirit broke as the girl continued to weep in her arms.

CHAPTER FORTY-FIVE

Alika's data pad lit up with a single word: *Ready.*

"Seth, if you'll assist me."

Seth nodded and turned to the others. "Stay here while we get Abigail, please."

Seth did a quick visual survey of the vessel as he followed Alika inside, and it appeared normal for the most part. He immediately spotted Abigail waiting for transport. He guessed the two students had retreated to one of the small quarters in the back. Although, today a spirit of overwhelming sadness, of grief hung as a tapestry over the metal walls of the ship. The walls should be soundproof. Regardless, Seth heard the sound of weeping escape through the door of the quarters. Alika looked away from it and used his cloak to wipe his tears.

"I'm sorry, Alika," Seth whispered, looking at Alika and then the door of the quarters.

"As I am to you, Seth," whispered Alika back, as his eyes moved from the quarter doors to Seth toward Dante. The two Elders gently wheeled Abigail from the ship and to the others. The ship door closed behind them.

"Dante," Lana's voice spoke softly as she touched her cousin's hand.

Dante stood there in a trance as he glimpsed his mother for the first time in so long. He didn't want to break down here. He whispered, "Please, let's get her in the room."

"Of course, Dante. As you wish," said Alika.

"We need to move her from the stretcher to the bed," said Seth as they got Abigail to the prepared room.

"I can move my mother."

"If you're sure, Dante."

"Yes, I'm sure, Seth." Dante gently reached out as if cradling a baby and lifted his mother from the stretcher. Pulling her securely to him, he softly placed her in the bed. He brushed the hair from her face and kissed her cheek. "I'm here, Mother," he whispered. He clasped her hand and collapsed in a chair next to her bedside. He bowed his head, weeping. Lana sat beside him, her arm encircling his shoulders. Seth and Alika stared at each other, both feeling the agony of being unable to provide solace to one in such pain yet again today. So, Seth lifted the one burden he could from Dante, the securing of his mother.

Seth drew Alika aside with Ryan and Caleb.

Alika listened and answered, "Well, we've an excellent security system. It proved necessary from the beginning, but I'm not sure it helps you. Limiting access is easy as there are only three people allowed to access anything."

"What about voice recognition?" said Ryan.

"It alone won't protect Abigail. This cloaked woman is an adversary to reckon with, but that doesn't begin to convey her power. You must put it in conjunction with handprint recognition."

"That could work," said Caleb.

"Under no circumstances should there be only a visual recognition for entry to Abigail. She won't be safe from the cloaked woman."

"Understood, Alika. What kind of time will this take?" asked Seth turning to Ryan and Caleb.

"It's not a quick thing, but we ... or maybe I'm mistaken," said Caleb, looking at Alika.

"We anticipated this before we left. My two students spent considerable time preparing for this trip." Alika produced a small bag he carried on his shoulders underneath his cloak and set it on a table. Inside revealed a couple of devices. "These should help the process go faster to set up the access you need for the handprint and voice recognition."

"Yes, this definitely cuts off our time," said Ryan looking at them closer.

"Does it contain a backup?" asked Caleb.

"Already built-in. It could even be a bit of a challenge for my student to get past," said Alika, smiling for one of the first times today.

"So?" Ryan looked over at Dante, feeling helpless as everyone else did.

"We'll make sure it's to his liking, and if so, you and Caleb will install it. He'll be ready again soon," Seth said.

"Seth's right. It'll keep coming in waves for Dante today. At some point, he'll no longer feel the waves crashing on him, and he'll find calm," sighed Alika.

—ele—

"I feel no more tears, but I find more. How is it possible?"

"We'll wait until you find rest from it, cousin."

"I have, Lana. Did they figure out how to secure my mother?"

"They discussed it, but they wanted to make sure with you before they pressed forward with it."

"I'm ready now."

Lana signaled to the others, and they walked over to Dante.

Dante felt better. His face almost appeared normal again. For a bit, he talked with the group about the best way to secure someone. He wanted for a few minutes to simply not feel, just think. He did, and he desperately needed it. They decided on fingerprint and voice access together. The five of them placed their fingerprints and voices in the system, so Ryan and Caleb could begin working on it. They completed it quickly with the devices Alika brought and noticed the system already consisted of three individuals in it. Caleb and Ryan looked at Alika, puzzled.

"We took the liberty of programming our information into the system. Hopefully, it proves unnecessary, but we want to be able to access her in time to prevent her from being recaptured. My spear-bearer could find a way in, but in such a situation, time is precious."

Dante smiled and said to Alika, "So their names are ...?"

Alika laughed. "Nice try, Dante. Younger spear-bearer and older spear-bearer. The voice part won't assist you either. All is encrypted. When someone wishes to enter, the computer only verifies it matches. It won't play any of the voices for you. It's built like that to reduce the likelihood of being compromised. I'm continually impressed by your persistence, young Dante."

Dante laughed too. "Alika, it's getting me nowhere."

Dante turned to the group. "I assume the other commanders are still unaware?"

"You're correct," said Seth.

"It would be best to brief them without me. One time of hearing this is enough for me."

"I agree. Caleb and Ryan can take the abbreviated version to the commanders and give them a night's sleep to process it."

Caleb and Ryan spoke with Seth for a couple of minutes to make certain of the shortened version for the commanders.

Seth came back and sat with Dante, Alika, and Lana by Abigail's bedside.

Seth asked Dante, "What else do you need, Dante? What would help you now?" Dante's spirit had finally quieted, so maybe he could answer.

"I'm not exactly sure, but questions are forming. It feels weird to know someone is having visions about my family and me. I'm not sure whether to feel strange or flattered or what. Hopefully, there's no embarrassing vision in there about me." Dante grinned.

"I don't get the impression there's anything to worry about, Dante," Seth said, smiling as he turned to Alika.

"You got me wondering, Alika, since I don't get to meet them."

"The spear-bearer told us nothing but good things about you and your family from the visions. We feel we know you and your whole family as well as your friends through what we've been told," He paused and patted Dante on the shoulder, "and everything I see confirms my spear-bearer's visions of you."

"Yet, I'm not meeting them, and you're not telling me why."

"You won't meet them on this trip. I can't say as far as the future. No, I can't tell you why, Dante. It's one of the few questions I won't answer, but it won't help you with anything from today, I promise you. I await your next question and hope to be more helpful."

"Seriously, you and Seth could swap places for the day."

"I'll take that as a compliment as well as to Seth's credit. After all, you're an impressive reflection of years of his training. He trained a couple of others I met with equal results."

Dante laughed and said, "All right. I'll move on for now. Your spear-bearer said I could do this task. When am I to do it? I can't just call up my father. We're not exactly on speaking terms."

"Another good question, but I don't have the answer, and neither did my student. The vision didn't show how you'd accomplish it or the circumstances. Think of it more as an impression or a voice, but clear like a message. For example, when they set out to rescue your mother, they didn't receive a vision on how to do it or even her location. Regardless, they clearly understood the task to rescue her belonged to them."

"Yes, Alika and I both agree it'll be apparent to you when it's time for you to do this operation. My task will be to prepare you for it, and it will be a different battle than you previously ever encountered."

"What if the Dark Lord is there with my father when I go? They're frequently together. It'll be hard enough to convince my father, but with the Dark Lord I don't see how it's possible."

"I thought of that too. The Dark Lord won't let Dante get to his father long enough to convince him," said Lana.

"We share your concerns. Believe me. We considered all of this for a while."

"Alika's student saw it. Dante will find a way because the Ancient One has commissioned this task to him, just as his students rescued Abigail from the facility. Just because the plan hasn't been revealed to us yet, doesn't mean there's no plan."

"I'll need to convince my father of what happened to my mother, but I can't bring her along."

"Dante, strangely today, an answer occurred to me or actually to my young spear-bearer, without my student realizing it. I'm not certain it'll work, but you may be able to use it in some manner."

"Go on."

"Approach your mother with me, Dante. Your mother still wears her wedding band. Many times the bands are inscribed on the inside. It would surprise me if it weren't in her case. There would be no mistaking it belonged to your mother. Also, we noticed a necklace your mother still wore. We didn't look closely at it, but I think I spied the symbols of your house on it. It'd be another way to identify your mother."

"You're right. They're both still there." He gently pulled the ring off, and it showed an inscription. "It says, Ethan and Abigail, enduring love." Dante slipped it back on his mother's finger. Then he examined the necklace. The outside of the locket displayed the symbols of his house on it, and on the back, it revealed Abigail's name. He opened it. Inside were two pictures, still in perfect condition, one of Ethan and Abigail smiling and on the other side one of Dante and Collin smiling. Dante stared at the photos for several seconds and then closed the locket. He closed his eyes and a tear rolled down his face. Then he sat back down, and the others followed him.

"My father couldn't deny those things belonged to mother," murmured Dante.

"You also could show the footage of where the Dark Lord held your mother," said Seth.

"True," said Dante.

"Surely, that would be enough to convince Dante's father," said Lana. "There's still the Dark Lord, though."

"Yes, and his threat is far more than a sword," said Alika. "Be careful. Remember, this sounds convincing to us. However, we couldn't comprehend how the Dark Lord swayed Ethan by all the lies years ago, but he succeeded. The Dark Lord takes something clear and twists it, so the truth is no longer seen. That's his greatest power."

Seth said, "Yes, what he did to Ethan years ago, he'll attempt to do again."

Dante sighed. "Yes, we can be sure he will," He paused. "We'll wait until Caleb and Ryan get back for more questions."

Soon Caleb and Ryan rejoined the others. Dante continued with his questions, "What about the black substance?"

"We gave you a sample of it to try to identify. There are specific instructions for handling it and time spent with it, all covered with Seth earlier. My younger student worked with it and felt strange each time. There's a strong darkness attached to it. My younger student picks up on that type of thing. It comes with the vision territory."

"No guesses at all, huh?" asked Ryan.

Seth looked at Alika and back at Ryan. Seth's troubled look matched Alika's face. "Nothing solid, but due to the source of the Dark Lord's power, Alika and I entertained disturbing guesses. The Dark Lord meddles in areas better left untapped and the connection to a person at some point in the operation ... So yes, we proposed theories to what the Dark Lord is conjuring."

"And the fact the student is picking up these ugly vibes from the sample makes you fear those may be closer to the truth," said Caleb.

"Thus far, the young spear-bearer's conclusions in this area are in the right direction, so yes," said Seth.

"Is there a possibility of additional answers at the facility where the Dark Lord imprisoned my mother? Perhaps another operation there could provide more intel."

"Out of the question."

"Alika's right. There's nothing more to find there. The facility is beyond alerted. The cloaked woman herself frequents it. It would be a suicide mission and for nothing."

Dante was taken aback at the firmness from both of them, but then he remembered Seth's previous comment. "Seth, you said something earlier, which makes me wonder if there was a problem during the rescue of my mother. Are the two spear-bearers, okay? Is that why we're not seeing them today?"

"No, it's not the reason." Seth answered, glancing at Alika. Alika nodded his approval. "The younger spear-bearer completed the rescue but returned severely injured in the process."

"Why didn't you say something?"

"My young spear-bearer is almost fully recovered. Our visit today is for you, Dante, and that's where we wished the focus to be. My young spear-bearer shared that desire as well."

"What happened, and how badly was your student hurt? I want to know."

"I tell you only to end all talk of returning to the facility. The only scenario I can see going back is to destroy the entire building from the ground up. Are we understood?"

Everyone nodded. It didn't get any clearer.

"They escaped to the rooftop to get Abigail out. The older student had just placed Abigail into the ship when the squadron began firing on them to prevent them from leaving. The younger became trapped fighting on the rooftop, ended up too close to the edge, and a failed cable later... my student fell from the rooftop." Lana gasped in horror at Alika's words. Dante turned pale, and the others shared his shock. Alika quickly continued, "The younger hit the side of the rooftop with great force, but a large eagle caught my younger spear-bearer before hitting the ground. It carried the younger safely into the woods. There was an issue with the ship, and it would not return for the younger. The older student observed the younger plummeting to the ground as the ship passed through the portal."

There was silence.

"Go on, Alika."

"The younger found a small group of smugglers in the woods, overpowered them, and took their ship. From there, we got my student back. We tended to the injuries, and my young spear-bearer is almost recovered now."

Dante stared at Alika, waiting him out.

Alika looked at Seth and remarked, "Your student is stubborn. We noted he reminds me of my own."

"All right, Dante, there's no point. The injuries included a concussion, a dislocated shoulder, removal of rock material and roof debris from the head area, a couple of broken ribs, and of course, all the injuries from my student hitting the left side of the building. Now you know. So, I repeat, no visits to the facility."

"Wow," said Caleb.

"How did your student possibly ..."

"You're the same one who continued fighting with a chunk from your back after you disabled the tank. Remember, we know about that one. My student is as much of a lousy and stubborn patient as you." Alika laughed. "Although, you will both continue to be trained as you both possess many redeeming qualities." Alika patted Dante on the back.

"Do you need the use of our medical?" asked Lana.

"No, Seth graciously asked the same. Due to the nature of the operations we run, our home, as we call it, is medically equipped. I hold the expertise to treat most injuries, and in this case, I did so. Time will do the rest. Let us go back to what started this conversation. My student would be most unhappy with us now. The facility will get us nowhere. While we tracked down where the Dark Lord held Abigail, we planted a tracking device on the cloaked woman's ship. My students are eager to check those places to see if they provide any clues to the Dark Lord's plans. Now that Abigail is safely recovered, they can pursue those leads."

"We could help them."

"No. At this time, your focus and that of your friends should be managing the attacks and preparing to carry out the operation with your father. You'll know if we discover anything valuable. This has been a long day for you, Dante. Perhaps you should spend time with Seth and the rest of your family and friends. If additional questions surface that you need my assistance, we can speak later."

"Of course, you must be tired too."

"Dante, stop. I'm not tired. I'll stay as long as you need this evening if it'll help you. Surely you know that, but I think you've run out of questions now which will assist you. Give yourself time to process what you found out today. Hopefully by tomorrow you'll know what questions to ask further. I'll resume answering any questions if I'm wrong."

Dante looked at him mischievously.

"Except for that one," Alika smiled and laughed at Dante. "My, you're curious and persistent. My young spear-bearer didn't convey that fully to us about you from the visions. I'll share that with them."

"What did your young spear-bearer share?" Dante laughed.

"Everything good, as said before. My young spear-bearer will be glad your spirit is calmer. We all worried about how you would handle the information you endured today. However, since my young spear-bearer is the one who sees the visions, the concern was greatly multiplied for you. Dante, are there any more questions for me this evening?"

"You're right, Alika. Nothing comes to mind. You can stay here for the evening if you'd be more comfortable."

"I appreciate the offer, but I'll stay on the ship with my two spear-bearers. I need to check on them. Perhaps they made progress on the information."

"Perhaps." For the first time, Dante didn't believe Alika when he gave the reason for returning to the ship.

Alika rose and said goodnight to everyone for the evening. "Dante, rest this evening. We'll all speak tomorrow before my two students and I leave."

"Dante, I'll return. I'm walking Alika back to his ship. Are you sure you will be okay?"

"I'll be fine, Seth. There are three people here to keep me company."

Dante turned and said to Lana, "I wonder what those two are talking about."

"Maybe they're exchanging tips on how to deal with stubborn students in training," Lana teased.

"Hey, you're one of his students too, cuz."

"But I wasn't called stubborn."

"Funny. I think Seth knows more about Alika's students than what he's telling us."

Ryan said, "You're probably right, Dante, but give it up. Alika isn't telling you, and if Seth knows, he's not either because Alika told him no."

⁂

Once Seth and Alika got out, they talked.

"Seth, he's better. I'm relieved."

"I as well. He's asking good questions, ones I'm wondering myself."

"I wish we provided more answers for him. I have concerns which he didn't directly raise."

"Like?"

"His safety during the attacks while his spirit is burdened with this. The other concerns aren't entirely about him. With Abigail no longer a prisoner, I wonder how it affects the Dark Lord's timetable of what he's planning. I thought we'd know by now what he's doing, but we don't. Also, I'm nervous for my students, for the increasing danger of their future operations. Abigail's rescue alerted the Dark Lord that someone endangers his plot. There's a possibility he's looking for a substitute. My two students appear back to normal on the surface, ready to storm the whole Black Dragon force with sunspears raised. Inside, the close call with Abigail shook them. Perhaps, it's not about them, but I'm the one who fears for them after the last encounter."

"I'd feel the same, Alika." Seth pondered Alika's words, but no solution crystalized. He didn't expect one after today's events. "How's your younger student?"

"I don't know, but I will soon. You heard how I left her with the other student. I hope her spirit is calmed as Dante's spirit. It's strange. Though they've not met each other, my young spear-bearer appears connected to Dante's emotions. I watched on the ship when you told him the news. Even if we couldn't listen to Dante, I would know Dante's state of mind and emotions through her reactions. I'm not sure what to make of it. She's the first student I've trained with the gift of visions to this extent."

"I hope they cross paths. It's already driving Dante crazy someone knows all about him, and he doesn't have a clue about them."

"I saw. I tried hard not to say she by mistake or let him notice I avoided using he or she like I did with you. The boy is persistent, though."

"Well, Alika, I'm concerned for your young spear-bearer, especially after today. I hope you find her calm like Dante. Somehow, I believe it'll be the case. We'll see you tomorrow."

"Thank you, Seth. I'll see you then as agreed. I share your hope for the evening."

CHAPTER FORTY-SIX

Alika entered the ship and found Alena sitting on the couch. He looked at her with the obvious question.

"She went to her quarters, utterly exhausted. She probably only fell asleep thirty minutes ago."

"Emotionally drained, like the other one. It'll hit Dante this evening."

"I expect so."

"What is it?"

"Alika. I thought I understood the power of her visions, but I'm astonished by them all over again. Maybe not the visions themselves, but how intensely it has tied her to Dante and his entire family. More than even that, the connection to Dante himself is becoming stronger, or maybe I'm just now seeing it. She mentioned for the past few months that the visions centered on him. I feel like she kept telling us, but we didn't really listen to her."

"I believe we both missed it, because I attempted to explain the same to Seth on the way here. The emotional connection between her and Dante the visions created, it's …"

"Yes, that. I can't come up with the word either. It's not bad at all. I didn't appreciate the depth of the connection the visions created either, and Dante hasn't even met her yet. I feel like there's something in the works besides rescuing Abigail and freeing Ethan."

"The Ancient One always has a plan, and it's often beyond what we see. I feel certain you're right, though. It may become apparent if or when the other part of the connection becomes known to the other. Dante is curious about the young spear-bearer who knows him so well but whom he knows nothing about. He was relentless tonight in his inquiries."

Alika got a drink, and then sat back down with Alena. "They will let me know tomorrow morning what else they need from us."

The girl perceived rustling in the other room and heard another sound, like a stream — the drink dispenser in use. Alika must be back. She got up.

Alika and Alena peered up at the sound of the door opening.

"Alika, you're back."

"Yes, how are you feeling?"

"I'll be fine. How are Dante and the others?"

"The others comforted Dante as you'd expect, and his spirit was calm when I left him. He even laughed toward the end."

The girl's face lit up in a smile. "Really? You don't know how much better that makes me feel, Alika."

"I'm finally beginning to understand." Alika smiled, and his eyes turned mischievous. "There's something you didn't tell me about young Dante in your visions, and I told him I'd tell you."

"I told you everything."

"Young Dante is persistent, and I didn't realize the extent until tonight."

"That's not my fault, Alika. You shouldn't need a vision to tell you that about Dante," laughed the girl. "What did he persist about?"

"He's intrigued by the fact someone sees so much about him and knows him so well, while he knows nothing about them. It's a mixture of fascination and insanity."

"It must feel strange. It does on this side of it too, but his questioning will get him nothing from you or Seth. I do feel sorry for him with that. Well, maybe a bit. I guess he turned in for the night. Rest will do him good after today."

"I believe he stayed up with the others to finalize securing his mother as far as the medical staff. Her doctors are hand-picked by Seth, ones he worked with for many years. With the others, they found ones they know personally and who possess both combat and medical training. There will also be guards at her door, and they'll be the same few guards. They also are known to Dante and the others. Everyone understood they must use the access device we've placed on the door, and there's someone out there who can change her appearance to seem like anyone. So even if it appears to be anyone with access, down to Dante himself, they must not enter unless they pass the door's access."

"It sounds covered," said Alena.

"I thought so. Dante appeared satisfied and assured that his mother would be secure."

"Which is what we hoped," said the girl. "What else do we need to do tonight?"

"Sleep. It has been a long day, child."

"I will, in a while. I feel better after what you said about Dante's mood as you left him. I'll look over some items for a bit. Maybe it proves helpful for tomorrow."

"All right then. I saw your smile and heard you laugh again, so my spirit feels better too," said Alika as he hugged her.

"Thank you, Alika."

"Don't worry, he'll be fine. The more time I spend with him, the more I understand why you like him so much." His eyes twinkled at her. Before she could respond, he walked away to the extra quarters on the ship.

Alena tried not to laugh. "Here, I'm not ready to turn in either. What are we doing?"

The girl turned her eyes from Alika's figure to meet Alena's eyes. "Oh, yeah. Not you too? Are you serious? I'm concerned. Okay, extremely concerned. I saw visions of him for months now. You two are enjoying this way too much." She didn't know how to react.

"You're right. You saw him for months in your visions, and it helped us get Abigail back. It looks like it will aid Dante in getting his father back too. Maybe that's it. I don't see visions. Nonetheless, I think there's more than what you see at present or you want to admit. I don't believe you're to remain a stranger to Dante."

"What happens then?"

"It won't be unpleasant like you make it sound." Alena laughed as she shook her head at the girl.

"We should see if we can find something to help Dante... and the others, of course, or none of it matters."

"Of course."

"You need to stop, Alena." The girl laughed.

"You know I'm right, but now I'm waiting on you. Tell me where we're starting."

The girl shook her head at Alena and gave up the battle on the discussion about Dante. "We gained so much information, but it's not what we need to reach our answer. Our time is running out. I know it somehow. Lana felt this way at some point in the process."

"Yeah, before the field trip or maybe after. I don't remember."

The girl displayed all the chemicals the Black Dragon army obtained over the past months and, on the other side, the list of items from the warehouses. She sighed as she scrolled through the massive inventory. "We poured over these lists, and we still don't know." She took a deep breath. "Alena, what do you think happens once they realize they left without the real chemicals and materials from the last time? The others only fooled them one time."

"Only guesses. None good."

"Tell me, Alena. I think we arrive at the same place."

"The least threatening option is they'll continue adding more individuals to the payroll willing to ship it to them for the right price. We know there are far more competent people than your late father to ship things. Another possibility is they get what they need from the colonies, whatever the means. The colonies finally bear the price in the lives of the colonists. Dante and his comrades pay as well because the attack doesn't go their way. Another guess is the Dark Lord is almost ready to execute his plan and goes with what he collected. He doesn't worry about the other operation with Abigail, or he attacks more severely because of his fury over the loss. Either way, he moves up his timetable substantially, and no one is prepared for whatever he launches in his rage."

"That covers it. There's probably another scenario, but we arrived at the same ones. We must unravel what they're doing with these supplies. Alena, I only see one way to finally know. I'm so…" the girl trailed off and stopped. "No, I'm awful saying it after what lays ahead of Dante. I can't."

"No, say it. It's okay."

"I'm afraid, but I can't be. The only way to get the information is to get inside, way close inside. It's been a while since we …" She paused, looking at Alena. "See, I told you. How can I think this way now?"

"You have good reasons to." She met the girl's eyes. "And because less than a week ago, you almost got yourself killed. Your mind and body remember that part. You're not the only one, though. I'm afraid too. Alika hasn't said, but I know he is as well. Our fear doesn't care how important it is that we must figure out the Dark Lord's plans. It's more dangerous now, so the fear is legitimate for what lies ahead. You're not terrible for feeling that on this next operation."

"I agree about it being dangerous and having a close call, but I can't feel like this now. It's not right. It's not the time. I need to be sharp. I can't be allowed to fear now."

Alena hated to do it, but she tried a different angle with the girl. "I suppose Alika should tell Dante that he's not allowed to fear about the operation ahead of him?"

"Alika can't tell Dante that, Alena. Dante has every reason to fear. There's no clear plan as to how he's to accomplish it. He may end up facing the Dark Lord and his father together."

"Before we left, you said though he would achieve it because the Ancient One gave him the task. Then why should he be scared at all?"

"It doesn't mean he's not going to be scared. It'll be dangerous, beyond dangerous." The girl stopped and stared at Alena with her mouth open in surprise. "How did you do that? You turned it around on me? And used Dante on me again?" She wasn't sure which annoyed her more, that she was so easily tricked or Dante entering back in the conversation. She blushed slightly at being caught in another discussion focused on Dante.

"Because I'm good, and I'm right. Why is it okay for Dante to feel scared about facing his dangerous operation, but you can't feel scared about going on an operation, especially since you almost didn't come back from the last one? Or, for that matter, I told you I felt scared about it too. Is it okay for me to be scared? I thought you died." Alena paused. "Come on, why can Dante feel scared, but you're not allowed to?" challenged Alena.

"Because, because... I don't know." The girl shook her head. "Yes, everyone can feel scared but me. I admitted it." The girl saw Alena still looking at her. "Okay, especially Dante. Are you happy? I don't know why. I can't apply the laws of logic to him lately. For the record, I don't like it. It may be driving Dante crazy not knowing who knows him, but I'm beginning to go insane being on the other end of this crazy vision part with him." The girl threw her hands up and looked at Alena, clearly exasperated with the conversation.

"At least you finally admitted it."

"What, I'm losing it?" She leaned back in the chair and ran a hand through her hair.

"If that's the way you want to look at it." Alena couldn't contain her laughter any longer.

"Can we please do something productive this evening?"

"I'm still waiting on your lead."

"Well, let me do a better job, Alena."

They both stared at the screen for a few minutes. "Alena, maybe we're going at this wrong."

"How so?"

"We established we'll end up doing another difficult operation to uncover their scheme. Maybe we can use the lists to help figure out where to go. There are places to visit from before. Doesn't pinpoint which place, though."

"You're suggesting using the lists as a filtering agent somehow, kind of like when we figured out where they kept Abigail. You relayed the vision, but it alone didn't give us Abigail's location." Alena's nodded as her eyes traced the projected list. "I see where you're going."

"The reality is the more places we break into, the greater chance of getting caught. You're right. There's every reason to be afraid. We must hit places to yield the most results, and we can't afford any wasted time."

"Because no matter how carefully we plan, it doesn't always work out like the blueprint, so we make each trip count. What's going on in your head?"

The girl grinned. "Tell me we brought a couple of our regular tracking devices."

"Of course. We always come prepared."

"It's time Alika calls in a favor to Dante and his friends tomorrow. Seth and Commander Gabe are doing the operation with the box swap, right?"

"Yes, and I know exactly where you're going with it. I like it."

"Hopefully, the Black Dragon doesn't figure out the ploy yet. Or if so, they believe it's a bad batch. Otherwise, we could run into issues."

"Like walking into a trap."

"Yeah, like that."

CHAPTER FORTY-SEVEN

"Everything is in place, Dante. Your mom will be secure," said Ryan as he strolled back in with Caleb.

"Ryan, thanks. I can always count on you and Caleb," said Dante, hugging Ryan.

"Not a problem. What else do you need? Name it." Ryan's eyes showed only concern.

"Location, when I'm supposed to do the operation, how am I supposed to do it. Any or all of that would be great."

"Give me something I can help you with, Dante. Maybe once we get a location, we can figure out how to get you in. You know I'd go in and help you in a minute. Unfortunately, everything indicates that part is up to you. I wasn't clear for sure."

"You're not the only one, so don't feel bad, Ryan."

They sat down again, and Seth spoke, "Any thoughts or questions, bring them tomorrow for Alika, as they'll be leaving after he meets with us. Alika wants to provide any assistance he can that will help us in the coming days and, of course, with your operation, Dante." Seth paused to look directly at Dante. "Yet, he feels the urgency to discover the Dark Lord's plan, and so do his two students. They'll resume operations to obtain the information, even as it becomes more dangerous."

"It's awfully fast after what happened to his student," Dante said with the implied question.

"He is aware. We discussed it on the way to his ship, but the gravity of the situation demands haste. His young student will be ready and recovered for the operation ahead. Alika says so. I met him only today, but I trust his judgment."

"Isn't there something we can do to help them?" asked Caleb. "This feels so..."

"One-sided," said Ryan.

"Yes, that's the word," said Dante, nodding.

"They indicated nothing at this time. Honestly, I don't expect any more help from them during the attacks. With the operations they'll be doing, it won't be safe for them to divide their attention."

"That's reasonable," said Lana.

"Seth, I know I was annoying when I kept asking about Alika's students. My real point is when do we work together? I trust them, Seth, so please don't get me wrong. I mean, they rescued my mother and almost died in the process. They gave me the knowledge to get my father back. They helped us in numerous other ways. Alika reminds me so much of you, it's crazy. Not to mention, one of his students decided I'm a nice guy through some visions, although I wonder why neither one wants to meet any of us. I'm puzzled why the separation, and I can't be the only one. It would be more productive if we worked together."

"Dante, I understand your confusion, as does Alika. That's why he teased you every time you attempted to extract an answer from him on the subject." Seth laughed. "Except that, I don't know if or when we work together as one. At present we need to control the attacks and concentrate on the task before you. They're to run the operations to get more information about the Dark Lord's plans. There are other factors in play currently that make this the arrangement. Alika made that clear."

"Will these other factors always be in play, Seth? You sound like you know."

"No, he didn't go into details. I made guesses."

"And you won't share those guesses."

"No, I won't. He told you the truth, including about the visions and what the young spear-bearer said about you. It's why Alika is already so fond of you and concerned for your safety. He may decide to take you on as his third student if I'm not careful." Seth laughed.

"It may be the only way to meet the other two students at this rate," Dante laughed.

"I'm sure we won't come to that, Dante. It's time we got sleep and see if more productive questions come to mind."

They walked out of the building to go around.

Ryan came over to Dante and laughed. "Seth is going to get you, Dante."

Dante laughed back. "Either that or I'll finally wear him down."

Caleb teased him, "He still trains you, Dante. You could get stuck doing one of those leisurely strolls in the woods for a whole day if you keep it up. He hasn't done that in a while."

Dante groaned. "You're right. I should behave." He laughed again.

Lana smiled at Seth and said, "He appears back to his normal spirits. It's good to see."

"Yes, it is," Seth replied, smiling as he squeezed Lana's shoulder.

The girl and Alena looked at the screen beside the cockpit.

"I don't know, Alena. I think two is good, one for an item in the warehouse and another for the lab. I'm paranoid about doing more than the two."

"We put a device on the cloaked woman's ship before. Everything indicated she didn't find it, but ..."

"Yeah, we both know the reality. By now, they must assume someone tracked her, so we ..." The girl gazed out the cockpit window and stopped in mid-sentence. Coming out of the building, Dante and the others headed to their rooms for the evening. Dante smiled, and she saw Ryan come up to him, followed by Caleb. The three of them started laughing.

Alena followed the girl's eyes. "He seems good, as Alika said."

"Dante does. I feared how his spirit would be left today. I'm sorry, Alena. We should work on the other." The girl still stared out the window, though, at Dante. Suddenly, he turned and peered through the darkness right at her. It didn't matter because the cockpit window setting allowed no one to see in. Yet Dante sensed someone completely entranced with him. He made a comment to Ryan and Caleb. They laughed, and one of them or both made a few comments back to him. He laughed back, shaking his head, as they continued walking. They finally went inside the building. "Alena, what's wrong with me?"

"You refuse to admit what's in front of you."

"What's that supposed to mean?"

"You said it earlier. All logic leaves you when it comes to Dante. Stop trying. It's okay. In the middle of a mission, no. Now, yes."

"Technically, we were discussing the … tracking device."

"Stop it. You know what I meant. You're fine, and you know it." Alena laughed. "Oh, and nice save even though you got distracted by the view outside."

"We haven't gotten anything done tonight."

"Not so. In fact, it turned out very productive. We stared at those lists countless times along with Lana and the others and got nowhere. Then you received inspiration tonight," the girl looked at Alena for her choice of words, "and came up with the tracking device for the supplies. I'm surprised we didn't come up with the idea sooner. Maybe you just needed …"

The girl cut Alena off and laughed, "No more from you, Alena. On the other hand, it felt good to laugh this much after earlier." She hugged Alena. "I'm tired. We'll get with Alika tomorrow before he goes."

"Definitely. He'll confer with us before he leaves. Sweet dreams, dear."

The girl looked at Alena as if to say something else but settled on saying, "Sweet dreams to you too, Alena." The girl went to her quarters and laughed.

❦

Dante had the strangest feeling of being watched as he walked with Ryan and Caleb. It originated from the direction of the ship hangar. He peered into the darkness, but he didn't see anyone. He looked over into the cockpit of one of the ships. He murmured, "That's the visitors' ship."

Ryan laughed. "Dante, are you still on that? Let it go tonight."

Dante retuned his laughter. "Ryan, I promise you I felt someone watching me from Alika's ship."

"Maybe they are. The one wanted to see if you look the same in person as in the vision. I'm sure you do, so you're good, Dante."

"Maybe I should wave to them."

"You're so curious to meet them, you're imagining it. Go get sleep, like they're probably doing," said Caleb as he laughed.

They continued laughing as they went inside.

Dante thought that he might have trouble sleeping after the day's events, but he found himself completely exhausted, and sleep overcame him.

The girl laid down and assumed, at first, it would be difficult to sleep. Yet her mind quieted, and she found herself drained from the emotional upheaval of the day. Sleep came easy for her.

CHAPTER FORTY-EIGHT

Dante slinked around the corner. It had changed enormously since the last time he stepped inside. He never thought he would return. So many memories created here. He concentrated on the task at hand. He turned the last corner, his sunspear drawn from using it earlier. He hoped the others were doing well, but he couldn't concern himself with that now. He would only get one shot at this, and he wasn't clear on how to accomplish it. Taking a deep breath, he knew what room stood next. Quietly, he entered the room. The tapestry with the Ancient One's symbol greeted him up ahead, tattered but still clinging to the wall. Countless hours he once spent here... He wondered which one elected to watch everything from here. He thought they'd watch it from the command ship, but no, this is what they chose. From their perspective, it made perfect sense why they decided to observe it from here, but the move still angered him. It didn't matter. Somehow his entrance wasn't quiet enough. The door closed behind him, and two figures emerged from the side entrances at the front. He knew them both.

"Well, young Dante, we didn't expect you today," said the Dark Lord.

"It has been too long, son," said the Black Dragon Commander to Dante.

Dante held his sunspear in the Dark Lord's direction.

The girl screamed, "Dante, no!"

⁓ℓℓ⁓

Dante awoke instantly in his bed. He didn't know why, but he brushed it off. He still felt tired. A glance at the display showed only 6:00 in the morning. He groaned and turned back over since he wasn't due downstairs until nine after yesterday's events. He went back to sleep.

—ell—

Alena and Alika ran to the girl's quarters. The scream mirrored the one like the nightmare with Collin.

Alika tried to shake the girl awake gently and urgently. "Child, wake up. It's only a nightmare."

The girl gasped, her body shook, and her eyes opened. She stood straight up in bed, trying to catch her breath. She looked at Alika and Alena like someone coming out of a daze and reached over to Alika. He wrapped his arm around her shoulder in comfort. Alena waited with a cup of water ready. The girl's body finally ceased shaking, and she took a deep breath. She accepted the cup Alena offered.

Alena asked, "Are you okay now?"

"Guess the sweet dreams didn't work."

"Appears not. Leave it to you."

"Actually, it depends on how you look at it."

"How is a vision that leaves you screaming ever a good thing?"

"Look at what the last one revealed and where it led us, Alena."

"Ah, I understand," said Alika. "I do hate the state you're in after. I'm sorry."

"It's a part of the deal with the current situation. Maybe one day, I can glimpse a happy vision. We can tell Dante before we leave where he'll face the Dark Lord and Ethan."

There was silence.

"That's what you saw?" asked Alika.

"Yes."

"You screamed. Was it not going well? I would not necessarily tell him that part, but it doesn't make me feel good," asked Alika.

"No, that wasn't it. The fighting hadn't started. I just saw him there, having to do it and knowing the whole confrontation was about to begin," said the girl unhappily.

"Where did you see?" asked Alena.

"Dante's home planet, in the Elders Hall where he trained in his childhood," said the girl.

Alika said, "Not on a command ship or one of their facilities. Are you sure?"

"Positive. Let me take you both through it, especially you, Alika, since you'll share it today."

The girl did so, piece by piece. Alika and Alena listened and agreed the girl saw the Elders Hall of Dante's childhood.

"Dante will not doubt the time to do this operation. I can't tell exactly what from the vision, but there's something else happening at the same time. It's another operation with the rest of the fleet or his other comrades. I don't know for sure, but it's substantial too. Dante finds the Dark Lord and Ethan there because they decided to watch whatever it is from the Elders Hall."

"From what you described, it also makes sense to Dante why they chose the location to watch it from," said Alika.

"It could be because it's personal for Ethan and the Dark Lord knows that," said Alena.

"I think that's part of it. It's also an Elders Hall. It represents everything the Elders stand for, everything from the Ancient One," said the girl. "Dante received his training there in the way of the Ancient One, along with who knows how many others."

"It could be either one of their ideas to be there or both," said Alika.

"Yes," said the girl. "They sound as if they don't know Dante is coming. I'm inclined to believe it, at least on Ethan's part. Whatever they're watching, if it succeeds, I sense it represents to them the end of many things. The location they chose is no mistake."

"You think it's all tied together, don't you?" said Alika.

"Yes," said the girl, "but it's not a part of the vision. It fits because whatever they're watching is significant. The completed operation was in the making for a while. So, it's a guess. The part which is not a guess is Dante's thoughts and feelings. He understands why they chose the place, and he's upset by it."

"I believe it's a good guess," said Alika.

"Do you want to try to rest again?" asked Alena.

The girl groaned. "I'm not going back to sleep after that interruption. What time is it anyway?"

"Around six-thirty. You started screaming around six," said Alika.

"People shouldn't be awakened at such an hour, especially like this. It's time to start a new day. Alena, can tell you Alika what we discussed last night."

"Which part? A lot of discussion took place."

"My, already this morning, Alena." The girl laughed. "Okay, you took my mind off my awful wake-up call this morning. On second thoughts, wait until I'm out of the shower and dressed. I need to be present for your briefing to Alika."

"Now I'm curious."

Alena smiled. "We devised a good idea for you to take to the others. The livelier discussion involved the stubborn, persistent student in the other camp."

"Ah, I missed an entertaining talk. I regret I went to bed when I did."

"They both will long be driven crazy by the time they finally meet each other."

Once all three were ready, they settled in the sitting area of the ship and talked. Alena and the girl told Alika their idea of putting the tracking devices on the shipments.

"It's a solid idea. Even if the Black Dragon discovers the previous shipment, we'll be fine. I'll take the idea to our friends."

The girl and Alena looked at him, puzzled.

"Unfortunately, it'll be apparent in the next attack if they discovered the trick. The attack would look different. Seth and Commander Gabe need to be careful they're not caught in a trap. Although, it goes for all of them."

"You're right," said Alena.

"Let's hope we get one more run out of it," said the girl as she handed Alika the two tracking devices.

"Anything else?" asked Alika.

"We won't be able to help them during the attacks now. Not with the operations ahead of us. I hate it, but it's the reality," the girl said, frowning.

"I'm sure they understand that, but I'll mention it," replied Alika.

"Say something to Lana today, too. She's doing well, but she feels the weight of her decisions lately. I sense it, Alika," said the girl.

"I will do so, child," said Alika, smiling. The girl didn't realize how similar she and Lana were. "You're right. She needs it now and for the decisions to come."

Alika waited for her finish, to move to the one person remaining whom there must be a message to give.

"Alika, remind Dante to stay focused during the attacks instead of on the operation ahead of him and the burden of everything he was told yesterday. He'll be able to do the task before him when the time comes. You must remind him of the Dark Lord's tactics. He's stronger than Dante fathoms and already binds Ethan. I ... we cannot let him take Dante as well. I am deeply concerned for Dante."

"I'll do so. I share the same concerns for him." Alika knew the girl understood how quickly the darkness could overcome one in a moment of weakness; he turned and left.

CHAPTER FORTY-NINE

Dante got up, showered, dressed, and went downstairs for their meeting with Alika. Dante met Ryan first as he entered the room.

"How are you feeling?" Ryan patted Dante on the back.

"I thought I'd have trouble sleeping with everything, but I was exhausted, Ryan. Something broke my sleep at around 6:00 this morning, but when I saw the time, I went back to sleep quickly," said Dante.

Lana came over and hugged her cousin. "Doing okay this morning, Dante?"

"I'm good, cuz. Slept most of the night. Woke up a few minutes this morning for no reason but went right back to sleep. I'm ready to get started again."

"He seems fine, Lana," Caleb said, smiling at Dante's response.

They all sat as Seth brought Alika over to them.

"Everyone is here," Seth looked over at Dante, "and looks well this morning."

Dante nodded and smiled at Seth and Alika.

"Any questions for Alika?"

There was silence, and everyone looked at each other. They couldn't think of anything still.

"Then I bring something to you. It ended up being a busy evening for my students after I left you. We'll start with the evening."

"How late did they stay up working?"

"I'm not sure, Dante. I went to bed, but they wanted to work for longer. They labored for some time, I believe."

"Sorry, it wasn't important, Alika. Continue."

"They tried to figure out a way to narrow down their search grid. The more places they go, the greater the chance they're caught before they find answers.

None of us wants to relive the incident they came through. We may not be as fortunate the next time."

"Scary that's the definition of fortunate."

"Yes, I understand, Dante, but my student came back alive and is recovered. In this case, the definition became redefined with the situation. They examined the list of items as you have, with the same frustrating result. Last night it occurred to my young student to look at it in a new light. Maybe it could help them differently. My young student said it reminded them of someone else recently, and it gave them the idea last night." Alika turned to Lana. "Lana, my compliments, as your wisdom stretched beyond your circle."

Lana replied, "Alika, I didn't do anything."

"Oh, you did, Lana. My student remembered your group being stuck with the data, and how you got them past it. Your method was unconventional, but it worked. Despite your doubts and frustrations, you tried something different and didn't give up. My student saw from afar, and now we uncovered a solution. it's not nearly as imaginative as your field trip, and we're rather surprised we didn't come up with it before. It's a good plan, though, and it's thanks to you. You're a wonderful leader, and you don't get told enough. I was also reminded to tell you that this morning."

"I don't know what to say. I'm overwhelmed by your words of kindness. Thank you, Alika."

"They're all true, Lana." He smiled at Lana and spoke to the whole group again. "My two students need your assistance with what they wish to do and asked me to come with their request."

"We get to help them for a change?" asked Ryan.

"Name it," said Dante.

"Whatever they need, Alika," said Caleb.

"I'll tell them I should've come with a list since you don't know the request yet, and you're so eager," Alika said, laughing.

Seth said, "It's because we received so much help from you and your students, but we see an opportunity to return the favor."

"I understand. They wish to slip two tracking devices inside the boxes during the box swap the next time there is an attack—one from the warehouse and one from the lab. It should only take seconds. Then they can track the two boxes' final destination. Hopefully, it leads to where the operation is going on or where whatever is being built. They want one from both places in case whatever is going on is being done at separate locations. I have the two tracking devices with me, and they are programmed and ready to go." Alika paused and turned to Seth, "You and Commander Gabe are doing the operation, so this task goes to you and him."

"Alika, I'll take care of it. It will be done."

"Is there anything else we can help with?" asked Dante. "It seems a small request."

"No, that was their only request. It will cut down their work and increase their chances of coming back to me after the operation." Alika sighed. "I'm sorry. I shouldn't say it that way. I've trained both since children. They're more than capable of carrying this out. Anything helpful it yields will come to you. Onto the next item. It has been a long morning, especially for my younger student."

"Something happened? Is your younger student, okay?" Dante asked, concerned.

"We now know the location for where you'll face your father and the Dark Lord to win your father back."

"How? Where? You still didn't answer about your student."

Lana glanced at her cousin as she touched his arm. "One question at a time. Calm down."

"My younger student is fine. My older student and I awoke early this morning to a loud yell from my younger student's room. My younger student received a vision, and it revealed the..." Dante's face held a strange look on it, and Ryan turned to Dante puzzled. Lana and Caleb turned to stare back at Dante too.

"Alika, what time did your student get the vision?"

Alika normally would think the question unnecessary, but Dante's face told a different story. "Around six this morning, Dante."

"How? It can't be a coincidence. Alika, I slept the whole night soundly until this morning at exactly six. I woke up startled by something, but I saw nothing. I brushed it off, and a few minutes later, I went back to sleep. I didn't know what to make of it."

"I don't know, Dante. My student has had the visions for as long as I can remember. This is the first I am aware the other person sensed the vision in any way, but I don't doubt it. I see how my student is left after one, as the visions are intense. I don't have an answer." Alika turned to Seth, seeing if he wished to add anything. Seth shook his head, signaling he could provide no further insight, or none he wished to share in this open discussion.

"How is your student left, Alika?"

"My student is fine now, Dante. However, the visions which awaken my student are terrifying, to say the least, so my student takes time to calm down from them. Once my student realizes it's not happening anymore, the morning or middle of the night goes better. It's not the desired wake-up call. Needless to say, we've all been up since six this morning. No one could return to sleep afterwards, but thank you as always for your concern for my young student. It's time to share what the vision revealed. You'll return to your home planet to face your father and the Dark Lord. It's a place you know well there, where you spent many days training as a spear-bearer as a child. It's the Elders Hall."

"Are you sure?"

"Yes. It was the first question I asked my young student. My young student went through the vision with us frame by frame. It's definitely the place."

"My father completely destroyed the planet in his rage. It's not this glorious place to build a fortress or command post. Why would my father go back there?"

"It didn't make sense to me at first either, but as we went through the vision with my student, it becomes clear. Let's do so. This process of taking a vision apart is new to you, but I have developed years of practice. Let's begin."

So Alika did. He became his young student for the time, showing them the vision through her eyes.

When he finished, everyone stayed quiet, letting the magnitude of the image sink in.

"I can tell you our thoughts after we went through it, or you can go first."

Lana glanced at Dante, and Dante nodded. Lana looked back at Alika. "You said it yourself. Your experience far outweighs ours in this area. Please, go first."

Alika did, and when he finished, they sat quietly again for a couple of minutes.

Seth said, "You're right. The significance of watching it there can be no mistake."

"Do you truly think they don't know I'm coming?"

"Yes, but we can't be sure. I don't believe your father knows. The Dark Lord is another matter. He's full of deception, so we could be mistaken. Don't go announcing your visit now. I'm sure it could change the vision, Dante."

"Although it seems from the vision, they're at the Elders Hall to watch whatever is going on at the same time. They're not there for Dante," said Ryan.

"Yes, but Dante knows their location because of the other," said Caleb.

"And we can't help Dante because we must deal with this other threat from the Dark Lord, and it takes all of our resources," said Lana sighing.

"Yes, that's what we gathered."

"Are the visions always so intense?"

"Yes, Dante."

"Your student didn't just see what happened. Your student shared in what the person felt and thought... got impressions, even... experienced it. That's a whole other level of seeing. Is it always like that too?" asked Dante, his face as someone finally seeing for the first time.

"Yes, Dante, always."

"Alika, no wonder your student knows me so well after all these months. You said you saw us through your student's eyes. I heard you, but now... if you care for us like this, just knowing us through what you're told, for your student..." Dante paused, "Your student didn't give a second thought to rescuing my mother, never questioned it?"

"No, not for a moment."

"And Collin and my father. With Collin, your student felt the grief as if your student lost their own sibling. My father is the same. Your student sees him as I see him. He's truly my father, Ethan, as I experienced in my childhood, not what he presents to the galaxy now."

"Yes, Dante, that's why everything unfolded as it has. My student truly sees through your eyes in every way."

"Then there's me, Alika. Your student sees me in the visions, I mean really sees me. They know me, like someone whose known me for years. They experienced …" Dante stopped, trying to grasp his own words but stumbling in the process. He looked back at Alika and asked, "How did your student react yesterday when I was told everything?"

"We monitored the proceedings, as we all worried about how you would handle the information. We were all upset for you as we expected how difficult the day would be for you, but you're right. My young student's visions create a unique perspective concerning you. So, it is very difficult for my young student to see you in the pain you experienced yesterday. It felt much more like your circle of friends around you felt—watching you, if that makes sense. My young student shared in your pain deeply. Does that help you, young Dante?"

"It does, Alika, thank you," Dante said softly.

"Are you sure, Dante? I gave you the best answer I can. I've seen my student with the visions, but there are times I'm still left with my own questions. Dante, I don't begin to understand the connection between the one who sees the visions and the one who is the focus of the vision or if there's any connection created. It seems there is in this case. It could be the result if the focus remains long enough on one person, or it may be in this instance there's something else beyond what we're able to see now."

"You're giving me the best answer you're able, and that's all I ask. It's strange for someone to know me this well. Sorry that doesn't capture it. For someone to experience so much with me, but I don't know them at all. I'm not sure what to do with that. I'm not afraid or worried because I know they care for my well-being. That's obvious from the moment we met you. I mean, you're not the student, but I'm sorry, I'm not making sense." Dante's face crinkled up, and he shook his head, still stumbling with his words.

"No, you're doing reasonably well, making sense of something perplexing to all of us. My student is not having any easier time sorting out any of this, even with all the experience with the visions. So, you should not be so hard on yourself for feeling mystified. It's a strange situation. Hopefully, in time the fog clears. And I understand what you mean about me. My older student and I feel we know you from what my younger student has told us. So, the way I approached you and seem to already know you and care for your well-being as your comrades who have known you for years, it's because I feel like in a sense I have, through my student's eyes. So yes, my student is genuinely concerned that you stay safe, so try to do so, Dante. You do not excel at that part." Alika smiled as he patted Dante on the shoulder.

"Anything else?" asked Alika.

Everyone shook their head. Alika looked at Seth. "Seth? I did all the talking. Your group is quiet this morning. Did you put a limit on their questions?"

Everyone laughed, including Seth. "I promise, I didn't, Alika. You are incredibly thorough," said Seth smiling.

"Then I have a few reminders for you and a couple of personal ones that my young student wanted me to convey. Unfortunately, we anticipate being of little or no help to you during the attacks. It's not our wish. It's just too difficult to divide our attention during an operation. It'll put them in too much peril."

"We figured as much already."

"We'll communicate anything we find which could help you. Nevertheless, it will become more dangerous to communicate with each passing day."

"If you do need our help, let us know. We will help," said Dante.

"I know you will. Hopefully, it won't come to that, as your focus needs to be elsewhere. If we need assistance, we'll make it known. Also, bear in mind our ship appears in several forms due to our operations. So, if you spot an unknown lone ship approaching, give it a minute before sending it crashing out of the sky. Neither one of my students wanted to make the pit stop in Ryan's territory, but it proved necessary. They made a couple of other stops which no one caught." Alika caught the looks. "The ship appeared as the friendly sort to you, so it didn't draw the attention the first stop did."

"Was that all? You mentioned a couple of personal messages."

"You listen well, Dante. We'll add it to your list of good qualities. I made a promise to my young student to relay those, and I'll do so personally to those they're intended before I leave."

Seth smiled. "I wish we had more questions for you, Alika. I've greatly enjoyed your company."

"I've enjoyed the time here as well. I wish it had been under better circumstances." He got up, turned to the others, and smiled at them. "All of you as well. You are everything I was told to expect and more."

The others rose too. Alika went to Ryan and put a hand on his shoulder. "You're a true friend, and you'll need each other more than ever as the time approaches. Dante will especially need you. Continue to be that friend to all here, Ryan."

"Of course, Alika, and we'll be here for Dante," said Ryan.

Alika moved to Caleb and said, "You as well, Caleb. I know you'll continue to be there for Dante. Also, continue to hold your wife close and lend her your strength. We all face tough moments ahead, and she'll need your encouragement."

Caleb smiled and said, "I will, and thank you for your help."

Alika moved to Lana and said, "Your message came from my young student. I gave you part of it earlier."

"But the visions are about Dante," said Lana.

"And those closest to him and the impressions drawn from his interactions with them by my student. I told you I don't understand all of it."

"Okay," said Lana, fascinated.

"You had many decisions to make lately, and more lie ahead. You feel the burden of them, but trust in the path you know to be true from the first. You're doing well. There are those around who care for you. Remember they stand with you to help and cling to the assurance you're not alone, along with what you were taught in the beginning." Alika paused and smiled at Lana. "It has truly been a pleasure, Lana."

Her eyes glistened with tears. "Thank you, Alika, and tell your student as well. I am eager for the day when we meet both of them." She hugged Alika goodbye.

Alika came to Dante last. "Dante, there are multiple messages for you from my young student as we've covered the unique viewpoint which exists for you. I understand how overwhelming this is, which is placed upon your shoulders, and it grieves me greatly to see your pain. You'll be able to do the task before you, for the Ancient One will be with you. Don't falter from that, Dante. In the meantime, before you must do your task, keep your head clear and focused on whatever the immediate task is before you. Don't let what's ahead of you or the burden of the information you received come to you. I do not wish to see you hurt. Then when it's time for the task with your father, be focused completely on that in the same way. Remember what you've been taught. Listen to it only. The Dark Lord still uses the same tactics as he used on your father. The Dark Lord is powerful. His voice is persuasive. He can be beaten, and your father returned to you, but you must let the Ancient One guide you in this. You won't be alone ever in any of this. And Dante, I'm glad your spirit returned to a happier state now as it lifted my spirit to see you smile and laugh again."

"The message from your student is ..."

"Yes, exactly. My student does well with that. There's been a few times my student stumbled around with words, but it's rare." Alika looked over Dante as if a thought occurred to him. "I suppose there's something that might change that. Anyway, I wanted to get the message right. I don't want to be in trouble with my young student when I return." laughed Alika. Then he smiled at Dante. "I meant what I said to you since I've been here, Dante. Everything I was told about you turned out to be true and more." He saw the look from Dante. "And all the more is good, despite how I teased you."

"Thank you, Alika, for everything, and tell your students the same and to stay safe. I look forward to meeting them one day. Tell your younger student especially, thank you for the kind words, and I'll heed them. I'll stay safe and accomplish whatever task is immediately before me. I'll get my father back, with the Ancient One beside me. I'm glad your student is happier again as well," Dante said, smiling and reaching over to hug Alika goodbye.

"I'll walk you to the ship, Alika," said Seth.

Alika nodded and said to the group as he walked out with Seth, "Goodbye, take care of each other, and stay safe."

"Strange. Her vision awakened Dante, Seth."

"You said she yelled. What did she yell?"

"She screamed his name. She knew the terror he would face in the vision."

"What does she think of Dante? You know your student, Alika."

"I do. She cares for him, and it's growing beyond what I'd realized. She glimpsed him last night coming out of the building with the others and watched him the whole time. She also denied it every second. We brought up the notion to her there's more at play here. She's confused, Seth. This is a realm unfamiliar to her. The circumstances are like no other. So, I understand her confusion. Is this depth of caring because she knows him through the visions, or are the feelings genuine of something else at work? There's a fear, but not like any she has ever encountered. She doesn't know how to handle it."

"You're sure it's not time for them to meet?"

"Yes, I'm sure, and so is she. It'll be clear if and when the time arrives. Believe me, when they meet, Dante won't have any complaints with my young spear-bearer on that account. He will be pleased, to say the least."

Seth smiled. The young spear-bearer's outer appearance must match the gentle spirit they'd seen so far. "I understand," Seth said, laughing.

"I'm worried about this timetable for what the Dark Lord is planning, Seth. My students feel it, and I do too. I'm afraid we won't figure it out in time to stop it."

"I know, but we'll get the tracking devices on. Something large enough to hit at the heart of the Elders and what the Ancient One stands for is frightening."

"We'll do what we can, Seth. There's serious work ahead of you for Dante to be trained for the challenge ahead. I know he'll be ready, but it'll be hard."

"Yes, it won't be a battle won with a sunspear in the end, I believe, and he must remember that."

"I fear you're right. The hardest battle my younger student fought involved no sunspear as well," Alika's voice became soft, "and it almost overcame her. Ethan long ago fought a similar battle, and there was no sunspear. He lost the battle. Here we are, sending his son to win him back in the same battle."

"The Dark Lord's weapons remain the same as you said. It won't be any easier," said Seth, concerned. If the battle his student almost lost left this mark on Alika, Seth could only imagine how it shaped his young student.

"Seth, the son must not fall as well."

They arrived at the ship that instant.

"No, he must not. We send them into battle another day."

"Yes, and may yours remain safe as the Ancient One stands beside them for the battles they face, my friend, Seth."

"The same to you for your two young spear-bearers, my friend, Alika. Until the next time we meet." The two men hugged, and Seth turned around and walked away. The ship door opened, Alika went inside, and the door quickly closed after him.

⎯⎯ℓℓℓ⎯⎯

The two came out of the quarters and walked to the cockpit window as they talked with Alika.

"Everything good?" asked Alena.

Alika smiled. "We're good." He turned to the girl. "I delivered all messages as promised, but I guess you heard."

"Yeah, we listened. They seem confident about getting the tracking devices on the shipments. It's a good sign," said the girl as she sat at the cockpit.

⎯⎯ℓℓℓ⎯⎯

Dante moved over to a window to watch Seth reach the ship, and Alika board it. "I'm going outside to see them leave."

"Dante," Lana said, but Dante already walked away.

Seth hadn't gotten back in the building, and Dante came outside. Seth looked at him. "Did you finally come up with a question, Dante?"

"No, I came to see the ship leave. This is as close as it gets," Dante said and shrugged his shoulders. He sensed it again, the same person looking at him from the ship as it lifted off, and he smiled.

Seth turned back to the ship and smiled to himself.

"It's time to go," said the girl. She didn't try to hide her sadness. She'd already said goodbye to Abigail, and she enjoyed seeing Dante's friends and family from the visions. But it came down to Dante. Though it was a few precious moments, she finally saw him. She worried they would leave, and his spirit would be broken. Instead, she recalled him smiling and laughing last night despite what they brought him. She would miss him, and she didn't feel like denying it to herself today. Almost as if he read her thoughts, Dante came out of the building to stand beside Seth. The girl watched an exchange between the two as they turned to watch the ship leave.

"I know you'll miss him," whispered Alena waiting on the girl to deny it.

"Yes, I will miss him," said the girl quietly.

"Are you sure you're ready to leave?" asked Alika, touching the girl's shoulder lightly.

"Yes, there's no reason to stay longer," said the girl smiling as the other two began liftoff. "Goodbye, Dante," whispered the girl and watched him until the planet disappeared from view.

ABOUT THE AUTHOR

Elizabeth Lavender is the author of the Sunspear series. Originally from the Alabama coast, she currently lives in the Dallas area with her husband, Jeff, and her two children. She has a Master's degree in counseling from Dallas Baptist University and has studied psychology and English.

She enjoys science fiction and fantasy and hopes to bring some of that same enjoyment to others. She also enjoys suspense novels. However, as long as the storyline is intriguing, she will give it a try. Her reading spans from Les Miserables to Shakespeare to the Percy Jackson series to anything written by Ted Dekker or Frank Perretti.

She works full-time and has been at the same company for over twenty years happily. She is a huge football fan and has a decent throwing arm, despite what her oldest son says when he practices with her.

Although she enjoys Texas, she does love going home to Alabama to visit. Besides visiting family and friends, it is nice to be back near the water again, where the seafood is the best.

Find more books by Elizabeth at:
https://elizabethlavender.net